RACHEL'S STORY

LEIGH RUSSELL

BLOODHOUND
— BOOKS —

Print ISBN 978-1-913942-39-7

ALSO BY LEIGH RUSSELL, PUBLISHED BY BLOODHOUND BOOKS

The Adulterer's Wife

Suspicion

For Michael

PROLOGUE
CLARE

One night we were woken by a faint tapping at the front door. Only the Guardians were allowed out on the streets after the curfew, but they would have kicked the door open and burst in. This was a tentative request for permission to enter our lodgings.

My mother's voice trembled as she whispered my name. 'Rachel? Are you awake, Rachel?'

Lying perfectly still, I pretended to be asleep. It was partly fear that stopped me from answering, but I was also curious. I had never heard my mother talking to someone else when she did not know I was listening. She stirred beside me in the darkness. A moment later her bare feet padded softly across the dirt floor, and the door creaked open.

'Clare?' my mother murmured. 'What are you doing outside after sunset? Have you lost your mind?'

There was a muffled response, and then I heard my mother speak again. 'Very well then, you'd better come in before they see you.'

In the flickering flame of a torch I watched our neighbour, Clare, glance over her shoulder as she slipped inside and shut the door. Her hair was covered by her cape, but I could see her eyes peering out from beneath her hood, and tears glistening on her cheeks.

'It's all right,' she muttered, setting her torch in a sconce on the wall. 'There's no sign of them out there. I made sure there was no one around to see me knocking on your door. The last thing any of us want is to cause trouble.'

'How can you say you don't want to cause trouble when you've come here after the curfew?'

'Relax, Mary. No one saw me.'

'Don't tell me to relax. You know perfectly well it's dark out there, yet you've taken it on yourself to risk both our lives by coming here like this,' my mother replied sternly. 'Now, tell me what's happened. Why are you out so late? Are you in some kind of trouble?'

Clare's mumbled response was inaudible, but I was old enough to understand that she was terrified.

'You know I'd help you if I could,' my mother said at last, when Clare fell silent. 'But you must appreciate there's nothing I can do. You can't hide here, not if they're already searching for you. It's not fair of you to ask that of me, not when I have a child to think of.'

In the flickering light of the torch, my mother looked grave. Her dark eyes stared intensely at Clare, who crouched on the floor and let out a low wail before raising her head and removing her hood. Seeing tears trickling down our neighbour's cheeks made me want to cry too, but I bit my lip and watched silently, trying to understand what was going on.

My mother squatted on the floor facing Clare, and the two of them leaned forwards so that their heads and knees were nearly touching. My mother had lowered herself to the floor with her back to me, and her matted hair stuck out from her head, obscuring half of Clare's face.

I wriggled silently in bed to change my position, so that I could see our visitor again. Wiping her tears away impatiently with the back of her hand, she pressed her lips together and shivered. For a moment the two women sat gazing at one another in silence, while I lay rigid, staring at my mother's back through half-closed eyes. At last, with a sigh, my mother reached out and placed her hand on Clare's shoulder.

'You have to tell me what's wrong,' she whispered. 'I can't help you if you won't tell me what's happened.'

Clare murmured so softly, I had to strain to hear what she was saying. Apart from my mother, Clare was the one person who ever spent time with me, and we had been friends for as long as I could remember. Although she was a grown-up, she was younger than my mother. She used to visit us when she could, and she sometimes kept me company when my mother went out. Her blue eyes twinkling, she would entertain me with fantasies of a bygone age. She told me that people once lit torches at the touch of a finger with flames so bright there was no way of telling night from day, and men rode across the sky in giant carts.

I had giggled at the idea of people flying through the air and asked, 'What happened if something dropped out of a cart, and it landed on someone's head?'

'I know you don't believe me, but it's all true,' Clare insisted, after spinning one of her far-fetched tales. 'My mother told me her parents talked to people who were many hundreds of days' walk away, on the other side of the world.'

'Hundreds of days' walk away?' I repeated, shaking my head in disbelief. 'Is the world outside the city really that big?'

'It's bigger than you can possibly imagine. You've seen how wide the sky is? Well, the world is even bigger than that. The sky goes right around it, because the world is round, like this.' She clenched her fist and held it up. 'If you travelled for long enough, you would end up right back where you started.'

That made a kind of sense, unlike many things she told me, even if it was not true.

'Those people who talked to each other from far away wouldn't have been able to hear each other if they were so far apart,' I pointed out.

'Their voices travelled through the air.'

'Then everyone else would have heard what they were saying, and it would have made so much noise, with everyone talking at the same time, they would never have been able to hear what the other person was saying.'

'Well, they did. Two people in distant cities were able to have a conversation with each other.'

It still made no sense. 'Even if they could hear one person clearly, how would they know who it was if they couldn't see them?'

'I don't know how it worked, but it did,' she replied. 'And they could see each other even when they were far apart. At least, I think they could. But oh, I don't know. I wasn't there. You ask so many questions! But you don't have to believe me if you don't want to. I'm only telling you what my mother heard from my grandmother.'

Concerned that she might be annoyed by my constantly doubting her, I begged her to tell me more stories about the old days.

'My mother said that her mother told her people travelled in carts that moved by themselves, with no one pulling them.'

That made me burst out laughing again. 'How did the carts know where to go?'

'And there were carriages that transported people under the ground as well as through the air,' she continued, ignoring my interruption, 'and trees grew on every street.'

'What are trees?' I asked.

Clare shook her head and admitted that she did not know. 'My mother talked about them but she never explained exactly what they were, at least not so that I could understand. But I think she saw one herself. Perhaps more than one.'

'What did she say? Tell me more,' I begged. 'I want to know about trees.'

'Well, she described the trees as alive, but they weren't human. They grew straight up out of the ground, covered in living green ribbons, and they always stayed in the same place. And people were allowed to walk out of their rooms at any time, day or night. They could go anywhere they wanted because—' she leaned towards me and lowered her voice so that her next words were barely audible. 'There were no Guardians.'

She pressed her lips together. Perhaps she regretted being so outspoken, even though she must have known I would never betray her confidence.

I gasped at her audacity. 'Who protected the people from monsters if there were no Guardians?' I asked, no longer attempting to conceal my incredulity.

Clare shook her head and put her finger on her lips. It was all fantasy, of course, but her stories were fun.

By contrast, my mother talked only about the real world, warning me of monsters that roamed the wasteland surrounding the city: huge creatures with sharp teeth and claws, and eyes that darted flames. Her dark eyes solemn, she told me they were the reason we were forbidden to stray outside the city walls. Even the Guardians were afraid to leave the protection of the city, and patrolled the streets in groups. At night, my mother told me, the monsters climbed over the city walls and lurked in the streets, stealing stray children and carrying them away.

'What happens to the children after the monsters take them?' I wanted to know.

'They die in the wilderness, torn apart by the monsters,' my mother replied firmly, pressing her thin lips together as though to indicate she had finished her account.

But I was not satisfied to leave it there. 'Why do the monsters want to kill children?'

'After the Great Sickness, the monsters living in the wasteland swore an oath to destroy everyone living in the city. Don't ask me why. The reasons for their enmity are lost in the past, and I don't think anyone even remembers how the hatred began.' She sighed and shook her head. 'There's no point in talking about it. That's just how it is.'

'But why do the monsters bother to take the children over the walls, if they're just going to kill them? Why don't they kill them here, where they find them, on the city streets?' I asked.

My mother shook her head and did not answer.

The night that Clare came to our house I lay in bed, listening to her talking urgently to my mother in a low voice, while outside all was silent. Between fits of sobbing, Clare confessed that her food card had been stolen. 'It was when I was on my way home from the clinic,' she explained. 'A dirty little street urchin knocked into me, and he must have taken it, only I didn't realise what was going on until afterwards and then it was too late.'

'Pull yourself together, and tell me exactly what happened.'

'Somehow, when he bumped into me, my pouch came loose and fell on the ground. We both reached for it but he got there first. I managed to snatch it back from him, and he ran off. Although I was shaken, I remember feeling relieved that the encounter was over. It all happened so quickly, I barely had time to feel shocked. It wasn't until the next day that I discovered my food card was missing.' She broke off, momentarily overwhelmed by her plight. 'The boy must have slipped my card out of my pouch without my noticing. He might as well have announced my death sentence on the spot.'

'I'm so sorry. That's terrible, but what can I do about it?' my mother asked, drawing away from our neighbour and sitting back on her heels.

Clare leaned towards my mother. 'You can share your pills with me,' she whispered.

My mother shook her head. 'You know I can't do that.'

'Just one every couple of days,' Clare begged. 'That's all I'm asking. There are two of you. That's two sets of pills. You won't miss a few.'

My mother rose to her feet and folded her arms across her chest. 'Clare, you know that's not possible,' she said coldly. 'We'd never get away with it. As soon as we started to lose weight they'd notice, and realise what was going on.'

'They wouldn't know, if we were careful. They'd just give you more. It's only for a few days, until my card turns up.'

'If it was only me, I'd think about it,' my mother answered. 'But you know I can't take a risk like that, not with Rachel to think about. I'm sorry, Clare, but there's nothing I can do.'

'You've got to help me,' Clare pleaded, standing up and seizing my mother's hand. 'There's no one else I can ask, no one. I'm all alone, and I'll starve to death if I don't take anything soon. I haven't had a hydration pill for three days. Please, I'm begging you, don't let me die, not like this.'

My mother snatched her hand away. 'You should not have come here. Go away and leave us alone. We can't help you. It's night-time, Clare. You shouldn't have left your home. What were you thinking of, coming here like this? Have you lost your mind?'

'Are you just going to let me starve, without doing anything to help me?' Clare asked. She had stopped crying, and her voice grew harsh. 'I thought we were friends.'

'A friend would not ask this of me. Find your card, Clare. That advice is the only help I can give you. There's nothing we can do for you, nothing. I wish we could help you, really I do, but we can't. I have to think of my daughter, and I can't risk her life, I just can't, not after everything that has happened. So many people died to preserve her life.'

If it had not been for me, my mother might have helped our friend. I wanted to leap out of bed and rush over to Clare and tell her she could share my pills, but I was afraid to risk my mother's anger by revealing that I had been eavesdropping. So instead of offering to help Clare, I closed my eyes tightly and pretended to be asleep, and a moment later I heard the front door open and close softly.

Two days later a new neighbour moved into the lodgings next door. We never saw Clare again.

1

DISASTER

Alarmed, I searched the pocket of my waistband, but my food card had gone. In a panic, I scanned every inch of the dirt floor of our room, staring into each of the five dusty corners, but there was no sign of my card. Flinging myself down on the bed, I hugged my knees, sobbing, but crying would not save me from disaster. Even as I wept, I was aware that time was running out. If my food card failed to materialise before my mother returned, it would not be long before she stumbled on the truth. And then, after all she had done to protect me, my mother would be forced to hand me over to the Guardians.

'Do you want to starve to death, like your father?' she would hiss at me. 'How do you think you are going to survive without a food card? Do you think I can support you, all by myself?' And then she would weep, tousled dark hair falling over her face. Raising her head, her eyes blazing, she would continue in a low voice. 'How could you be so careless? This is your life we're talking about. What am I supposed to do now? You know the law. You leave me no choice.'

She would be right. If she attempted to share her rations with me, we would both be seized by the Guardians. The

Council took good care of us, keeping our enemies outside the city walls during the day, so that we could walk the streets in safety, but without our regulation pills we would starve. The responsibility for taking our pills rested on our own shoulders. Every day Guardians patrolled the streets, their announcements loud enough to be heard from indoors: 'Keep your card safe', 'No card no pills', and 'Without your card you starve'. If my mother tried to share her pills with me, it would not take the nurses at the clinic long to detect that something was amiss. As soon as my mother's weight dropped, she would be investigated, and once they discovered that my weight had also fallen below the prescribed limit, our transgression would be exposed.

Frantically I tore off my tunic and shirt and trousers and felt every inch of them between my fumbling fingers, but my food card had not slipped into a fold of the fabric. I shook them violently, but nothing fell out. Quickly pulling my clothes on again, I scrabbled through the bed covers, and searched the rest of the room, crouching down to peer under the bed. I even pulled the door open in case my card had somehow become lodged in the dirt underneath it. My red and black food card should have been easy to spot, but all I could see were piles of dust in the corners of the room. My mother swept the mud floor every day but whenever the door was open, flecks of grit blew in from the wasteland beyond the city walls.

As I hunted desperately for my card, I tried not to think about Clare, who had lived next door to us, the sole friend of my childhood.

As a last resort, I pulled the sacking off the trestle bed that my mother and I slept on and shook it. To my surprise, a small white card fluttered out and landed at my feet. Dropping to my knees, I picked it up, and stared in amazement at an image of an odd face. On the back of the card there was a row of indecipherable symbols. I looked at them for a long time, hoping their meaning would mysteriously become clear. Eventually I gave up and turned the card over.

The woman's face bore a marked similarity to my own reflection, which I had seen in polished metal trays at the food clinic where we went to be weighed and measured. Although she was approaching middle age, and her cheeks were oddly puffed out, she had my round blue eyes, turned up nose and slightly protruding upper lip. Given our resemblance, I guessed we must be related. Apart from my mother, every other member of my family had died before I was born.

Those who had survived the Great Sickness had starved to death in the subsequent World Famine, so it was hardly surprising that my father had died before my mother bore me, his first and only child. With the whole world starving, family members had been forced to pool their limited food supplies so that at least one of their number could survive. As she was expecting a child, my mother had been the person our family had chosen as their sole survivor. Since then, more than twelve years had passed and, along with other survivors, we were looked after by The Council. Although it was not my fault that my birth had saved my mother's life, I do not think she ever forgave me.

The picture my mother had kept hidden under our mattress was disturbing. The woman's face was oddly distorted, her cheeks so full and round that no bones showed through her skin, and her arms looked unnaturally thick. She appeared to be bloated with some horrible disease, yet her skin looked healthy, and she was smiling. Her protruding tongue was attached to a shapeless pink blob in a tapered conical cup, and I could not imagine why she might want to touch it with any part of her mouth. Presumably she was using her tongue for protection, but it would have been far easier to have simply shut her mouth. Even if nothing passed between her open lips, whatever her tongue was touching must be dirty, yet she was smiling, as though she was enjoying herself. It was unnerving.

Absorbed in looking at the picture, I had not noticed how fast the daylight was fading and, just before dusk, the front door opened. My mother was home. In a panic, I threw the sacking back on our bed and slipped the picture into my waistband.

As I did so, my fingers brushed against my food card which had been there the whole time, concealed behind a slit in the fabric. Shaking with relief, I looked up and greeted my mother. I wanted to ask her about the woman in the picture, but was afraid she would be angry with me and take the card away.

'What have you done to the bed?' she demanded.

'Nothing.'

'If you lie down, you must tidy the bedding when you get up. You can't always expect me to do everything for you.' She paused to study my expression. 'You have that guilty look on your face. What have you done?'

She was bound to discover the absence of the picture sooner or later. Defeated, I explained that my food card had been temporarily mislaid, and in my search I had come across a picture of a woman. Ready to defend myself against a scolding for losing my food card, albeit briefly, I was surprised when she fixated on my discovery. The safety of my food card ought to have been of paramount importance, yet she did not even mention that.

'What picture? What are you talking about?' she demanded, scowling suspiciously at me.

'It's just a picture.'

'Picture? What do you mean, "a picture"? Give it to me.'

Reluctantly I drew the card from my waistband, and she snatched it from my hand. 'Is that my grandmother?' I asked. 'What's she putting in her mouth?'

Without warning, my mother slumped down on our bed, her

shoulders bowed. 'Where did you find this?' she asked in a low voice. She was no longer angry. This was not like my mother at all.

'Is that my grandmother?' I asked again.

My mother turned away, but not before I had seen the glint of tears in her eyes. It was the first time I had seen her cry. Even so, her voice was devoid of emotion as she answered my question. 'You're right. This is a picture of your grandmother.'

'I knew it!'

'You look like her.'

'That's just what I thought!' I sat on the bed beside my mother, and we stared at the picture together in silence for a few moments.

'Every time I look at you, I see her,' she said at last, with an odd catch in her voice.

'Why is her face so fat?' I asked. 'Was she sick?'

'No, she wasn't sick.' My mother paused for a moment, a distant look in her eyes. 'This picture was recorded before the Great Sickness struck. Your grandmother was young, and life was very different then. It's hard to explain.'

'What has she got in her hand? She's holding it up to her mouth. What's she doing that for?'

My mother did not respond.

'She looks happy, doesn't she?' I asked.

'Yes, she does. She looks happy,' my mother agreed. 'I think people were happy in those days. They had no idea what was about to happen.'

'Do you mean the Great Sickness or the World Famine?'

'Both. But the sickness was the start of it all.'

'The start of all what?'

'The destruction of the world.'

'What do you mean?'

She sighed. 'The world your grandmother grew up in was a very different place to the world you know.'

There was a lot more I wanted to ask her but, before my mother had a chance to answer any further questions, we heard a loud crash outside in the street, followed by the sound of heavy boots marching past. It was the night patrol. Working for The Council, the Guardians carried out their duties after dark, smashing down doors and dragging transgressors away in huge prison carts. No one knew exactly what happened to people when they were taken away; very few were ever seen again, and those who did return never spoke about their experience.

My mother sprang to her feet. 'Hide!' she hissed at me. 'Get into bed, pull the covers over your head and keep quiet! They're looking for someone.'

I reached out and clutched her hand. 'What about you?'

'Don't worry about me. Just do as I say and hide yourself and don't make a sound.'

I could feel her hands shaking with fright as she tried to push me towards the bed, but before I could scramble under the covers there was a deafening knock, and a deep voice shouted at us to open the door. In a desperate bid to protect my mother, I grabbed my grandmother's picture and slipped it through the slit in my waistband. With my food card safely back in the pocket in front of the picture, it would be impossible to feel a second card through the fabric. Unless my waistband was physically torn apart, the picture would remain safely hidden.

'Go!' my mother whispered urgently. 'Hide yourself.'

But it was too late. The door flew open and a Guardian appeared on the threshold, one hand resting on his blow pipe, the other holding a flaming torch. I had never been so close to a Guardian before and stared up at him, mesmerised.

Thin lips and a square chin were the only parts of him that were visible beneath the visor of his black helmet. His colossal torso and limbs were encased in a shiny black uniform, and his massive hands and feet were concealed by black gloves and enormous gleaming black boots. A second Guardian immediately blocked the doorway behind him, as though they were afraid we might try to outrun their swift darts. With lungs trained from birth, the Guardians could send their poisoned missiles through the air so fast their flight was scarcely visible. Ducking his head to fit his helmet through the door, the first one strode across the room and kicked our bed, which toppled over onto its side. The cover slipped to the floor in an untidy heap. It was fortunate I had not had time to hide there.

Our unwelcome visitor swung round to face us. The ceiling of our lodging was barely high enough for him to stand upright. His huge gloved fist pointed at my mother, while his stentorian voice echoed around the room. 'Woman, state your name.'

'Mary Lincoln,' my mother stammered, 'my name is Mary Lincoln, sir. Mary Lincoln.' She hung her head and stared at the floor, as she held out her identity card in a hand that trembled violently.

The Guardian barely glanced at her blue and white card before switching his attention to me. 'Child, state your name.'

His booming voice scared me so much, I could not utter a word.

He took a step towards me and his huge boot stamped on the floor, throwing up a small cloud of yellow dust. 'Child, state your name,' he repeated.

'Rachel Lincoln,' I mumbled, fumbling with the card in my waistband. For a moment I was afraid I had handed over my grandmother's picture by mistake. Unable to tear my eyes away from the Guardian's lips, I held my breath as he seized my red and black card and stared at it. A long time seemed to elapse while he studied it, but at last he turned away from me and I breathed again.

Her face pale, my mother was gazing up at the Guardian. He made a gesture with one hand to usher us out of the room, while his other hand rested on his blow pipe. With a cry of alarm, my mother leapt in front of me, as though her frail body could offer me any protection against the might of a Guardian.

'Not the child!' she cried out. 'Please, I beg you, leave my child alone. She has done nothing wrong, nothing. Take me, but leave her alone. She's just a child!'

As the Guardian reached for her, I thought of all the people who had died so that my mother could live to give birth to me. After their sacrifice, surely her life could not end here, in one instant of pointless cruelty. Transfixed with horror, I watched the Guardian's fingers encircle my mother's neck and lift her off her feet. Her arms flailed helplessly, while her legs scrabbled for a foothold and her eyes fixed on me with a despairing glare. Her mouth opened as though she wanted to tell me something, but no sound came out. At last she let out a faint rasping breath, her head fell forward and she hung limply from his huge hand, as though all her energy was spent. The Guardian let her drop, without swivelling his head to glance at her as she landed on the floor with a faint thud.

In stunned silence, I stared at the dark smudges on her neck where his fingers had bruised her flesh, while her dark eyes stared at the ceiling, unblinking, her face grey in the flickering light of the Guardian's torch. A few yellow specks swirled in the air and came to rest on her inert figure. All I could think was how vexed she would be at the amount of desert dust disturbed by her body hitting the floor. Involuntarily, I glanced over at the broom propped against the wall.

'Come with me,' the Guardian barked.

'The floor– I can't leave yet, I have to sweep the floor–' I stammered stupidly. 'She always sweeps the floor.'

He lunged forward and gripped my arm so tightly, I yelped

in pain. My shock at the attack on my poor mother quite possibly saved my life, because I was too dazed to remonstrate when the Guardian propelled me towards the door. Everything had happened so quickly, I had not yet registered that my mother was not going to clamber to her feet and start sweeping the floor, grumbling under her breath about the endless grains of dust that drifted in from the desert beyond the city walls.

Even when chains were snapped on my wrists and ankles I did not complain, merely wincing when the Guardian seized me by the arm and dragged me out of the room, leaving my mother lying on the floor. A fog descended, shrouding my thoughts, but I was dimly aware that if I resisted, he would kill me. It flashed into my mind that death might be preferable to whatever fate the Guardian had in store for me, but a fierce instinct to survive kept me from protesting.

Stupefied, I followed the Guardian meekly out of the only home I had ever known. This was my first experience of loss, and I had no idea how to react. An image of my grandmother had brought tears to my mother's eyes, but I did not know how to cry over my own mother's death. I only knew that she had been snatched away, without warning, leaving me to fend for myself in a terrifying world, and all I felt was emptiness, as though nothing mattered anymore. So many people had given their lives to bring me to this moment, in this place, and it was all meaningless. My mother was dead and I was utterly alone in a hostile world.

2

THE CITADEL

Outside, an unfamiliar black sky seemed to smother me as I was dragged along the street, my hands and feet chained. All year round, the sun beat down mercilessly throughout the day, and I was accustomed to the heat. Now, at night, in the glow of flickering torchlight, everything felt different. I had never stepped outside after the sunset curfew before, and was surprised by the coolness of the air, and the absence of shadows cast by the buildings during the day. Nothing in this strange dark street looked familiar. Torches flickered, illuminating several Guardians patrolling the street, as my captor propelled me up a steep ramp into a large waggon with sides higher than a man's arms could reach. Once I was inside, the ramp was raised to form a fourth wall for our moving prison cell.

A single torch flickered above us, illuminating several people crouching helplessly on the floor of the cart. Only one man was on his feet, waving his fists and yelling at the Guardians. He stared wildly at me as I joined the other prisoners and I trembled at the desperation in his eyes. Tangled hair framed his face that was ruddy and curiously rounded, as though his cheeks were swollen with some terrible disease. He reminded me of my grandmother's image.

'You have no right to keep us here,' he bellowed as the floor vibrated and we started to move, pulled along by a team of Guardians yoked to the front of the cart. 'Let us go. You can't keep us locked up like this. Let us out of here at once! You have no grounds for arresting us. We demand to be released. The Council will hear of this!'

An old woman was seated on the floor, leaning against the side of the cart, her scrawny legs stretched out straight in front of her. 'Shout as much as you like,' she said wearily, 'we all know it won't make any difference. No one's listening. You might as well save your breath. They're not going to release us, just because you make a nuisance of yourself. All you'll do is provoke them, and how is that going to help?'

'Leave him alone, he's an addict,' someone else called out. 'He can't help himself.'

We hurtled round a corner and I was thrown against the side of the cart. Gritting my teeth against the pain of the impact, I lowered myself awkwardly down beside the old woman, cradling my bruised arm. Specks of dust that had been disturbed as we swung around the bend settled back on the floor as we continued along a straight path.

'Where are they taking us?' I whispered.

Hunched over, the woman did not respond. It was possible she had not heard me above the rattling of the cart.

'Where are they taking us?' I repeated, raising my voice.

'Where are they taking us?' the plump-faced man echoed. 'Where are they taking us? Where do you think they are taking us? To the citadel of course. Where else would they be taking us?'

He turned away and began beating a loud tattoo on the side of the cart with his chained hands. After a few moments the cart jerked to a halt, and the back wall fell away. As the end of the ramp hit the ground, a Guardian tramped up the slope and stood at the top, blocking our exit. He raised his blow pipe to his lips and his head swivelled slowly, staring at each of us in turn. The protestor stood perfectly still, watching, his arms poised to strike the side of the cart again. With a sudden roar, he whirled round and launched himself straight at the Guardian.

One shot was enough. The man's outstretched arms had not even reached the Guardian when he fell to the floor where he lay sprawled, his eyes rolling, the chains on his wrists jangling with the twitching of his limbs. The Guardian turned and marched back down the ramp. The wall closed up and we began to move again, further away from my home and everything I had ever known.

'I warned him, didn't I?' the woman beside me remarked listlessly.

No one else took any notice of the dying man. Leaning back against the side of the cart, I closed my eyes, trying to shut out the memory of what had happened. The stranger had meant nothing to me. We had never set eyes on one another before that night. I just happened to be the last person he had spoken to before he died, the last human face he ever set eyes on. He seemed to take a long time to die, but at last he stopped writhing and groaning.

For the first time, the reality of what had happened that night overwhelmed me, and I wondered how I was going to survive without my mother. Constantly worried about my future, she had warned me that she would not live forever, but the plans she had discussed related to a distant future, when I would be old, and I had paid little attention to her concerns. Neither of us had expected her to die while I was barely more than a child. She must have known it was possible she would be taken before her time, but she had chosen to shield me from the truth.

The hard wall rubbed against my back as the cart jolted on the uneven surface of the road. I sat there numb with horror, desperate for this ordeal to end, yet fearful of what might follow. The night was cold and dark, as well as dangerous, and I yearned to go home and curl up in the security of my mother's warmth in bed beside me. Even though I had seen her die it was hard to believe that I would never go home to her.

At last, after travelling up a steep incline, the cart stopped, and we prisoners were herded down the ramp into a courtyard bordered on every side by high stone walls. Tall towers rose up at intervals along the battlements, with sentries positioned on a platform at the top of each tower, while yet more Guardians paced along the top of the crenelated walls.

Somewhere down in the streets of the city, far below the citadel, my mother's body would be gathered up, tossed into a communal death cart, and taken away to be consumed by fire. Not knowing whether her corpse had yet been consigned to the flames was upsetting, but it made no real difference to me. Knowing when it happened would not ease my grief. Resolutely, I thrust these thoughts of my dead mother from my mind and refused to weep for her as she deserved. It was important for me to remain alert so that I could contrive to stay alive. If I was killed, it would be as though my mother had never existed. Preserving my own life was all I could do to honour her memory.

One by one the prisoners were led away. Some accepted their fate quietly; others raged against their captivity. The Guardians dragged them all off, impervious to protests and pleas. Finally, a Guardian grabbed my arm and marched across the courtyard, forcing me to run to keep up with him, while my chains scraped painfully against my ankles. Frightening though the journey through the streets had been, this was worse, because at least there had been other prisoners with me in the cart. Now I was alone. Bending down to enter through a low opening in the wall, the Guardian propelled me along a winding corridor lit by occasional flickering torches, until we reached a dank stone dungeon. The Guardian shoved me and I stumbled through the door. By the light of a torch in the passageway, I glimpsed the interior of the cell and saw nothing: no bed and no pisspot, and no handle on the inside of the heavy metal door which clanged shut, leaving me in darkness. Feeling my way around the wall to the door, I pushed against it, and succeeded only in bruising my shoulder. The metal did not even quiver. Squatting on the floor, I stared into the darkness and wept until my eyes stung.

Being left alone in absolute darkness was truly terrifying. My mother had always been at my side, scolding me and looking out for me. Whenever she had to leave me alone, she was never gone for long. Now, not only would I never see her again, I might never see another living face before I died. The prospect filled me with horror. In desperation, I felt for my grandmother's picture in my waistband. There was no point in taking it out since I could not look at it. Even so, just knowing it was there gave me some poor comfort. My mother had told me that people had once been happy. Recalling her words seemed to offer some faint promise of hope that at least happiness was possible. But as the time passed, with no sign of relief from my dark cell, I cursed myself for wanting the Guardians to preserve my life when they could so easily have killed me, along with my mother. For the first time I understood her bitterness that her life had been saved. Only then did I remember that the Guardian who had killed my mother had also kept my food card. Even if they released me from captivity, I would starve to death unless they returned it to me.

After what felt like never-ending solitude, I was actually relieved when the door opened to admit a Guardian. His thunderous voice echoed round the cell, making my ears throb after the long silence.

'Come with me.'

He led me along an ill lit corridor, my shackles chafing my ankles as I shuffled behind him. After many twists and turns in the narrow corridor, we entered a large square chamber where two chairs faced each other across a table. The Guardian pushed me down on one of the chairs where I sat, the manacles on my wrists rattling as I shivered with fright. The Guardian left the room without removing my fetters, and I was alone again.

Time crawled by. I struggled to reassure myself that they would not have brought me to this room only to leave me seated there, but it seemed they had forgotten about me. I was unaccustomed to sitting on chairs and after a while my back started to ache. However much I wriggled, it was impossible to find a comfortable position, but when I attempted to stand up I discovered that my ankle chains had been wound around the legs of the chair, securing me in place. Groaning, I lowered myself back onto the seat. Telling myself that what was to come might be even worse than this, I tried to focus on the positive aspects of my situation. At least I was alive, and had a chair to sit on, even it was uncomfortable. But it was difficult to hope for anything other than a swift end to my misery.

Eventually the door swung open to admit a Guardian who stepped into the room without speaking, and positioned himself beside the door. A second Guardian entered the room and approached me. All I could see of his face were his thin lips and square chin, as he towered over me.

'You communicated with the woman, Clare?' he demanded.

I nodded. There was no point in denying what they already knew.

'Speak!' the deep voice thundered.

'Yes, I knew her,' I mumbled. 'She was our neighbour.' My mouth felt dry and my voice sounded hoarse.

'The woman, Clare, was your friend?'

I hesitated. If I confessed to a friendship, the Guardians might condemn me for fraternising with her. At the same time, I had already admitted to knowing her, and if the Guardians thought I was lying to them, that would also be considered a transgression. In my panic, I could not think what to say.

'An answer is required! Refusal to comply is not an option.'

'We weren't friends exactly,' I blurted out at last. 'She was never my friend. She was our neighbour. My mother knew her. My mother was her friend.' It made no difference to my mother if they believed she had been friends with a transgressor. Nothing could hurt her anymore. Even after her death, my mother was protecting me. In that moment I realised that I was not clinging to life merely to honour my mother. I wanted to live for myself. I wanted to feel the cool of the night air on my face once again. And I wanted to experience happiness, like my grandmother before me.

'Clare was older than me,' I said, hoping the Guardian would appreciate my effort to be obliging.

'The age is known.' His words reverberated around the room, seeming to resonate inside my skull, until I felt my head would explode.

'Where is the woman, Clare?'

'I don't know where she is,' I stammered. 'I thought you took her away. How would I know where she went?'

'When did you last see the woman, Clare?'

As it happened, I remembered very clearly the last time I had seen her. How could I forget the night she had come to our home to beg my mother to save her life by sharing our pills with her? But I had no intention of telling a Guardian anything he might not already know. As my thoughts whirled, he repeated his question.

'I can't remember when I last saw her,' I muttered. 'It was years ago.'

'Where is she now?'

'I don't know. She disappeared a long time ago.'

'What do you mean by that? Humans do not disappear. They live or they burn. There are no other options. Where did she go?'

'She lived next door to us, until one day we discovered someone else had moved into her room. That was how we knew she had been taken away and wasn't coming back.'

'Where did the woman, Clare, go after she left her home?'

'I don't know,' I insisted.

My interrogator did not seem to be listening to me and I replied to his questions with growing unease, aware that I could not give him the answers he was seeking. 'We thought you had taken her, because she went away without any warning. I thought she was my mother's friend, but she never told us she was leaving. She just disappeared.'

Like me, I thought. I too had disappeared, without warning, in the middle of the night. The only difference was that no one would notice my absence.

The Guardian growled, a horrible, guttural sound that seemed to grow louder as it echoed around the walls. 'Tell me where the woman, Clare, is.'

Terror made me bold. 'Not until you tell me what you are going to do with me.'

'Your fate is unimportant,' he roared. 'We need to find the one called Clare. Humans cannot disappear. It is not an option. Where is she? Tell me now.'

'I can't tell you where she is, because I don't know.'

With a grunt, the Guardian who had been interrogating me

turned stiffly on his heel and left, and the other Guardian marched me to an unlit cell, identical to the one where I had spent the night. It could have been the same cell.

As the Guardian began to close the door, I shouted out in panic. 'What do you want with me?'

After the heavy door clanged shut, a fit of crying shook me until my eyes again felt raw. Exhausted, I lay down on the hard floor, too weary to sleep, and tried to make sense of what had happened. Ever since her disappearance, I had assumed Clare was dead, but with the Guardians so keen to find her, it seemed she had left home before they could apprehend her. It was even possible she had survived, and was living in the city, evading capture. Although I could not seriously believe she was still alive, the thought of her escaping from the Guardians' clutches lifted my spirits. Just the idea that she might be free seemed like a glorious blow against the power of the Guardians, meaning they were not invincible. But I knew that was a foolish thought.

I must have fallen into an uneasy doze because I was woken by noises that reached me from the corridor outside my cell. Heavy boots tramped past and deep voices bellowed. The door swung open and a Guardian shouted at me to get up. Weak with hunger, I followed him along several long passageways, and right out of the building. Daylight blazed painfully in my eyes as we walked across a walled yard and through a high gate to the street, where a cart was waiting for us. The Guardian shoved me inside the conveyance, the ramp was raised, and we set off, jolting along the street. A handful of other captives were already in the cart, all of them in chains, most of them slumped against the sides of the cart, their eyes vacant. A white-haired old man lay on the floor beside me, muttering that he wanted to die. In the dim light I saw that his hands were bound behind his back, and his skinny legs were shackled together.

'What happened to you?' I asked, but he did not answer.

Staring into his eyes, I wanted to ease his distress but could think of nothing comforting to say. Meanwhile, the other prisoners stared straight ahead, paying no attention to one another. I shivered, no longer locked in a cell by myself, yet still isolated. We descended a long incline, away from the barricaded citadel, and then travelled along level streets through the city.

After a long time, the cart stopped and I was dragged out into the street where my shackles were removed. Two of the Guardians began pulling at ropes to raise the ramp, preparing to continue their journey.

I ran over to the nearest Guardian and asked where we were. He ignored me. I dashed over to his companion. 'Where am I? Where's my home? What's going to happen to me? Why are you leaving me here?'

Like his companions, he took no notice of me. With the ramp secured back in place, they strode to the front of the cart, their boots beating a loud tattoo on the ground. Slipping yokes around their broad necks, they rejoined their team and prepared to pull. The leader barked an order, and the cart set off, jolting down the street. Uncertain whether to feel relieved or terrified, I watched it disappear round a corner, leaving me outside a large grey building in a strange part of town. The sun beat down on me as I gazed around, trying to work out where I was, and why the Guardians had left me there. It was a relief to know that they had lost interest in me, but I was alone in an unfamiliar district of the city, with three pills left in my pouch, only one of which was a hydration pill. At a stretch, I could make my supply last six or seven days, but if I did not find a food clinic soon, I would starve, if the monsters that roamed the streets at night did not find me first. And I had no food card.

The buildings that surrounded me rose higher than those in the area where I had spent my childhood, but they were constructed of the same dull grey stone. From a distance the walls appeared smooth and clean, but close up they looked pitted and dirty, like the walls of my home. The windows were also familiar, narrow slits placed high above eye level, so that although they admitted light into the rooms, it was impossible to peer through them from outside. Pressing my back against the wall of a large building to shelter from the blazing sun, I wondered how to find my way home, if my home still existed. Perhaps a stranger had already moved into the room where my mother and I had once lived, while I was left to starve to death on the street.

3

THE FACILITY

While I stood, numb with indecision, an unfamiliar figure appeared, walking with an agile grace that gave the impression he could run very fast when he chose. From a distance, I was puzzled to see that his steps did not appear to disturb the dust that lay everywhere on the ground. Too small to be either Guardian or monster, when he drew near I saw that he was not much older than me. I watched him warily, and his grey eyes gazed back at me with bold curiosity.

'Hello there,' he greeted me with a friendly smile. 'I haven't seen you out on the streets before. Where did you spring from? Are you lost? You look lost.'

Never having spoken to a boy before, let alone a stranger, I was uncertain how to respond, but his confidence was reassuring, and I made no move to run away. He could easily have outrun me had I made the attempt and, in any case, I had nowhere to go. He obviously belonged to one of the feral gangs that roamed the streets, dodging Guardians and stealing from food carts and clinics, pilfering and haggling to survive, and I had nothing on me that was worth stealing. If he took my last three pills, it would only shorten my life by a few days.

'Don't be afraid,' he went on, taking another step towards me. 'My name's Gideon. Who are you?'

'Rachel,' I replied, hoping he might be able to explain what was happening to me. 'Did the Guardians abandon you here too?'

'The Guardians?' To my amazement he burst out laughing, without a hint of fear or deference in his voice. 'I'd keep well away from those monsters if I were you.'

'The Guardians aren't monsters,' I blurted out, shocked by his heresy; everyone knew the Guardians protected us from monsters.

'Aren't they?' he replied, with a mischievous grin. 'Are you sure about that?'

Remembering how Clare had been robbed in the street, I backed away from him.

Gideon smiled at me. 'There's no need to be scared. I'm not going to hurt you.'

'That's easy to say,' I replied, 'but I know you rob people on the street. It happened to my neighbour and she was left to starve.'

'You have no right to jump to conclusions about me, and judge me, when you don't even know the first thing about me,' he replied indignantly. 'Your neighbour must have been attacked by one of the gangs that run wild on the streets, scrounging and stealing, but you can't blame me for something I didn't do, and would never do. I'm no parasite, and I'm not a thief.'

'Who are you then?' I asked. 'Where do you live?'

He was about to answer, when a woman's voice called my name urgently. I spun round to see a stranger beckoning to me from the imposing doorway of the large grey building behind me.

'Rachel, you are welcome.' She smiled at me with

extraordinarily red lips. Reaching out, she grasped my hand firmly. 'We have been waiting for you. Now come inside, you must be tired, my dear.'

She was right, I was exhausted. All I wanted was to go home and lie in my own bed and think about my mother, and make plans about how I was going to manage on my own.

'Come along, Rachel,' the red lips mouthed, as though she could read my thoughts. 'This will be your home from now on.' The woman was short, around my height, and her greying hair was scraped back off her face and wound into a tight bun at the nape of her neck, giving her a sharp look, as though her eyes were about to bulge out of her face. But what struck me most about her was that she appeared to be unnaturally clean. She half turned towards the building behind her, my hand gripped firmly in hers, and her eyes still fixed on me. Unnerved by her intensity, I tried to pull away but she held on tightly when I attempted to free my hand.

'No, this is a mistake,' I protested. 'This isn't my home. I already have a home.'

Her smile did not waver as she pulled me towards the open door. 'Come along, Rachel. This is your home now.'

'What do you mean? What is this place? How do you know my name? Please, I just want to go home.'

'Don't think about what has happened. You will never find peace until you learn to put everything that has happened to you before this moment out of your mind. Memories belong in the past. Forget them. Now come in and see your new home. This is your future. Come on,' she urged me. 'It will soon be dark, and you don't want to be out on the street at night. If the Guardians don't pick you up, there are others who come out at night.'

I glanced over my shoulder, but the grey-eyed boy had vanished, and the woman was right when she warned me about dangers that lurked in the darkness. My mother had told me about them often enough. Finding my way back home would have to wait until the morning. Shivering, I allowed the woman to usher me into a wide entrance hall, where the air was heavy with a rich and potent scent. I reeled at its sweetness, and would have lost my footing if the woman had not been holding my arm. For a moment I struggled to breathe, overwhelmed by a giddy sensation. Until that moment, the only smells I had encountered were the stale odours of my home and the public baths, the tang of the food clinic where I had gone every month to be weighed and measured, and the stench of the dungeon in the citadel.

For the first time in my life, I discovered that a fragrance could be exquisite, and I wanted to stand in that hallway forever, transported by every heady breath.

Observing my expression, the woman's watchful expression relaxed and she let go of my hand. 'It is time I introduced myself. My name is Vanessa,' she said. 'I will be responsible for your welfare from now on, until you are ready to leave The Facility.'

Several white doors led off the wide vestibule, with nothing to indicate what lay behind them. Further away, a bright pink door opened to admit a group of young women dressed in white overalls. They nodded at Vanessa before ascending a wide white staircase and disappearing. All of them were clean and well groomed, like Vanessa herself.

'Those women are so beautiful,' I murmured, filled with awe. 'Have you brought me here to serve them?' In that moment, I could think of nothing more wonderful.

Vanessa smiled. 'On the contrary, my dear, they are here to serve you.'

That made no sense, but before I could question Vanessa further, something else caught my eye. Facing the front door, the gigantic black mask of a Guardian was displayed on a massive white plinth.

'Having a mask guarding the front door makes everyone here feel safe,' Vanessa explained, following my gaze. 'And it stays there to remind us that we're never alone. Whatever we do, the Guardians are always watching over us. That is why we must show our gratitude, however hard it may be,' she added with a shrewd glance at me, as though she could see fear in my face.

Struggling to conceal my trepidation, I nodded. Clearly Vanessa had never watched a Guardian seize an innocent woman by the neck and casually squeeze the life out of her, nor had she been thrown into a cart and incarcerated in a prison cell for no reason. A stranger in the street had warned me that the Guardians themselves were monsters, a claim that contradicted everything my mother had taught me. Yet a Guardian had killed her in what had surely been a wicked act. I was so confused, and overwhelmed with the trauma of the past few days, that I stumbled and nearly collapsed.

'Come with me, my dear,' Vanessa said.

Even my mother had never spoken so kindly to me. Too confused to resist, I let her take my hand and lead me along a gleaming white corridor and up a wide flight of stairs.

'Tread carefully,' she said. 'The floor has been polished.'

Looking down, I realised there was no dust anywhere, nor any other sign of dirt. The white walls and floor shone as though they had been scrubbed. At the top of the stairs was another plinth, with a mask identical to the one by the entrance. Hiding a shudder, I followed Vanessa through a white door and was dumbfounded at the sight of a row of pink baths supported on elaborately curling golden legs.

My mother took me to the city baths once a month to immerse my body in rancid oil, brown and musty, but the liquid here was a delicate pink, and it gave off a wonderful soothing scent. Vanessa instructed me to remove all my clothes before entering the bath, which was as comforting as a warm embrace. I could have lain there forever, feeling the tension ease away from my aching muscles and bruised flesh. All my recent troubles seemed to fade away as I breathed in the sweet perfume of the oil. Even my mother's death felt like a strange dream that had happened to someone else in another life.

While I lay there transported by wonderful new sensations, the door opened to admit a woman holding two large jugs of steaming oils. Kneeling beside my bath she told me to lower my head in the bath. Too tired to protest, I let her clean my hair. The task completed she left, taking her oils with her. By now the liquid in my bath was soiled and had begun to cool. Reluctantly I hauled myself out of the tub and wrapped a soft white towel around my body. Against the surprising pallor of my flesh, the sparse hairs between my legs looked strangely black. Until now, they had merged with the grime and grease on my body so that I had scarcely noticed them. My clothes had been removed, so I pulled on a fleecy pink gown and matching slippers that had been left for me. They felt unbelievably soft against my skin, like a gentle caress. I wondered whether Vanessa would allow me to keep the gown when I went home.

As though she knew I was ready, Vanessa returned to escort me out of the room. Enquiring what had happened to my clothes, I learned they had been taken away.

'You won't be needing them here,' Vanessa explained.

'Where have you taken them?' I demanded, upset by this unexpected development. 'I want them back.'

'I'm afraid that's not possible. But don't worry. You will have lovely new clothes here.'

'What about my waistband?'

Vanessa smiled. 'Don't fret about that. You won't be needing it anymore. Believe me, you will be well looked after here.'

Dismayed at the loss of my grandmother's picture, I wondered whether to mention it to Vanessa, but decided the safest option was to keep quiet about it. 'I want my clothes back,' I insisted, but Vanessa told me they had already been disposed of.

'Don't worry, my dear,' she repeated. 'Everything's been taken care of. There's nothing more to discuss. Now come along, it's your bedtime and, goodness knows, you need your beauty sleep.'

I had no choice but to follow her down a long white corridor. We passed several white doors before she stopped, rapped once, and then opened a door without waiting for a response. Four tall white cupboards stood in a row along one wall. Each had a full-length shiny metal sheet on the outside, and in the clear reflection I saw four beds covered in frilly pink lace. Three girls who looked about the same age as me were lying on three of the beds. The fourth bed was empty and looked as though it had never been slept in.

With a flutter of unease, I turned to Vanessa. 'Can you please give me back my clothes and tell me how to get home? I don't belong here.' If I left right away, the boy with grey eyes might still be outside in the street, and perhaps he would be able to help me. He had seemed friendly.

Two of the girls sat bolt upright in their beds as I spoke and looked at one another, giggling. They both had sleek blonde hair which they wore straight and loose, and their faces were exquisite, with clean pink skin and bright eyes. The third girl remained lying supine on her bed. Her dark hair had fallen across her face, so that all I could see of her were untidy curls hanging past her shoulders. For a second I was reminded of my mother and had to struggle not to cry out. As I watched, the girl flicked her hair off her face, staring at the ceiling all the while.

'You'll be sleeping in here,' Vanessa said, ignoring my request for my clothes to be returned. 'I'm sure you'll all get along fine, won't you?' she added, turning to the other girls. 'You know it's an essential part of your training to learn to behave courteously at all times.'

'Yes, Vanessa,' the two blonde girls chorused. 'We will all get along, Vanessa.'

Their dark-haired room-mate lay quite still with her eyes closed, but her eyelids flickered as though she was listening.

The prospect of a soft place to lie down was tempting, although any bed at all would have felt comfortable right then, after the floor of my cell at the citadel. Besides, I had no clothes other than the fleecy pink gown I had put on after my bath, and no proper shoes. 'I think I can live with this for one night,' I said, sitting on the empty bed which bounced invitingly.

'One night?' the dark-haired girl echoed, without opening her eyes.

'Yes. I'll stay here tonight, seeing as it's after the curfew, but I'll be off tomorrow. I want to go home.'

'In your dreams,' the dark-haired girl muttered. She half sat up. Leaning on one elbow, she smiled sadly at me. 'I'm Hester. What's your name?'

After introducing myself, I explained that my arrival there was a mistake that was bound to be discovered and put right in the morning. 'It's not that I've got anything against any of you,' I added hurriedly, afraid of alienating all three of them when we were forced to spend the night in the same room.

'You're the one who's making a mistake,' Hester replied. 'If they bring you here, it's because they want you here. They don't make mistakes. And they won't let you leave. You can't just walk out.' Flinging herself back down on her bed, she added, 'You'll find out soon enough that nothing's like what you're expecting here. It's all very different.'

Before I could enquire what she meant, one of the other girls spoke. 'Why do you have to be so crabby all the time, Hester? You're so ungrateful. You may think you're being original, but it's not in the slightest bit charming.'

Hester sat up and folded her arms across her chest. 'I'd rather not be here, that's all.'

'Where would you rather live? Out there?' the other blonde girl joined in. 'At least we're safe in here. And you can't pretend they don't look after us well.'

Her blonde companion agreed. 'It's very nice here. We don't have to queue for pills, and they keep us clean and make us look pretty.'

'What's the point of looking pretty if no one ever sees us?' Hester retorted crossly.

'We can see each other. And it's important for us to learn how to look pretty. Or it will be soon.'

The two blonde girls giggled, and Hester flopped back down on her bed again and hid her face in her pillow.

'Don't take any notice of her,' one of the other girls told me. 'She's always in a bad mood.'

Recovering from their laughter, my blonde room-mates introduced themselves as Naomi and Judith. They told me they were both fourteen, a year older than me. Naomi told me she had been living with Vanessa for five years. 'I'm an orphan,' she explained.

When I said I was sorry to hear that, she shook her head vehemently.

'Don't be silly. I'm much better off now.'

Judith had been living there for as long as she could remember. So far as she knew, her parents were dead. Right now, they confided, they were both waiting impatiently for their fifteenth birthdays.

'And we all know what that means,' Naomi giggled.

Judith beamed. 'We're going to be married and live in luxury for the rest of our lives.'

'Because our husbands will be rich, and they're going to buy us gorgeous gowns and we'll have beauty treatments every week,' Naomi cried out.

'Every day, more like,' Judith said.

They both fell back on their beds, giggling hysterically, and I could not help smiling. Naomi and Judith seemed to be having fun, and their glee was infectious. When I told them I would come back and visit them as often as I could, even Hester laughed. Naomi and Judith were still chattering and giggling as I fell asleep, too tired even to climb under the soft covers on my bed.

Daylight was streaming in when I opened my eyes to see Hester sitting up, watching me intently.

'Hello,' I said. 'Why are you staring at me?'

She did not answer.

'Tell me about this place,' I said, sitting up. 'Have you been here long?'

Hester turned and glanced over at the other two girls before leaning towards me, so that they could not hear her whisper. She told me that the place was called The Facility, and she had been there for three years. 'Before that I lived with my mother, but I was brought here when she disappeared.'

'What do you mean, "she disappeared"?'

'Exactly that. The Guardians came for us in the middle of the night and locked me in a cell, and the next morning they brought me here. I never found out what happened to my mother.'

She was going to say more, but Naomi leapt out of bed and bounded over to us. 'Is Hester at it again? She's always grumbling. She can be a real drag, and she's always going on about her mother. Don't let her get you down.' She turned to

Hester. 'How many times do you have to be told that you don't need your mother in here, you dummy.'

After a good night's sleep, I was feeling cheerful enough to agree with Naomi. Of course it was desperately sad that Hester had lost her mother, in much the same way as I had lost mine, but there was nothing either of us could do about it. In any case, I was not planning to stay around for long enough to hear more of Hester's complaints.

'Well, I'm leaving today,' I announced brightly.

'Leaving?' Naomi asked, looking puzzled.

'Yes, I'm going home.'

Hester shook her head. 'That's what I used to think. For weeks I waited to leave, but I've been here for three years now. The truth is, they weren't interested in my mother. This is all about us. We're the ones they want.'

'I don't understand,' I replied. 'What would anyone want with me?'

'Isn't it obvious?' Hester replied. 'It's the same reason they brought the rest of us to The Facility. We're here for The Programme.'

4

THE PROGRAMME

Hester seemed to like speaking in riddles. Before I could ask her to explain what programme she was talking about, a bell shrilled. At the piercing tone, Naomi sprang to her feet and hurried over to one of the cupboards, while at the same time, Judith scrambled out of bed and dashed to another.

'It's time to get dressed!' Naomi cried out. 'Come on! You too, Rachel. You need to get a move on! We can't be late.'

'A trainee is never late,' Naomi and Judith chorused in unison, as though repeating a rule they had learned by rote.

Their excitement puzzled me, until I saw the clothes they were taking out of their cupboards. Naomi held up one magnificent gown after another in front of her mirror, swaying her hips and extending her neck, trying to decide what to wear. Judith's wardrobe was similarly packed with brightly coloured clothes which she began rifling through.

'The end wardrobe is yours,' Naomi told me. 'Choose an outfit and get dressed, Rachel, and for goodness sake hurry. Vanessa will be here soon, and we have to be ready. We're not allowed to be late.'

'A trainee is never late,' she and Judith chorused again.

Opening my wardrobe, I gazed at a multitude of dresses of different lengths and colours, that formed a dazzling rainbow of varied fabrics, some shiny and flowing, others soft and fleecy, and yet more, lacy and gauzy, or sparkling with tiny gems. On one side of the hanging space, shelves were filled with frilly undergarments of every colour imaginable, and the other side of the wardrobe was stacked with pairs of shoes in different styles and colours, all of which had long narrow pointed toes. Some of the shoes were decorated with ribbons and bows, others with gems and embossed patterns. Until that moment I had never felt shabby, but now I was ashamed of my customary threadbare grey clothes and tattered sandals.

'Go on,' Naomi urged me. 'What are you waiting for?'

'Those dresses are for you,' Hester explained, with a curious smile. 'That's why they're hanging there, waiting for you to take them out and wear them. You're going to stay here, whether you like it or not, so you might as well accept the bribe gracefully. All you have to do is smile and look pretty. That shouldn't be too much of a challenge for a girl with your looks. Don't look so anxious. Nothing about the life here is hard if you remember your orders, and never question anything. Just copy Naomi and Judith, and you won't go too far wrong. All they think about is their dresses, and their hair, and their shoes. They're perfect role models for you because they always do exactly what they're told.'

Busy looking at the dresses hanging in her wardrobe, Judith took no notice of Hester's mockery, but Naomi spun round and shook her head, her hands on her hips.

'Careful, Naomi,' Hester sneered. 'You nearly frowned there. Don't forget it will give you wrinkles on your forehead. We can't have that, can we?'

'Don't you ever give it a rest, Hester?' Naomi snapped.

'What's so bad about following The Programme? Aren't we looked after well enough for you?'

'Remember not to let your anger show in your face,' Hester replied. 'You don't want ugly lines spoiling your pretty face.' She turned to me and spoke very rapidly in a low voice. 'Naomi and Judith will tell you we should be grateful to Vanessa for taking care of us, because that's what we're taught to believe. But we don't have to agree with everything they say, do we?'

'We appreciate our good fortune in being chosen, if you don't,' Judith replied primly, still rifling through her gowns.

'Good fortune?' Hester retorted, her voice rising with indignation.

'Why don't you leave, then, if that's what you want?' Naomi asked, glaring at Hester. 'Go on, starve on the streets, or be carried off by monsters and ripped limb from limb in the wilderness beyond the city, if you prefer. Because we all know that's where you're going to end up if you carry on like this.'

'Yes, do stop being an idiot, Hester,' Judith chimed in, strutting across the room in high-heeled shoes, with a glittering gown over her arm. 'We're safe here and, like Naomi said, we're well looked after. There's no way you really want to leave. For a start, where would you go?'

'You're just showing off in front of the new girl,' Naomi added. 'It doesn't make you look clever or interesting. It's just stupid and boring.'

Distracted by the colourful clothes hanging in my wardrobe, it was easy to ignore their squabbling. Slipping into a bright yellow dress, I watched the skirt swirl around my legs as I twisted my hips. As if the dress was not gorgeous enough on its own, Naomi helped me to find matching yellow shoes. They pinched my toes, but she assured me that we would not have to walk far.

'They're really tight,' I complained.

'You get used to it,' Naomi assured me.

'After a while you'll hardly notice you're wearing them,' Judith agreed.

'And these are definitely the right shoes for that dress, no question about it,' Naomi said. 'You can't possibly wear any others.'

'The shoes must match the dress,' Naomi and Judith chorused together.

Studying myself in the mirror, I smiled, despite my discomfort. My reflection was nowhere near as glamorous as the other girls, with their shiny hair, clear skin and bright eyes, but I looked lovely all the same. My elation was only diminished by the thought that my mother would never see me wearing such beautiful clothes.

'Now it's just your hair and nails to go, and you'll be one of us,' Naomi said, stepping back to admire my outfit. 'Go on, swing your hips and turn around. You know you're going to be stunning, Rachel, absolutely stunning.'

Suddenly I was not sure I wanted to look stunning. Everything that had happened since my arrival at The Facility felt weird, as though I was playing a part in someone else's fantasy. But there was no time to examine my bewilderment, because as soon as we had finished dressing, there was a sharp rap at the door, and Vanessa entered. We were instructed to line up against the wall while she inspected us.

Naomi was dressed in a short pink frock with matching stockings and shoes, and a large matching bow in her hair.

Judith had chosen a bright blue outfit, with long gauzy skirts that looked as though they were light enough to float away.

Even Hester had made an effort, and was wearing a striking green gown, with a matching band around her head that had strings of sparkling green beads hanging from it.

After nodding at the other three girls, to indicate her

satisfaction, Vanessa studied me carefully, from head to foot. She smiled when she saw my shoes. 'Well done,' she murmured approvingly. 'I see you learn fast.'

'Naomi helped me choose the shoes,' I replied.

'Good, very good.' Vanessa nodded again. 'Modesty is a prized virtue. But tell me,' she went on, turning suddenly to Hester. 'What do you have on your feet?'

Naomi and Judith gasped. In all the fuss over my clothes, neither of them had noticed the grey ankle boots whose long, pointed toes were poking out from below Hester's green dress.

'I asked you a question,' Vanessa said coldly. Her eyes seemed to bulge dangerously, as though they were about to pop out of her face. 'What are you wearing on your feet?'

'Boots – grey boots–' Hester stammered, all trace of her former surliness gone. 'I thought the outfit might – I thought it might work with a grey belt,' she stammered. 'I was looking for a grey belt when you arrived.'

Vanessa drew in a deep breath. 'Very well,' she replied, sounding somewhat mollified. 'There's nothing wrong with trying something different once in a while, girls, but now can you please find the green shoes that match your dress, Hester, and keep those grey boots for a grey winter outfit. Remember, no one wears boots in the summer.'

'Clothes must suit the season,' Naomi and Judith trilled in unison.

These remarks struck me as curious, since the heat outside was consistently fierce all year round. I nearly asked Vanessa what she meant, but everything in this place puzzled me and, besides, I was feeling increasingly uncomfortable. Vanessa was cross, my shoes were painful, and I was not convinced that Hester's criticisms of The Facility were not justified, despite what the other girls said. So I kept silent.

'The boots are more comfortable,' Hester objected, with a resurgence of her earlier sullenness.

Vanessa's eyebrows shot up, so that her forehead creased. 'Now look what you've made me do,' she complained, lowering her eyebrows and smoothing her forehead with her fingers. 'Never raise your eyebrows, girls,' she told us earnestly. 'It causes unsightly lines that will make you look old. Now listen carefully, especially you, Hester. It doesn't do to be too adventurous in your choice of shoes and accessories. If you are sensible, you can't go wrong. But if you try to be original, or different, you risk making a dangerous blunder. Remember, your future security depends entirely on your appearance, so don't take unnecessary risks.'

'Yes, Vanessa,' Naomi and Judith chorused.

Muttering under her breath, Hester changed her footwear and we all lurched and limped along the corridor.

'Walk tall,' Vanessa chided us. 'Hold those heads up, girls.'

Our shoes were not only painfully narrow, but they had very high heels which Vanessa told us were called stilettos. Never having worn shoes with heels of any kind before, I teetered precariously, twisting my ankles as my feet lost their grip on the slippery floor. Each time I stumbled, Vanessa exhorted me to keep walking with my head held high, and reminded me not to scowl.

'You do not want a lined face as well as thick ankles,' she said. 'You will attend additional classes, Rachel, to help you learn how to walk elegantly in heels.'

Before I could retort that there was nothing wrong with my natural gait, which had never been a problem before I entered The Facility, Vanessa added that my daily bath would soothe my aching ankles. The memory of the fragrant oils of the bathroom silenced my protest.

Before long, I discovered that the programme we followed on my first day at The Facility was a daily routine. We spent the morning in a salon with gleaming white walls and floor, where we bathed while women rubbed scented lotion into our skin, and applied balm to our blistered feet, and soaked our hair in perfumed oils. They pasted grainy gum on our faces and scraped it off again, leaving the skin feeling fresh and alive, and removed all the hair from our bodies. After a few treatments, my dry hair became sleek and shiny, and was trimmed to the same length as Naomi and Judith's hair, and coloured a dark blonde. Judith and Naomi clapped their hands and squealed with excitement when they saw me, and Vanessa beamed and congratulated me. Even Hester said that my new hair style suited me.

Once our physical appearance had been attended to, we were given our pills and escorted to a spacious hall for lessons in deportment. We were trained to smile while walking in shoes that pinched and rubbed our feet, followed by lessons in facial expression, where we learned how to lower our eyes and look quietly cheerful while we were subjected to unpleasant noises and smells, designed to develop our ability to maintain our composure regardless of what was going on around us.

'Husbands do not like wives who complain or appear discontented,' our instructress explained. 'Serenity is paramount. Feel it from within.' She laid her hands on her chest to demonstrate. 'Breathe deeply and let the feeling flow through you, while you repeat "I am happy, I am happy, I am happy," to yourself. In silence, Naomi. There is no need to say the words aloud. Your serene smile should be enough, and remember the less you say, the better.'

Another woman instructed us in manners. 'Remember at all times that your role is to be looked at, not to be heard, unless a man invites you to speak. Never speak to a man, under any circumstances, unless it seems necessary, as in answering a question, for example, when it could be construed as disrespectful if you refused to respond. Men do not want to hear original thoughts from you, only the ones they have presented to you themselves. This protects you from making mistakes, and you must always express gratitude for the care that is showered on you.'

After our lessons, Vanessa lectured us. 'Never forget that you are the lucky few, chosen for this great privilege, to be lifted out of a life of poverty and suffering and adversity. The Programme will fit you to be wives. It is your duty to work hard to make sure you look beautiful at all times. Remember, your goal is to please the man who chooses you, so that he keeps you as his wife. The training is arduous, but the rewards will make all the hard work worthwhile.'

There was a lot more along those lines. Naomi and Judith appeared to listen attentively, smiling all the while, but Hester looked solemn throughout. As for me, I had very little idea what Vanessa or anyone else was talking about most of the time, and the speeches washed over me in a stream of meaningless words. They could have been addressing us in a foreign language for all the sense they made to me. The other girls seemed to understand what was meant by 'husband' and 'wife', but no one had yet explained to me what any of this had to do with our futures, or what was expected of us, and I did not want to look foolish by asking anyone to explain what our training was actually for. In the meantime, I did my best to dismiss my unease. We were kept clean and well fed, and slept in soft beds. For the time being, I was content to stay at The Facility. It was not as if I had any other choice.

Vanessa's occasional threats to throw Hester to the Guardians as a punishment for her insolence made it perfectly clear what my fate would be, if I failed to obey the rules of The Facility. Lying in bed at night, I tried to focus on how comfortable my situation was. In silence I repeated the words to myself, 'I am happy, I am happy, I am happy,' until the words lost their meaning and I was no longer sure what happiness meant. Vanessa had advised me to forget the past, but the truth was I had not felt truly happy since my mother's death. Once something good has been carelessly snatched away, it is difficult to trust that anything worthwhile will last. As I drifted off to sleep each night, in my comfortable bed, I would have gladly forfeited all the luxuries of my new life for the sound of my mother breathing softly beside me in the darkness of my childhood home.

5

THE WIFE

One evening, Vanessa informed us that we were to receive a very important visitor the following day. Hester looked faintly agitated, Judith grinned and clasped her hands together, and Naomi burst into tears.

Vanessa raised her hand in admonishment, clearly irritated by this outburst of emotion. 'No, no, no,' she berated Naomi. 'Stop this unseemly display at once. I cannot allow it, I simply cannot. Have some respect for your eyes, you foolish girl. Have you forgotten the importance of your appearance? You know very well that if you cry, your eyes will become red and swollen.' Her smile became fixed. 'Do you really want to look ugly? Such thoughtless damage can be irreparable, you stupid, stupid girl.'

'Is a future husband coming to view us tomorrow?' Judith gasped, her eyes alight with excitement. 'Oh, Naomi, do stop crying, for goodness' sake. You'll make your eyes look hideous.'

'No, of course it's not a viewing,' Vanessa snapped. 'That would be premature. You are nowhere near ready.'

Naomi dabbed at her eyes delicately with a dainty piece of cloth. 'When *will* we be ready?'

'When your education is completed, and you reach your

fifteenth birthday,' Vanessa replied. 'Until both those conditions are met, your training will continue exactly as it always has done. No, none of you is yet ready to be viewed.' She paused and looked at each of us in turn with an encouraging smile. 'But you are all well on your way, and that is why I have arranged for you to enjoy the privilege of meeting a real wife tomorrow. You must look your best, and watch and listen and learn as much as you can from our esteemed visitor. Soon you will need to emulate her success.' Her smile broadened. 'It will not be long now.'

Naomi and Judith seemed satisfied, but Hester looked uncomfortable. For my part, I remained perplexed about our expected visitor. The next morning, while Naomi and Judith were preoccupied deciding what to wear, I attempted to pry some information out of Hester. Seeing her seated on her bed, pulling on shiny stockings, I went and sat beside her and spoke very softly so that the others would not overhear my whispered questions.

'Hester, I want to ask you something,' I began. 'But I don't want the others to hear.'

She grunted.

'What did Vanessa mean when she said a wife is coming to visit us?'

Hester shook her head, and her long curls bounced against her shoulders. 'What does Vanessa ever mean?' she replied sourly. 'She means we have to behave ourselves and look our best. All you have to do is keep quiet, and put up with shoes that make your feet hurt, and you'll be all set for a life of luxury. That's what you want, isn't it? You and those other airheads. Don't worry. You must be by far the most beautiful pupil this Facility has ever trained, so you're bound to be chosen by one of the most important Council Members. I'm sure Vanessa's relying on your success to secure her reputation. We have to listen to everything we're told, and say nothing, so today won't be any different to any other day. Seriously, all you have to do is keep your mouth shut, and smile, and smile, and smile. That's all Vanessa wants us to do, smile and look beautiful. You shouldn't have any problem with that. So just keep smiling and don't say a word to anyone about anything. Got it?'

There was no time to press Hester for clarification. Of course I understood her advice about keeping quiet and looking cheerful. Modest contentment was expected of us at all times. But Hester had not explained anything, and I remained in the dark about the nature of the impending visit. The other girls were getting dressed, so I abandoned my attempt to coax information out of Hester, and hurriedly chose my attire for the day. It was never advisable to make such momentous decisions in a hurry, but time was running out and, if I was not careful, I would be late for Vanessa. The centre piece of the outfit I selected was a turquoise gown with a flatteringly tight bodice and an elegantly flared calf-length skirt. The matching shoes were as uncomfortable as all the other shoes in my wardrobe, but my feet were growing accustomed to the pain which was no longer quite as agonising as when I had first arrived, thanks to the ointments and gels that were applied to my feet night and day. Not only that, but the muscles in my face had grown accustomed to constantly smiling so there was no point in Hester taunting us about the expressions expected of us. As for her scornful tone, that was nothing new, and if her comments had not been illuminating, neither had they succeeded in making me share her negativity.

The wife surprised me. Her face was neatly but extravagantly painted, and she wore her mane of shining golden hair in a curious intricate fashion, twisted high on her head. It must have taken a long time to perfect that look. Her clothes were the most elaborate I had ever seen. Beneath the tightly fitting upper section of her frock, flounced skirts floated up and down as she glided into the room. Her expression did not alter as she took her seat, although her bodice must have been extremely uncomfortable. Her shoes were narrower and more pointed than any we trainees were expected to wear. She wore her nails very long and painted crimson, and jewelled rings sparkled on her fingers. Clearly she took great care over her appearance, yet she was so bloated, she hardly looked human. She resembled a small doll's head stuck on top of a giant torso with swollen limbs. She reminded me briefly of the photograph of my grandmother, and the rebel who had died in the cart on the way to the citadel after my mother was killed.

Vanessa did not seem to notice anything strange about our visitor, but introduced her with the utmost deference. 'This is Claudia, and she is the wife of a Council Member.'

Claudia sat completely still while Vanessa was speaking, her eyes downcast, a smile on her lips. She looked like a painted statue.

'Claudia was with us from the age of four, and became a wife when she was just fifteen,' Vanessa went on, nodding at our visitor with a proprietary air.

Naomi and Judith gazed in awe at the wife, who sat quietly on her chair, gazing modestly at the floor. At last she raised her head. A gold chain sparkled at her throat and bracelets jingled on her thick white wrists. 'I am happily married to a Member of The Council,' she said in a soft low voice, her eyes sliding past us without seeming to register our presence, although we were sitting right in front of her. 'I am his principal wife. My life as a wife is wonderful. Present yourselves well, girls, and you too could become wives. I have a wonderful life as a wife. I have lovely clothes, new perfumes are brought to me weekly, and my hair is oiled every day.'

She raised one hand to point elegantly at her head, as though we might not understand what she meant. 'My husband takes good care of me,' she went on. 'I am lucky to be a principal wife. I have a wonderful life. Work hard and you too could have wonderful lives as wives.'

She closed her painted lips, and rearranged her smile, and we all clapped enthusiastically. Vanessa cheered sedately. Even Hester was smiling dutifully. I wanted to ask why we were applauding Claudia's stupid speech, but Claudia was a wife, and that meant she was a success. Copying the other girls' perfect smiles, I joined in with their applause, and tried not to think about Hester's words, 'You might as well accept the bribe.'

One thing I had not realised before I joined The Programme, was how drab and colourless my life had been before I came to The Facility. As the weeks passed, I grew accustomed to my luxurious new environment, and the pain of losing my mother faded. My mourning could bring no comfort to her now, and she would not have wanted me to suffer on her account. Making a success of my new life was the only way I could honour my mother's memory and ensure that her death had not been for nothing. So I put aside my reservations, and came to embrace The Programme. Every morning, when we gathered to thank Vanessa for the blessed life she had given us, no one's gratitude was more heartfelt than mine.

When I had first arrived, my room-mates' chatter had bored me, but gradually I started to join in their discussions about clothes, shoes, hair, nails and make-up, and learned to understand that beauty was more important for a woman than anything else. Only the black helmets at the top and bottom of the staircase reminded me of a world outside The Facility, and I learned to avert my gaze when I walked past them. Days slipped into weeks and months. I scarcely noticed that my lips felt thick when I pressed them together, and my inner thighs brushed against each other as I walked, the skin soft and silky. One morning the buttons on my yellow dress would not fasten. Studying myself in the mirror, I saw that the fabric was stretched very tightly across my chest and hips.

'What has happened to this dress?' I cried out in dismay. 'How can it have shrunk like this?'

The other girls sniggered at my bewilderment. 'Haven't you noticed, we're all developing curves?' Naomi giggled.

'Curves in the right places,' Judith added smugly.

The changes had been taking place so gradually, that I had not noticed how our bodies were growing. Stupidly, I had attributed the differences in our appearance to the constantly changing fashions in gowns.

'It's because we're being prepared for breeding,' Judith explained. 'Don't you ever listen in lessons? As soon as we're fifteen we can be put on show, but no Member of The Council is going to be interested in viewing us if we don't have curves in the right places.'

'It's no good living like the women out there on the streets,' Naomi added, her habitual smile growing smug. 'None of them can ever become wives because they're underfed and that's why their bodies don't develop properly. We have to be fit for breeding, or we'll never be chosen, however beautiful we are.'

As we were getting ready for bed that evening, I glanced at the other girls' bodies as they undressed, observing their curved hips and swollen breasts and buttocks.

In the bath next morning, I studied myself. My lower parts were hidden in pink oils, but by resting my legs and forearms on the sides of the bath, I was able to lift my body above the surface. My thighs were plump and, below my swelling breasts, my stomach rose above the surface of the oil, smooth and round.

Without really noticing, I had developed from a skinny child into a well-fed woman.

Naomi and Judith had developed the same broad hips and large breasts as me. Only Hester had kept her childlike figure. One evening Vanessa summoned her for a chat. Above their constantly smiling lips, Naomi and Judith's fleetingly raised eyebrows registered their astonishment at my suggestion that Hester's family might have come to take her back home.

'You're not still harping on about leaving The Facility, are you?' Naomi said. 'That's such a stupid idea. Honestly, Rachel, how can you be so dense? No one leaves here to go back to their family. This is our home now, until we are chosen as wives.'

'Vanessa's reprimanding her,' Judith added. 'It's been coming for a while.'

'It must be about her weight,' Naomi added.

'How do you know?' I asked.

With exaggerated patience, Judith smiled at me as she explained that we had to reach a certain body weight before we could breed.

'That's what we're training for, dummy,' Naomi said. She sounded irritated, but her smile did not falter throughout the conversation. 'As soon as we're fifteen, and heavy enough to breed, we'll be put on display so someone on The Council can choose us as a wife. If we're lucky, he'll be rich.'

'And young. Don't forget our husbands must be young,' Judith replied, as though this was a familiar discussion.

'And good looking,' Naomi added.

'We'll be married in long white gowns smothered in jewels.'

'I'm going to continue having a bath every day for the rest of my life. Sometimes twice a day.'

'And we'll live in big houses with servants to keep us looking beautiful!'

They clapped their hands, giggling with glee. Grabbing hold

of one another's hands, they jigged around the room, dodging up and down between the beds. Laughing, I pulled my legs up onto my bed out of the way.

'That's why Hester's in trouble,' Naomi said, breathlessly, collapsing on her bed.

Neither Judith nor I criticised her for forgetting to sit down in a dignified manner, as we had been taught.

'If Hester doesn't reach the right body weight she won't be able to breed, and all the time she spent here will be wasted,' Judith said. 'Vanessa will be furious, after all she's done for her.'

'Hester's in serious trouble,' Naomi reiterated solemnly, her smile fixed.

Judith lowered her voice. 'I don't think she's even begun to bleed yet, she's so light.'

'If Vanessa has too many failures, she'll be replaced and end up starving on the street, like all the poor people out there,' Naomi said.

'It's not Vanessa's fault,' Judith protested softly. 'She does everything for us.'

'Think about it,' Naomi muttered. 'The medical team weigh us every day, and we are given the right pills to make us grow exactly as we should. If Hester isn't growing enough, well, you know what that means.'

She did not need to explain that Hester had not been taking her pills. In subdued tones, my room-mates discussed the possible reasons why Hester might not want to breed, and whether she was trying to kill herself. All the while, they both carried on smiling at one another while I listened, horrified. It had not occurred to me that Hester might be genuinely unhappy living at The Facility.

'I thought she just likes to complain,' I murmured.

'She's always so miserable,' Naomi said.

'Either way she's done for, if Vanessa can't persuade her to take her pills,' Judith replied.

'If you ask me,' Naomi said, 'it's already too late. Vanessa should expel her right now. Why let it drag on like this? If Hester doesn't appreciate what it means to be a wife, she shouldn't be here. If it was up to me, I'd get rid of her without any more ado, and give her place to someone who deserves to be here. It's not fair on us. We're working hard to make ourselves as beautiful as possible, and she's just messing around, taking advantage of all the luxury we enjoy here. Face it, she'll never be accepted as a wife looking like she does, so why waste money and effort on her?'

'It's not our money,' Judith pointed out.

'No, but someone's paying for her to be here, and the opportunity's being denied to another girl who might be really pleased to take advantage of the training.'

Judith's smile broadened. 'One less girl to compete against us for a husband.'

Naomi gave her a playful slap on the arm and they both laughed. Their joking touched on a question that had been bothering me. Although no one had ever said so, I suspected that not all of Vanessa's girls were successful. There were too many of us. Besides, Vanessa's was not the only Facility in the city. Yet no one ever talked about what would happen to us if we failed. When I asked my friends what provision was made for girls who followed The Programme and were not chosen as wives, they both promptly turned their backs on me.

'Shut up,' Naomi snapped, flapping one of her hands in the air.

'I don't even want to think about it,' Judith said.

It was clear we could not all be chosen to become wives, yet our training had made us fit for little else. If we failed, we would be thrown out on the street or taught to spend our days attending to other trainee wives, watching them pursue the dreams we had once cherished, until we grew too old to be of use.

'We have to find husbands,' Naomi said firmly. 'We just have to.'

'Of course we'll find husbands,' Judith agreed.

I hoped she was right.

The next morning, Hester was not in her bed.

'Better late than never,' Naomi said briskly. 'I told you Vanessa would get rid of her.'

'She didn't fit in here,' Judith agreed. 'It's a shame, really, after all that Vanessa did for her. I wonder what was wrong with her?'

'They never should have given her a place. We're supposed to be carefully vetted. Huh! Whoever selected Hester could hardly have got it more wrong. What a disaster! Poor Vanessa. I hope she doesn't get it in the neck for this.'

'What will happen to Hester now?' I asked.

'Who cares?' Naomi replied.

'Good riddance, if you ask me,' Judith said. 'She never should have been accepted on The Programme in the first place. I saw this coming ages ago.'

'We all did,' Naomi agreed.

'She tried to contaminate me with her corrupt ideas,' Judith said.

'Me too,' Naomi answered.

They both turned to look at me, and I confessed that Hester had frequently complained to me about The Programme.

'Not in so many words,' I added quickly, in case they challenged me to repeat some of Hester's sedition.

Naomi and Judith did not seem to care about our former room-mate, but Hester's absence upset me. Finally, I could bear it no longer, and asked Vanessa where she had gone.

With a bright smile, Vanessa told me to hurry or I would be late for the hair stylist. 'A trainee wife does not keep other people waiting,' she added, a hint of reproof in her voice.

With my thoughts in turmoil, I smiled and hurried to the salon.

6

THE CHOSEN

I was beginning to have an inkling about what having a husband meant. One day a man was going to take control of our lives, like Vanessa had done. Naomi and Judith were both better informed than me, and they both seemed extremely happy about the coming change in their lives. According to what they told me, having a husband was going to be wonderful. I looked forward to the future with excitement tinged with slight apprehension, because the unknown is always daunting.

Once a week we were given lectures to expand our general knowledge, in case our future husbands wanted a wife who was informed about the world. We were encouraged to learn about international affairs, while at the same time accepting that we must never express views of our own.

'It's best if you don't actually think about these matters for yourself at all,' our teacher explained. 'That way you avoid any risk of expressing an independent opinion. You need to be aware of what happened in the past without reaching any conclusions, allowing your judgement to be moulded purely by your husband. Imagine how difficult it would be if you held opinions different from those held by your husband.' Still smiling, she gave a fake shudder. 'What would he think of you? But at the same time, you must be a fit companion, should your husband turn out to be interested in the governance of the city.'

Hazel was a dried-up little woman whose age was difficult to judge. She recited lectures by rote, keeping her eyes fixed on a point above our heads. Her face was narrow and although she was not exactly ugly, she was certainly not attractive or even faintly interesting to watch. She had a small pointed nose and pale eyes, and wore her hair in a tiny bun, like Vanessa's. Her monotonous voice made it hard for me to concentrate, and I could not have been the only pupil whose mind wandered during her classes. Besides, understanding the causes of the Great Sickness was not as important as learning to walk gracefully in heels, or selecting the right shoes to complement a gown.

So I only half listened as Hazel told us about a global conflict that had erupted many years ago, between three territories called Korea, China, and Russia. The rulers of these three powerful states fell out over another territory called Middle Eastern. Hazel also talked about something called a World Wide Web, which made very little sense to me, although she devoted a whole lecture to it. From the little I understood, it provided a system that allowed people to communicate across long distances. The description of it stirred a vague memory of something our neighbour, Clare, had told me when I was a child, but I remained sceptical of such fanciful ideas. Naomi and Judith appeared to be attentive, but they were not really listening to our teacher either.

'What is the point of all these stupid history lessons?' Judith whispered when we were all in bed one evening. 'Hazel drones on and on and I don't know about you, but I barely understand half of what she says.'

'She makes it confusing because she doesn't understand it herself,' I replied. 'I switch off whenever she opens her mouth.'

'It's not as if it has anything to do with us anyway,' Judith complained. 'What do you think, Naomi?'

'I think you should both shut up,' Naomi replied. 'I need to get my beauty sleep, and so do you, if you've got any sense.'

I did not believe the ancient legends, and I was convinced our teacher did not believe any of it either. Some of her lectures were as fanciful as the stories Clare used to tell me about people flying across the sky in carts. According to our teacher, while Korea, China and Russia were struggling to gain power over each other, a territory called America joined in. There was a lot more about a contentious area called Middle Eastern that had somehow acted as a catalyst for all the troubles. By the time Hazel reached that part of the lesson, I had completely lost interest in the conflict between distant lands which, as far as anyone knew, no longer existed. She told us the conflict only ceased when all the peoples of the world were struck down by the Great Sickness that poisoned every form of life on earth. Only then, our teacher told us, did the enemy territories attempt to bury their differences and work together to save humanity from extinction.

'But by then it was too late,' she concluded sombrely. 'The land was poisoned and the human race was almost eradicated.' She looked at us with her practised smile. 'Almost but not entirely, of course. Billions of people died, but we survived to fulfil our destiny. You should feel proud of yourselves for being so special.' She paused.

'How many people died?' I asked. My smile hid my horror of her calm dismissal of the catastrophe.

Hazel nodded her approval of my question. 'Billions and billions,' she replied.

'What is billions?' Judith enquired.

'A bigger number than you can possibly imagine,' Hazel smiled.

'What would have happened if we hadn't been saved?' I asked.

'A wife does not speculate,' Hazel replied. 'Listen and learn, but do not ask questions. Remember, a wife's duties do not require her to think for herself.'

Clare's stories had been enthralling, but now I was too old for childish tales, and besides, there were more pressing matters to consider. Myths about legendary places were frivolous compared to the real-life problems we faced, worrying about our deportment and how to wear our hair. Meanwhile, Hazel's account of world history grew increasingly far-fetched. Even gullible Judith forgot herself and raised her eyebrows when we were told that people once lived without pills.

'It was only a few years after you were born that The Council gained control of the situation and life in the city settled down. Before that, everything descended into chaos, and people had to fend for themselves, without pills.'

'But that's impossible,' Naomi blurted out. 'Everyone would have starved.'

'No one would have survived without pills,' Judith agreed, her smile securely back in place. 'We wouldn't be here. No one would. Naomi's right. Everyone would have starved.'

'Not if they had other sources of nutrition,' Hazel pointed out.

'There aren't any other sources of nutrition,' Judith replied promptly.

'There aren't now, but before the Great Sickness, the population of the world was far too large for everyone to be issued with pills. How do you suppose they all survived? It's only in the last ten years that we have been so well looked after by

The Council. People back in those days were not issued with pills. They had to scavenge for nutrition.'

We all stared at Hazel, astounded. Although it was almost impossible to believe what she was telling us, in a way it made sense. She told us the problems had started with the conflict between Korea, China, Russia and America. The struggle between the leaders of the most powerful territories on earth had culminated in a series of scientific experiments that had resulted in the Great Sickness, which in turn had led to the World Famine that had killed off almost everyone who had survived the virulent sickness. Before the earth itself had been poisoned, Hazel told us people had taken their sustenance directly from the ground.

'You mean they found pills just lying around?' I asked, curious in spite of my incredulity. 'How did the pills get there?'

'They didn't have pills back then,' Hazel explained patiently. 'They obtained their nutrition from what they called "foodstuffs".'

'Foodstuffs?' Naomi repeated, giggling. 'What does that mean?'

'What you have to appreciate is that foodstuffs were everywhere back then, on the ground, above the ground, and even under the ground.'

Naomi, Judith and I gazed at each other in smiling bewilderment.

'Who put the foodstuffs there in the first place?' I asked.

'They were just there, in the same way that we are here,' our teacher replied.

'But if these foodstuffs were just lying about on the ground, or in the ground, how did the rulers control what people ate?' I asked.

Hazel inclined her head, acknowledging my question. 'Rachel has identified a major problem they faced back then,' she announced, and I felt a flicker of pride at this praise. 'The government couldn't exercise any control over what people ingested.'

'Then how did people know how many foodstuffs to swallow?'

'The answer is, they didn't. Most people swallowed either too little or else too much. Almost no one swallowed the correct amount to maintain a healthy body weight, because there were no food clinics to supervise what they ate. Many people were sick, suffering from some sort of problem caused by poor nutrition. It was bedlam. Half the population of the world ate more than was good for them, while the other half starved, because some territories were rich in foodstuffs, while others had very little, and there was no one to control the distribution of the available nutrition.'

'Why didn't the ones who had plenty share their nutrition with the people who were starving?' I asked.

Hazel shook her head. 'It is hard to believe, I know, but people were not prepared to share what they had. Those living in well stocked territories grew greedy and did not care that other people were dying, a long way from them.' She smiled. 'We are fortunate to have rulers who take care of us and don't expect us to be responsible for our own diet.'

'That's daft,' Naomi said. 'We can't know how many pills to swallow without being told. We're not scientists.'

'Just so,' Hazel said. 'The system was deeply flawed before our government took control. When the World Famine arrived, after the world was poisoned by sickness, no one had any foodstuffs any longer, and the entire human race would have perished if The Council had not stepped in and saved us all.'

I was not convinced any of this was true, although it tied in with my mother's story about a World Famine in which all her family had perished, including my father. Hazel went on to explain that the old types of foodstuffs were destroyed by the spreading sickness which destroyed foods from the ground as well as the creatures who lived on it. Fortunately the pill had already been invented to help people who experienced difficulties with foodstuffs. There were a number of problems with foodstuffs, the most common of which were obesity, suffered by people who ingested too much, and anorexia caused by people not eating enough.

'Why didn't they just eat the right foodstuffs so their bodies would stay healthy?' I asked. 'Why would some people eat too much and others not eat enough? It doesn't make sense.'

'If they ate too much they would die, and if they didn't eat enough they would die,' Judith said. 'It's a wonder anyone survived at all.'

'Exactly so.' Hazel sounded pleased with our grasp of the lesson. 'It was almost impossible to get the right balance. After the Great Sickness, people who had been used to ingesting too much began dying of malnutrition, alongside the people who had been starving before the sickness. We are fortunate The Council stepped in and now all the problems caused by foodstuffs have been eradicated.'

Hazel smiled at us; she embraced any opportunity to praise the ruling Council. 'Our Council set up the National Sustenance Service to ensure we all ingest the nutrition our bodies require, and here we are today, all living happy and healthy lives.'

In my experience, people outside The Facility were neither happy nor healthy, but I refrained from contradicting Hazel. As future wives, we were not allowed to disagree with our instructors. Learning to be permanently agreeable was part of our training, so I smiled and nodded, along with Naomi and Judith.

'The other benefit to come out of all the troubles,' Hazel went on, 'is that we now have an army of Guardians, who were originally developed as a land defence force during the aftermath of the Great Sickness. As it turns out, they have been more useful in protecting us against the creatures living in the wastelands beyond the city walls than against our enemies from overseas who were all wiped out, if not by sickness then by starvation. But it was because of the threat from distant territories that scientists worked on chemicals to enhance the growth and power of the Guardians, and those same chemicals now create the pills that ensure our survival.' She beamed. 'So thanks to the foresight and wisdom of The Council, we are all alive and thriving.'

Not long after Hester disappeared, we returned to our room to find a stranger sitting on the empty bed. Thin and scruffy, she was fidgeting with her fingers and looked terrified. I went over to my own bed and sat down facing her. As a glamorous future wife nearly ready to breed, I welcomed the street girl kindly. Her voice sounded coarse, and she smelled disgusting. It was hard to believe that on my arrival at The Facility I must have been equally repellent, unwashed and stinking of sweat. But nearly three years had passed since Vanessa had first welcomed me into The Facility, and I was now civilised enough to be reluctant to share my room with a foul-smelling newcomer. She had no place sleeping beside a sophisticated trainee wife like me, not after I had worked so hard to make myself beautiful. It was one thing to allow her to live at The Facility, but it did not seem fair to expect Naomi, Judith and me to share a bedroom with her.

Naomi and Judith expressed no surprise on seeing a stranger in our room. On the contrary, they seemed pleased to see her, and bombarded her with questions. I remembered they had expressed no surprise on my arrival at The Facility. For the first time I wondered who had slept in my bed before me, and what had happened to her. The newcomer relaxed under their scrutiny, and smiled a lot, apparently enjoying the attention. We learned that her name was Leah. Her parents had disappeared when she was very young, since when she had lived with a neighbour who had recently vanished. A Guardian had found Leah wandering on the street.

'You poor, poor thing,' Naomi said kindly. 'Left all on your own like that. And your poor neighbour. I wonder what happened to her.'

Leah snorted. 'Don't waste your tears on that bitch. I hope she's dead. She only took me in because she wanted someone to look after her. She treated me like a slave all the time I lived with her. Believe me, I'm better off without her.'

Soon after that, Vanessa appeared and took Leah away to the baths.

'That one's yours,' Naomi called out, as Vanessa led the new girl past Hester's wardrobe.

When I expressed surprise on learning that Leah was thirteen, Judith pointed out that I had looked a lot younger than twelve when I had first arrived at The Facility.

I smiled at my pearly nails and stroked the curve of my hips with my fingertips. 'Which means that I had three years to develop,' I murmured. 'Leah only has two.'

'That's true. It could be a problem,' Naomi agreed.

'Perhaps she's a fast learner,' Judith pointed out. 'And no doubt her pills can be adapted to speed up her growth.'

We saw nothing more of Leah for a few days. In the meantime, Naomi, Judith and I discussed her when we had a free moment. While I refused to believe Leah could ever become beautiful enough to become a wife, Judith insisted on irritating me by pointing out I had looked far worse when I first arrived.

'That's different,' I insisted, feeling my smile tighten on my lips. 'I was a child then. Leah's already thirteen, and her body should be nearly ready to breed, but look at her.'

After a few days Leah rejoined us, and the following morning Naomi was summoned to Vanessa's office for important news. The new girl forgotten, Judith and I waited, half jealous and half relieved. We all wanted to be chosen first, but at the same time, we were nervous about becoming wives. Judith fidgeted with her shoes, straightening them in their rows, when they were already tidy, while I lay on my bed, smiling and whispering under my breath, 'I am happy, I am happy, I am happy.'

At last, Naomi came back. Her eyes were shining, and she was beaming. 'I've done it,' she cried out, and burst into tears.

'Stop it. You mustn't cry,' I warned her, afraid her eyes would turn red and puffy.

'You've got to look your best,' Judith agreed. 'You might be displayed soon.'

Tears welled up in Naomi's eyes again. 'It's tonight,' she whispered. 'The display is happening tonight.'

'They don't give you much notice, do they?' Judith replied, smiling nervously.

Judith and I helped Naomi choose what to wear for her display. She was shaking so much, we had to assist her in trying on about twenty dresses before we were satisfied. Then Vanessa joined us and made Naomi change her clothes all over again. At last she was ready, dressed in a white blouse stretched tight across her breasts and a black skirt that barely covered the tops of her thighs, beneath which black suspenders could be seen holding up her sheer black stockings. The outfit was neither colourful nor pretty, but Vanessa declared herself pleased. Naomi smiled, casting a longing glance at the diaphanous silver gown she had chosen and been ordered to discard.

'Admittedly it's not very elegant, but The Council Member

requested a short skirt,' Vanessa said, almost apologetically, as she stood back to study her protégée. 'This strikes the right balance between sexy and demure.'

Not for the first time, Vanessa was using words that I did not understand, and I felt almost as apprehensive as Naomi. Vanessa hurried her away before we had time to say goodbye, which Judith and I later regretted. Naomi did not return the next day, nor the day after that. For several days her bed remained empty, and Judith and I began to experience an anxiety that was not good for our faces. If Naomi had been chosen as a wife, we thought the tidings would have reached us straight away, but we dared not ask Vanessa about our friend.

Finally, Vanessa told us she had news. We gathered in the entrance hall, in front of the black mask, where we were joined by all the women who helped to train us. Above her smiling lips, Vanessa's eyes looked grave.

'I'm pleased to tell you that Naomi has been chosen to breed.' Although the news was good, Vanessa did not sound happy. 'This time next year she will be a mother.'

Leah clapped her hands and gave a cry of excitement.

'But is she going to be a wife?' Judith asked quietly.

Vanessa carried on smiling. 'Naomi has been chosen to be a mother,' she repeated firmly. 'That is good news. It means she will be taken care of while she carries her child.'

'But what will happen to Naomi after the baby is born?' Judith insisted, with an intensity I had not seen in her before.

'We are hoping the father will marry her when he sees the child.'

Judith and I looked at one another, our fixed smiles no longer hiding our dismay. I felt sick. No man could want a more beautiful wife than Naomi. If she had failed to win a husband, what hope was there for the rest of us? Vanessa's was not the only Facility grooming girls for breeding. Other trainers might offer girls who were more attractive than us. There were only a finite number of men on The Council. Most of them were old and already had enough wives. Vanessa had assured us that a man could always be tempted to take another wife, but at the same time she had warned us the competition was tough. We all thought she had said that only to scare us into working harder. We were so beautiful, we had been certain we could not possibly fail. It seemed our confidence had been misplaced.

7

ESCAPE

That night my sleep was disturbed by strange dreams in which I wandered unfamiliar streets searching for my mother. She alone could save me, but even in my dream I knew she was dead. I overslept and, in my panic, put on shoes that did not match my dress. There was barely enough time to run back to the bedroom and fetch the right shoes, before my appointment with the hair stylist. Telling Judith to go on without me I scurried back upstairs, past the empty helmets which no longer scared me. My childish terror was a distant memory. Other fears troubled me now.

To my surprise, Naomi was in our bedroom. For a moment I thought she had come back to us, but then I saw that she was folding clothes and stuffing them into a large bag. The change in her appearance was devastating. She was wearing no make-up at all, and had clearly been crying. Her bloodshot eyes peered at me through swollen eyelids and her hair was a tangled mess.

Glancing up, she caught sight of me watching her, and dropped a bundle of shimmering dresses on the floor before dashing over to fling her arms round me. 'My life is over,' she sobbed. 'Everything is ruined.'

Fortunately my hair had not yet been styled for the day, or her tearful snuffling might have disturbed its arrangement. I extricated myself from her damp embrace as gently as I could. 'I'm so sorry he didn't choose you to be his wife,' I said. 'You poor dear. But really, he must be mad. No one could be more beautiful than you.'

Naomi shook her head. 'No, no, no, you don't understand. It wasn't like that. It was me. He wanted to marry me, but I couldn't do it.'

My careful smile concealed my dismay, but I was afraid she had lost her mind in all the excitement. We had spent years training to become wives. That was our sole aim in life. No one could deliberately refuse the honour, or the luxury, that such a life offered. Besides which, there was no viable alternative open to us. We fulfilled our privileged role as wives, or we starved.

'Naomi,' I urged her, aware that I risked being late for my hair stylist. 'Listen to me. You have to stop crying before you ruin your face, and please stop frowning like that. It makes you look unattractive. Now please, sit down and let's talk frankly. You don't know what you're saying. It's just the excitement that's thrown you into turmoil, but you have to accept this. You have to be a wife. That's what we've been trained to do. It's all we can do.'

'You don't understand,' she wailed, tears spilling from her eyes. 'I couldn't put up with that man for the rest of my life. I just couldn't. I'd rather die.'

'Naomi, you're not making any sense. What are you talking about?'

She sat down on her bed, her fit of crying over, and stared at her feet. When she spoke, her voice was barely louder than a whisper. 'My future husband was old, and flabby, and ugly. I felt sick every time he came near me and forced me to breathe in his foul odour. And when he touched me—' She shuddered. 'It made me feel sick. I could have put up with all of that, but he hurt me, Rachel. He really hurt me. It was horrible, like a knife slicing into my flesh. When it was over, I told him I'd rather die than be his wife, and he beat me until I begged him to stop. Then he forced me to do disgusting things to him until I threw up, and after that he beat me again.'

She stepped out of her gown and I gasped in horror on seeing dark red weals across her breasts and belly, and dark bruising on her thighs. She half turned to show me more injuries on her back. 'This is what he did to me. This!'

'Naomi, you have to show Vanessa.'

'She wasn't interested.' Naomi raised her eyes to stare at me in despair. 'She told me a wife must submit. But it wasn't only the pain. He enjoyed watching me suffer. The more I cried out, the more excited he became, and then he forced himself on me again. He held me down until I thought I would suffocate, with my face pressed against his stinking bed. He was too strong. I couldn't stop him.' She shuddered. 'He chose me as a wife, but I couldn't. I just couldn't. I would rather be taken by the Guardians and banished from the city to be torn apart by monsters. That would be a merciful escape.'

I sat beside her on the edge of the bed, appalled by her confession. Not knowing how to comfort her, I patted her hand gently. Naomi had always been a cheerful optimist. Seeing her so upset made me feel like crying too, but I had already put on my make-up. I struggled to keep smiling.

'Don't cry, Naomi,' I said, finding my voice with difficulty. 'With your looks and talent other men are bound to choose you. You'll find someone young and smart and kind, like we always hoped.'

'No, no, you don't understand.'

I wished she would stop saying that. 'You can't let one man

ruin your life,' I insisted kindly. 'You're far too beautiful for that. There will be someone else. Vanessa will make sure of that. There must be plenty of men who will want you as a wife. You have a wonderful future, you'll see. All you need is a bath and a visit to the hair salon and the make-up parlour, and you'll look as beautiful as ever. You just need to remember to smile.'

'You don't understand,' she insisted. 'I refused to be his wife, but I couldn't refuse to breed with him, not after he'd chosen me. After that first night, he tied my hands and forced himself on me again and again for weeks, until he knew I was ruined. No other man will want me as his wife now that I am going to bear a child. They'll take my child from me, won't they? If it's a girl, they'll give her to Vanessa. I can't bear it,' she wailed, 'I can't bear it.'

I stared at her in horror, as the reality of her situation dawned on me. 'What will happen to you?'

She shrugged. 'They'll take my baby away and abandon me on the street. I'll have no one to help me, and I'm not fit to look after myself. No one has taught us how to survive on our own. I don't even know where to go for a food card.'

It was true. Vanessa always did everything for us.

'I only hope I don't have a girl,' Naomi said fiercely. 'I hope my baby dies before it's born.'

Too shocked to speak, I stared at her, my smile fixed on my lips while my world fell apart. Naomi had pushed her fringe off her forehead and her hair was all dishevelled, sticking out from her skull like a shattered halo. Remembering how proud she had been of her golden hair, I struggled to comprehend what had happened to her. Naomi had always been the good humoured one of us, laughing and kind. She would have made a wonderful wife, or so we had all thought.

'Naomi,' I stammered, 'I don't know what to say.'

With a sniff, she stood up and resumed stuffing clothes into her bag, cramming them down to make room for more. Many of the fabrics would crease, but I said nothing.

'I might be able to sell them,' she explained.

It was time for me to go and see the stylist. I left Naomi bundling clothes into a bag, with tears streaming down her flushed cheeks. A few moments later, I was smiling at my own painted face in the mirror, while a stylist snipped at the ends of my hair. There was no doubt that I looked lovely, but that no longer felt important. The more I considered Naomi's plight, the more desperate the reality of my situation seemed. The harsh truth was that there were too many of us in training for us all to be chosen. Even if we were successful, there was almost no chance we would end up with a husband who would treat us with respect. Realistically, the Members of The Council were bound to be old, because no young man was rich enough to join The Council and acquire trained wives. We were competing for a prize that would sentence us to a life of subjection to the whims of an old man.

All the luxury we enjoyed suddenly seemed pointless, because we were destined to endure a lifetime of misery. Even if we were fortunate enough to be married to a benign old man, no one had mentioned what happened to wives when their aged husbands died. Naomi's visit shocked me out of my dream of being happy as a wife, and I understood that Hester had been right all along. Our training was a trap, Vanessa's house a prison of perfume and lace. It was time to stop fantasising about becoming a wife, and plan my escape.

'You really ought to smile more steadily,' the hair stylist chided me, pausing in her snipping. 'You know it's necessary to practise as much as possible. If you're growing impatient with how long this is taking, then it's a perfect opportunity to practise smiling when you don't really feel like it.'

In the mirror, I watched her resume her work, her fingers deftly brushing through my hair as her scissors trimmed it. Before the news reached us that Naomi was not going to be a wife, I had enjoyed having my hair styled. Even as recently as one day ago, I would have been content to sit quietly smiling while the hair stylist worked to alter my appearance. Tending to my hair was her responsibility, as mine was to study to look beautiful. Each of us had our proper path in life. But hearing about Naomi's experience had changed everything.

There was nothing I could do to help Naomi, but Judith and I might still be saved. When I did not share her excitement about her imminent birthday, she accused me of being jealous because she would reach fifteen first, and she flatly refused to listen to anything negative, although Naomi's fate had shown me that our future might not be as wonderful as we had hoped. Convinced that Judith would not believe me, I decided against telling her the details of Naomi's horrific experience. I would not have believed the story myself, if Naomi had not told me in person. Even then I hadn't believed her until she showed me her injuries. On balance it seemed best to hold back from talking openly to Judith, in case she betrayed me. Once Vanessa heard about my heretical views, she would throw me out on the street, or hand me straight over to the Guardians. Either way, I would end up in prison. Reluctantly, I gave up trying to warn Judith. She would never know that Naomi had returned to The Facility to collect a few colourful garments to exchange for pills.

So we carried on with our daily routine, discussing nail varnish and make-up, ribbons and bows, and the accessories which had once seemed so important. And all the time, I was thinking about Naomi, and Hester who had not taken her pills as a result of which her body had not grown enough for her to breed. I wondered whether to follow her example, but that would be risky. Firstly, it might already be too late since I was already fertile. There was no way of finding out whether it would be safe, or even possible, to reverse the development in my body. Secondly, we had no idea what had happened to Hester. She could have been cast out on the street to fend for herself, or she might have gone straight to prison. Whichever it was, she would have died in misery. There had to be a better way out of my predicament.

With no clear plan in mind, I began to save my pills, taking care to do so without attracting attention. After escaping, it might take me weeks to work out how to survive, and I would need pills to keep me alive until I somehow managed to acquire a food card. It would be too dangerous for me to use the one that had been issued to me by The Facility, because Vanessa was bound to report my flight, and the Guardians would be searching for me. Alone, I had no hope of surviving for more than a few weeks. Without a supply of pills, I would not even manage to live for that long. Meanwhile, the hope of escape was all that kept me going, but collecting pills was a slow process requiring patience. One week I hid three days' worth of pills, claiming I had a stomach upset to explain my loss of weight. Those pills would keep me alive for ten days. A couple of weeks later I hid a few more pills, concealing my spoils in a small bag hidden inside the long toe of a shoe. But I could not keep pretending to be ill to explain my weight loss.

When a new nurse at the food clinic asked me how many pills I needed, I seized on the chance to say I was down to my last one. She handed me a whole packet, unwittingly adding two week's supply to my hoard, which was now enough to keep me alive for nearly a month. With any luck she would keep quiet about her blunder, if she ever discovered it. For several days afterwards I trembled whenever Vanessa approached me, terrified that my lie had been exposed. I started biting my pills in two, and saving half of each one. By the end of a month I had saved enough to last me three months, but with every passing day there was a danger my secret hoard would be discovered. I might have been paranoid, on account of my secret activity, but it seemed to me that Vanessa was giving me suspicious glances, and had taken to hovering nearby whenever I went to be weighed and measured. If she stumbled on my secret, the punishment would be harsh. Worse, I would lose any hope of escape.

One day, Vanessa accompanied me right inside the clinic and questioned the nurse who had increased my supply of pills. 'Rachel's dose has been stable for a long time,' Vanessa said, with an accusing glare above her smiling lips. 'Why has it suddenly changed?'

'Yes, we raised her levels last month, but that doesn't signify anything serious,' the nurse replied, clearly thinking Vanessa was concerned and in need of reassurance. 'Individuals develop at different rates, and it just means that her body's preparing to breed.'

Pills were not my only problem. Should I succeed in slipping out of The Facility unseen, my survival would depend on my ability to blend in with the poor of the city. My gorgeous clothes would instantly mark me out as a future wife, as would my carefully tended hair and make-up. Nothing in my wardrobe was dull and dirty, but there was a long brown dress covered in shiny gems. While the other girls were asleep I stayed awake under my bed covers, picking off the bright jewels and hiding them beneath a pile of frilly underwear. When the dress was completely free of decoration and hidden beneath a shiny satin gown, I removed several rows of pearls from a square black scarf. By the time I finished it was torn, and there were threads hanging from it.

Over three years had passed since I had been recruited into The Programme, and Judith had been there even longer.

Vanessa often allowed us to go to the food clinic to be tested, accompanied only by an instructor. Leah's arrival had put an end to that limited freedom, because she was too new to go out without Vanessa there to keep a close eye on her.

One day Leah started her monthly bleeding and was allowed to spend the day resting in bed. Wanting to tend to Leah, Vanessa arranged for Judith and me to go to the clinic without her. I struggled to contain my excitement on realising this might be my opportunity to escape. Hurrying back to our room ahead of Judith, I checked that Leah was asleep before pulling on my plain brown dress, quickly covering it with a bright red and yellow dress. I was only just in time, because a moment later, Judith entered our room.

'You look beautiful,' she said, in our customary greeting.

I smiled graciously at her and told her that she looked beautiful.

We put black capes on over our clothes, so as not to attract undue attention on the street, and set off, accompanied by an instructor. When we were halfway to the clinic, I grabbed Judith's arm.

'Don't say anything, but I've forgotten my card,' I hissed. 'If Vanessa finds out, I'll be in trouble. I'm going to run back and get it. You go on and don't say anything, and I'll see you there.'

Judith looked anxious. 'You know we're not allowed out on the street alone.'

'Don't worry. It'll be fine. Don't forget, I lived in the city for years before I joined The Facility. I can take care of myself.' That was not really true. I had grown up in the city, but had never been out on the streets alone. 'Just tell her everything's fine, if she asks.' I jerked my head towards the instructor. 'I'll be back before you know it.'

Before Judith could remonstrate, I darted away. This was my chance. Judith would spend a couple of hours being tested by the nurses. Afterwards she and our instructor would wait for me outside the clinic, on the mistaken assumption that I was still undergoing tests. Eventually, when I did not join them, they would hurry back to The Facility without me. Finding I had not returned, Judith would panic and tell Vanessa everything that had happened. As I hurried away from the clinic and The Facility, I tried to imagine what would happen next. Hazel had reprimanded me once for speculating, but she no longer had the power to stifle my thoughts.

Vanessa would probably not report my absence straight away. The Council must already be questioning her judgement. The ignominy of Hester's failure as a trainee wife had been followed by the calamity of Naomi's refusal to take up her position as a wife. If another one of Vanessa's girls caused a scandal by running away, Vanessa herself might be replaced. My guess was that she would wait for a while, desperately hoping I would turn up. In the end she would contact the clinic to find out what time I had left. Finally, discovering that I had never arrived at the clinic, Vanessa would have no choice but to report my disappearance to the Guardians, by which time I would be impossible to trace. That was my plan, and it was a good one, except that I had nowhere to hide.

The previous week we had worn thick black rings around our eyes, and bright red lipstick, impossible to conceal, but fortunately the fashion for make-up was light that week. Leaving the clinic behind me, I scanned the streets for a place to hide. Spotting a narrow alley between two buildings, I scurried along it until I could not be observed from the street. No one saw me remove my cape and colourful dress. Before leaving my hiding place, I wiped my hands along the ground. When my fingers were covered in filthy grey dirt, I rubbed them against my cheeks, and dragged my cape along the ground. Wrapping my tattered black scarf around my head, I returned to the street, dressed in a brown gown and soiled black cape, my hair hidden beneath a ragged scarf. Taking a deep breath, I began to walk, aimless and terrified, yet filled with unaccustomed exhilaration. If I did not find shelter before dark, the Guardians would find me. Until then, for the first time in my life, I was free.

8

MATTHEW

While it was still light, it was vital that I move as far away from The Facility and the Clinic as possible. A few people passed me on the street, but they all hurried by with their eyes averted. Like me, everyone seemed keen to avoid being noticed. A group of Guardians strode past and I looked down, wondering if they were already hunting for me. Even supposing Vanessa had not yet reported my absence, if the Guardians searched me they would find enough pills in my pouch for several months, more than anyone was entitled to carry. Glancing up, I thought one of them was staring straight at me. My breath caught in my throat, but he turned away and marched on. Resisting the temptation to look round, I continued on my way, trying to walk steadily on shaking legs.

For years Vanessa had taken care of me, keeping me healthy and training me to be beautiful. Now we would never see one another again, but I felt no regret at leaving her. Even the thought of abandoning my friends did not trouble me. All that mattered to me was avoiding capture. I was wearing my most comfortable shoes but they were not designed for walking far.

They squashed my toes, and after a while my feet began to hurt. Slipping off the shoes, I left them under a broken handcart that lay abandoned at the side of the road. Walking barefoot proved even more painful, but I could not turn back.

In the vast darkening sky I noticed one brilliant star sparkling down at me from afar and, unaccountably, my spirits rose. It made no difference where I wandered, because no one was waiting for me at the end of my journey. If that was a terrifying thought, it was also liberating.

Walking for so long was tiring, and after a while I began to feel sick, worn out with pain and fear. It seemed inevitable now that the Guardians would find me. I had been a fool to think it was possible to escape their all-seeing eyes. Right now I could have been sleeping soundly in a soft bed. Within a month I might have been a wife, living in luxury for the rest of my life, instead of which I was alone, with only my fears for company. Longing for someone to come along and rescue me, I imagined my mother walking past. 'Rachel!' she would cry out. 'What are you doing here? Come home and let me bathe your poor sore feet.'

There was another daydream in which my saviour was a stranger. Young and handsome, he would carry me in his arms all the way to his lodging. My fantasy man would be poor, but we would be safe and comfortable in his imaginary home, and that was good enough for me. I had experienced luxury in my life, and the price was too high.

But no one came to rescue me, and I spent a long time, alone and terrified, cowering in a dark lane. Only Guardians were permitted to walk around after sunset. They patrolled the streets at night, protecting the city from monsters that lurked in the darkness. Aware that a Guardian or a monster might seize me at any moment, I was forced to stay out of sight until morning.

Noticing a hut by the roadside, I stole out of the lane and limped towards it as quickly as I could. The Guardians used these huts to store tools for levelling off the roads after a sandstorm. They could pull their carts more easily over even ground. Hardly daring to breathe, I opened the door a crack and peeped inside. To my relief it was empty, so I slid inside. With barely enough space to curl up on the floor, I lay down and folded my scarf as a pillow. It was hardly the most comfortable of positions, but I was exhausted enough to sleep soundly, despite my aching legs and stinging blisters.

I woke up in the morning, feeling stiff and cold, just as day was breaking. Trembling, I swallowed half a hydration pill. There was no going back now. Somehow I had to find a way to survive alone. I knew it must be possible, because Vanessa had often talked about people who lived on the streets. One of her catalogue of threats was that if we disobeyed her, we would end up with the people she called 'outsiders'. Now I wondered who they were, and how to find them. It was not safe to linger in a hut where Guardians might come to collect their tools at any time.

With nowhere to go, I had to keep moving. People only went outside to go to the clinics. Anyone who appeared to be loitering would soon arouse suspicion. Preparing to go back out on the street, I ran my fingers through my hair. It had not been cleaned for twenty-four hours and felt dry, but it might still give me away. Covering my head with my scarf, I peered out of the hut at an empty street, before sneaking out of my shelter. With a thrill of terror, I noticed a scruffy man watching me as I limped hurriedly away. Reaching the corner, I glanced over my shoulder and saw that he was following me. Despite his lean build he looked strong and wiry, and he strode behind me with the lithe grace of a man accustomed to moving swiftly. Like a boy I had once encountered outside The Facility, the man seemed able to walk along the street without disturbing the dust and dirt that lay on the ground. As he drew closer, I saw bright blue eyes peering at me through his straggly hair. Nervously I hobbled on. My blistered feet burned when they touched the ground, making it impossible to run. Too scared to stop, I staggered on as fast as I could, but when I turned the next corner and looked back, he was still behind me. Attempting to escape would achieve nothing beyond further injuring my feet. In any case, whoever my pursuer was, he was neither Guardian nor monster, so I halted and waited for him to reach me, my heart pounding and my feet smarting. When he drew level with me, he started back in surprise.

'You're not Hannah,' he murmured in surprise.

'Who's Hannah?'

'Who are you?' he demanded, sounding annoyed.

We heard the cart before it came into view around the corner. Shuddering, I lowered my head and pulled my scarf forward over my temples as the wheels rumbled past without drawing to a halt. As the noise of the cart receded, I kept my head down until the sound of the Guardians had faded completely. When I looked up, the man was watching me inquisitively.

'Who are you?' he repeated, more gently. 'Don't be afraid.'

My fear of the Guardians had softened his attitude, and he came closer, staring at me.

'You look as though your face has recently been painted,' he said wonderingly. 'Is that possible? Where do you come from?'

Feeling uneasy again, I backed away from him with a polite smile. 'I'm sorry I'm not Hannah, and I hope you find her.'

I turned away, but the urgency in his voice arrested me. 'Wait! Tell me who you are.'

Reason urged me to run away from this man, who could be a

Council spy. Yet he had not betrayed me to the Guardians and, apart from any other consideration, my feet hurt. Too tired and dispirited to resist, I nodded submissively. If this stranger was going to kill me, at least the fear and agony would stop. Hopefully my decision to trust him would turn out well but, whatever transpired, this chance encounter would decide my fate. I took a step towards him and he noticed me wince.

'What's wrong? Are you in pain?'

For answer, I raised my skirt above my ankles to display my blistered and bleeding feet. They looked dreadful, but he merely remarked, quite casually, that my feet were a mess. 'We need to clean them before they get any worse,' he added. 'It is not good for dirt to enter the body through broken skin. You are not used to walking barefoot,' he added, raising his eyes to study my face.

He held out his arm so that I could lean on him as we walked, and I noticed one of the fingers on his left hand was missing. Catching me looking at the stump, he slipped his hand inside his long sleeve to conceal his deformity.

'What are you running away from?'

His question was so direct, it startled me, but I had decided to trust him and there was no point in trying to hide the truth. 'The Guardians are looking for me.'

'They just walked straight past you,' he pointed out.

'That's because they didn't know it was me. This is a disguise.'

'Why are they looking for you?'

'I was training to be a wife. I've run away.'

He stopped in his tracks, and turned to stare at me. 'Are you really training to be a wife?'

I glanced quickly up and down the empty street before pulling the scarf off my head.

'Put it back on,' he said quickly. 'Someone might see you.'

My hair was dirty and dishevelled after my night on the floor of the Guardians' hut, but it was still obvious that it had been dyed and styled.

'I may not look like a trainee wife now, but that's what I am, or at least it's what I was.'

'I believe you,' he assured me. 'I noticed your face. Keep your head covered. We need to go. They will be looking for you. It's not safe for you to be out on the street.'

While we walked, he told me his name was Matthew, and he lived a long way from the town. My spirits sank, knowing I could not walk far on my blistered feet, but his next words raised my hopes again.

'You can't walk there yet, not with your feet in that state. We'll get you to a house not far from here, where you'll be among friends. Don't look so worried. You'll be safe and well looked after until you are able to walk to the camp.'

'What camp?'

'The camp of the outsiders.' He smiled at me. 'We are society's outcasts. I'll tell you about it as we go. Now come on, it's not far to the safe house. Where are your shoes?'

I shook my head, too tired to explain what had happened to them. They were no use to me now. In fact, it was probably just as well I had discarded them, because one of the Guardians might have spotted them when they passed us, and stopped to investigate. As I hobbled along at his side, Matthew told me that The Council knew about the existence of the outsiders' camp beyond the walls of the city, but had been unable to discover its location. The Elders of the community would only allow me to join their camp if they were sure they could trust me.

'It's necessary for us to be cautious,' he explained. 'If anyone gives us away, The Council will destroy us.' Powerful men on The Council wanted to stamp out the outsiders, he said, viewing them as a threat to the safety of the city and its rulers. If The

Council discovered where the camp was, they would send Guardians to kill everyone they found there.

'So you see why we have to be careful. I have no wish to insult you, if you are who you say you are, but we cannot risk revealing the location of our camp to anyone who might betray us to our enemies. For all we know, you could be a spy.'

I bristled. 'That's just what I was thinking about you. How do I know you're not going to hand me over to the Guardians?'

Matthew inclined his head, acknowledging my question.

'I guess we just have to trust each other,' I added, afraid he might abandon me. 'But why do you want to live in the wastelands outside the city walls? Isn't it dangerous? Wouldn't it be better to ask The Council to let you come back and live here in the city?'

'I'd rather die,' he replied fiercely. I was startled by the sudden anger in his voice. 'Conditions may be primitive in the camp, but at least we are free there. We will never return to the city and be slaves to The Council.'

'People in the city aren't all slaves to The Council,' I replied.

'Are you sure? What are the Guardians for then, if not to keep everyone under control?'

'The Guardians keep us safe.'

'Safe from what?'

'From the monsters that live outside the city,' I replied, shocked by his blasé attitude towards the danger he must face, living in the wastelands outside the city walls.

Matthew laughed. 'There are no monsters out there,' he assured me, 'only us, the outsiders who refuse to obey The Council. Don't you understand? The monsters are a fiction invented by The Council to frighten citizens into blind obedience. That kind of scaremongering is nothing more than a cynical manipulation of people's minds. We refuse to be cowed into bondage by their lies and propaganda. We have defied the dictatorship of The Council, and its draconian use of Guardians to keep citizens under their control. But in any case, things have gone too far for us to return. You must be aware of the punishment for disloyalty? The Council are our judge and jury, and they do not forgive. We could not slink back into the city, and apologise for our defection, even if we wanted to. Nor could you,' he added gravely. 'You have rebelled, and must throw your lot in with us, or else survive alone. There is no going back for either of us.'

I began to bleat about the monsters being real, but he continued, ignoring my stammered response.

'We have chosen liberty over subjugation. If the cost of that decision is to forfeit the protection of the Guardians, that is a choice we have made willingly, and would make again.'

'Why would anyone want to disobey The Council?' I asked, clinging to my beliefs, yet unable to suppress a flutter of excitement at his words. No one at The Facility had ever mentioned individual choice or freedom.

'Because we value our freedom. What right do The Council have to determine what we may and may not do? We had no say in their appointment. We do not even know who most of them are. What about your training as a wife? Are you telling me you were free to do whatever you wanted? Was it even your own choice to be trained, or were you selected because of your lovely face?'

'I was lucky to be chosen. The Council takes care of us.'

'Yet you ran away,' he replied, and I had no answer to that.

He strode on in silence for a while, while I hobbled at his side. At last, he turned into a narrow winding lane where he rapped a rapid rhythm on a door. It was opened at once by an old man with white hair, a wrinkled face and a bulbous nose. His was perhaps the ugliest face I had ever seen, but his eyes were kind. He held his arms out to Matthew, hustling him inside.

'Come in, quickly,' he said. 'We don't have much time.'

Seeing me standing behind Matthew, he frowned and I felt a flicker of fear. My only companions were complete strangers who might refuse to shelter me, or worse.

9

SAUL

The old man ushered us into a room similar to the one I had shared with my mother. Although I had grown accustomed to far more luxurious surroundings, I immediately felt at home with the bare walls and dirt floor. I had not thought about my mother for years, while I had been living at The Facility, but now I half expected to see her walk in and begin sweeping the floor. Grief gripped me, threatening to overwhelm me, but this was no time to indulge in nostalgia.

Matthew introduced me to the old man, Saul. He must have heard many strange tales in his long life, because he evinced no surprise when Matthew told him I was a trainee wife, but merely led me to a corner, pointed to a pile of earth covered with sacking, and told me to rest. Soon after our arrival Matthew left, promising to return for me in a few weeks, after my feet had healed. Lying on the bed, I listened to the two men talking quietly by the door. Their muttered exchange reminded of when my mother had refused to help our neighbour, Clare. But that was a long time ago, and right now I needed to stay focused and resist the temptation to weep for the loss of the only two women who had ever cared about me.

'Don't worry, she doesn't know anything at all,' were the last words I heard Matthew say before he disappeared.

When I woke up, an elderly woman was talking to Saul in a fierce whisper. Like him, she was tall and gaunt. Like him, she had white hair, a large nose, and a wrinkled face. Closing my eyes, I listened to their whispered conversation.

'There is nothing to suggest she *can* be trusted,' the old woman was saying in response to something the old man had said.

'You can see she was a trainee wife,' Saul replied. 'Look at her.'

'That doesn't mean she wasn't sent here to infiltrate the camp.'

'But she wasn't to know that Matthew would come across her, or that he would bring her here.'

'He wouldn't be the first man to be hoodwinked by a pretty face,' the woman replied sourly. 'You know that as well as I do. And even if she is telling the truth, how do we know she wasn't seen, coming here?'

'No one saw her,' Saul replied.

'How can you be so sure?'

'Don't you think Matthew would have known if he was being followed? And in any case, if they had seen her they'd be here by now.'

'Unless they sent her, you old fool.'

It seemed wrong to eavesdrop after Saul had been kind to me, so I sat up, pretending to have just woken. He introduced the woman as his sister, Helen. She looked even older than her brother, and her back was bowed as though she could no longer stand upright. She was clearly suspicious of me but she treated me kindly, washing my feet very gently in foul-smelling oil that made my blisters sting, and afterwards applying healing balm to soothe the pain. Having finished her ministrations, she spread an old cloth under my feet, which were slimy with ointment and burst blisters, and told me to lie still and rest.

Vanessa had mirrors in every room so we could watch ourselves constantly. I spent an entire day with Saul and Helen without once looking at my reflection. At last, I could bear it no longer, and asked Helen how I looked.

'You're starting to look less like a wife,' she replied, giving me an encouraging nod. 'Although you must stop your incessant smiling. It's not just irritating; it looks strange and may give you away if a Guardian sees you in the street.'

With an effort, I forced myself to scowl.

'That's better,' Helen said. 'Now you don't look so much like a wife. We're getting somewhere at last.'

That should have been a cause for jubilation, yet I could not suppress a pang of regret. Years of hard work to ensure I was beautiful had come to this. Still, I had made my choice and, as Matthew had said, there was no going back.

That evening, Helen offered me a pill but I shook my head.

'You must eat,' she insisted. 'Don't worry, we can share our pills with you for a few days. Matthew brings us additional supplies for emergencies like this and, in any case, the clinic don't care if old people like me and my brother lose a little weight now and again. It happens. It wouldn't be the first time and, believe me, no one even notices. At our age, we don't attract attention.'

'No, it's not that. I've got my own supply.'

There were enough pills in my pocket to keep me alive for months. Helen looked frightened when she saw them, until I reassured her that they were neither stolen, nor a gift. No one else knew about them. She smiled warily when she heard how I had saved them.

'It took many months,' I added.

'That was enterprising,' she admitted, with a grudging respect. 'If it's true.'

'It is,' I assured her, and she nodded uncertainly.

That night I lay in bed puzzling about everything that had happened since I had abandoned Judith at the clinic. According to Matthew, there were Members of The Council who wanted to eliminate the outsiders altogether. Did that mean there were others on The Council who wanted them to survive? It seemed unlikely. The outsiders were rebels who posed a threat to The Council's power. Why would anyone on The Council want to protect them? Something about Matthew's account did not quite add up and, not for the first time, I wondered if he was actually a spy planning to hand me over to the Guardians. Helen was helping to heal my feet, but that might simply be because I would be more valuable to the Guardians if I was able to walk properly. Perhaps she was only keeping me with her to stop me from running away again. Matthew might have gone to arrange to hand me over to the Guardians. Although I trusted him, and Saul and Helen seemed to be genuinely concerned to help me, I remained wary. Vanessa had once appeared to be my friend. Had there been anywhere else for me to go, I would have stolen away in the night, but I was friendless and lost.

Slowly my feet healed. Once I could walk without pain, Helen gave me a pair of loose trousers, a long-sleeved tunic, and a hooded cape for the journey ahead of me. They were the colour of sand and stank of sweat, but I put them on without complaining. Compared to the corsets and tight bodices worn by trainee wives, my sand-coloured outfit felt wonderfully light, allowing me to move without restraint. The old woman also gave me a pair of shoes which were open at the back and did not rub against my sore heels. They looked battered and scuffed, and smelled rank, but they did not hurt my feet, and I was grateful for her consideration.

'Don't thank me,' she replied. 'I'm just being practical. If you can't walk, you will never be able to leave, and you can't stay with us forever. Who knows when another fugitive will need our help? We can conceal one outlaw, but two might attract attention.'

Matthew smiled approvingly when he saw me, and complimented Helen on the transformation she had achieved in so short a time.

'You're going to fit in with us a lot better now,' he told me.

It was time to leave the safety of Saul and Helen's home. With a stab of fear, I followed Matthew outside.

'Don't worry,' he murmured as we stepped out into the street. 'No one will suspect you were once a trainee wife now.'

I pulled my hood up and tried to feel pleased at knowing that I was no longer beautiful. The sky darkened as we hurried through a labyrinth of narrow winding streets. Without warning, Matthew halted in the middle of a narrow lane where we were not overlooked from any direction. After peering around, he knelt down and brushed at the dirt with his hands, to uncover a large disc in the ground. With a final glance in both directions, he drew a hooked tool from his belt and raised the disc to reveal a ladder leading down under the ground. Without a word, he gestured at me to descend.

'Hurry,' he urged me when I hesitated.

He held my elbows to steady me as I swung my legs over the side and searched blindly for the first rung of the ladder. Trembling with fear, I climbed slowly down into a black chasm. Staring at the barely visible rungs of the ladder, I forced myself to keep moving.

The ladder shook as Matthew climbed onto it, somewhere

above my head. A moment later there was a clang as he pulled the heavy metal cover back in place. Shocked, I clung on in sudden absolute darkness. It was an effort to continue, but I dared not stop, with Matthew descending above me in the darkness. If I stopped, even for an instant, he might kick my head and send me plunging into the abyss. One step at a time, I climbed down. One step at a time, I developed a steady rhythm. One foot after another. One foot after another. The motion was mesmerising. Had the metal on the side rails of the ladder not felt painfully cold against my hands, I might have lost focus and let go.

'We're nearly there.'

Matthew's voice broke the silence, startling me so much I nearly lost my grip.

'You should reach the ground any time now. Take two steps directly backwards and then stand absolutely still. Whatever you do, don't move to the side.'

Even though I was prepared for the impact, I stumbled when one of my feet reached for the next rung and landed flat on the floor. It was terrifying letting go of the ladder, unable to see anything. For all I knew, there might be a deep hole or ditch in the ground just behind me. Perhaps my guide had brought me there to eliminate a potential risk to the security of his community. But that was speculation. What was clear was that Matthew would soon be on top of me if I did not move aside. Taking a deep breath, I took two steps backwards into the unseen. Without Matthew's specific instructions, I might have remained rooted to the spot and been kicked in the head. Matthew must have landed beside me silently, because a second later I heard him strike a flint, and was almost blinded by a few dazzling sparks followed by a bright light. Behind his torch, Matthew's face quivered in the flickering flame.

We were in a long tunnel with a lofty arched roof. Near

where we were standing, I saw a deep drop. Matthew had warned me not to step sideways for a reason. At the bottom of the lower level, parallel metal struts lay in a row across the floor, stretching into passageways in both directions as far as my eyes could see. I breathed in a musty smell, as though the dust and ash of many years had lain festering down there.

Strangest of all was the silence. At home in the city, there was always noise: footsteps scurrying by outside, a cart rattling past, and Guardians' voices echoing along the streets, while indoors there was the soft swishing of my mother's interminable sweeping, and the low drone of her voice. At night there were distant sounds of marching feet and trundling carts, and the muffled bellowing of Guardians about their nightly patrols, mingling with occasional shouts and screams of people resisting arrest. In The Facility the noises had been different, but equally constant. Heels tapping along corridors, voices, and at night the gentle breathing of my fellow trainees and the quiet sounds made by the cleaners as they polished the floor. Here in the tunnel there was only a silence that seemed to ring inside my head.

'What is this place?' I whispered.

'No one knows. We think people once pulled carts along these metal rails.'

'How did they get the carts down here?'

'We think they must have brought them down the ladders in pieces, and assembled them when everything was here.'

'Why did they do it?'

'Perhaps they used them to carry people across the city.'

'Why would they want to move people around under the ground?'

'Maybe they wanted to transport them in secret, but no one really knows what went on down here.'

The tunnel reminded me of the words of our neighbour,

Clare, who had described carriages that transported people under the ground, and I wished I had not been so dismissive of her stories.

Matthew gazed around, and in the glimmering light I thought he looked sad. 'So much of the old city was destroyed,' he murmured. 'These tunnels only remained intact because they are below the surface. Most of what has survived down here is an enigma, and we have no way of unlocking the mystery. All we really know for certain right now is that the people who lived back then destroyed their civilisation, wiped it out completely.'

It was hard stepping across the metal struts that resembled the rungs of a ladder lying on the ground. At first I wondered whether what we were walking along had originally served as a ladder, like the one we had descended earlier, but it became apparent that this metal walkway was far too long for anyone to have climbed it vertically. As we walked, I fell into a regular stride. Matthew was keen for us to conserve our energy, so we travelled without talking. With nothing to distract us, it felt to me as though we were walking forever. Every now and again one or both sides of the tunnel opened out into a wide platform with doors leading away into darkness. Sometimes we saw other tunnels branching off into the shadows. This was not merely a tunnel, it was a vast network of interconnecting underground passages.

'Who made these tunnels?' I asked.

Matthew did not answer, but paused by an opening in the wall and held his torch above his head so the flame illuminated a different passageway. There were raised platforms on either side of the horizontal ladder which was blocked at this point by a colossal construction, painted in flaking red and grey.

'What is that?' I whispered, stepping in front of my companion, my curiosity stronger than my caution.

'It's a kind of vast carriage,' Matthew replied. 'We think it might have been moving people along the tracks, because some of them are still in there.'

I spun round to look at him and we nearly collided.

'Watch out,' he said. 'You nearly knocked the torch out of my hand.'

'What do you mean, there are people inside it?' I demanded. 'Shouldn't we rescue them?'

'Go ahead and take a look,' he replied quietly, holding up his torch. 'I'll follow you so you can see what's in there, but be careful not to touch the openings in the walls. Their edges are protected by transparent splinters which are difficult to see unless the light shines directly on them. We think they were put there to keep intruders out.'

Warily I advanced along the narrow walkway, until I was standing alongside the carriage.

'Remember not to touch the edges of the openings,' Matthew called out. 'The shards are difficult to see, but they will cut your hands to shreds if you touch them.'

Carefully I leaned forward and peered into the carriage, which was larger and longer than I had first realised. Inside were rows of scorched benches, more or less intact, running along either side of the carriage, and several poles holding up what must have been the ceiling. The whole of the interior was dusted with white ash. But what arrested my gaze was a desiccated figure of a woman, lying on her back on the floor. Her yellow skin was stretched taut across her face, exposing her teeth in a macabre grin, and her eye sockets were empty. Matthew moved along the platform beside me, illuminating more shrivelled bodies inside the carriage. Most were merely bones, but the ones that were vaguely recognisable as human appeared to be drained of blood, their clothes in tatters.

'Are they...? Who are they?' I murmured. 'Did the monsters get them?'

Matthew shook his head and the torchlight wavered with his movement. 'No one knows exactly who they were, or what happened to them. Now come on. We can't stay any longer.'

In silence we made our way back to the tunnel we had originally been following, and continued on our journey. At length we stopped to rest on a wide platform. Matthew's torch lit up an image on the wall: a red circle with a blue stripe across it, in which white symbols were inscribed.

'What does that mean?' I asked.

Matthew shook his head. 'It's a red circle and a blue line, but what the symbols mean is unknown. Some people say it's an ancient religious incantation. Others think it's a sign of some kind, perhaps identifying the tunnel, because there are different symbols in other tunnels. But no one really knows.'

'It could have something to do with the tunnel running in a straight line but having a rounded ceiling,' I suggested, studying the circle intersected by a single line.

Matthew smiled at me. 'I never thought of that!'

Thinking about the picture of my grandmother, and the symbols scrawled on the back of it, I wondered if there could be any connection between that and the sign in the tunnel. Could my grandmother have lived in a tunnel like this one? Perhaps she had slept where I was now squatting.

Matthew crouched on the ground, facing me. 'I guess you've been wondering about this?' He held up his hand with one finger missing.

'I hadn't noticed it,' I lied.

Ignoring my reply, he told me what had happened, while we rested our legs in the dark tunnel. As a young boy living a feral existence on the streets, Matthew had been arrested by the

Guardians. On their way to the citadel, they had stopped the cart to arrest a group of malcontents who were protesting on the street. The rioting citizens were caught and shackled, and dragged into the cart. While the Guardians were busy apprehending the troublemakers, Matthew had seized his chance to slip down the ramp, unseen. His hands were still manacled, and the only way he had been able to free himself was by slicing off one of his little fingers.

'If I had been any older, that would have been impossible, because my hands would have been too big. Helen found me and she saved my life,' he concluded.

I listened, horrified, as he told his story.

When he had finished, we set off in silence once more. The tunnel seemed to be interminable and I fell into a kind of trance, moving one leg at a time. Left foot, right foot, left foot, right foot. At last, Matthew turned off the main passage into a side tunnel.

'Here we are,' he said, waving his torch around.

We were at the foot of a vertical shaft only this time, instead of a ladder, we mounted a steep spiral staircase. Matthew went ahead, and before long he had vanished in the shadows above me.

10

SAND

My knees were aching by the time Matthew called down to me to halt, and I clung to the stair rail, afraid my legs would give way when I stopped moving. Overhead I heard him heave aside another heavy metal disc, allowing sunlight to pour into the shaft. Dazzled, I dragged myself up the rest of the steps and out of the tunnel. With a groan I pitched forward onto the ground and recoiled as my mouth filled with gritty sand. Matthew helped me to my feet, choking and spitting. He had pulled up his hood and he snapped at me to do the same.

'It will give you some protection from the sun,' he explained.

Down in the tunnel I had been afraid of losing Matthew. Without him to guide me, I would have been lost forever in a maze of underground passages, stumbling around in a black void until I died. Daylight should have been a welcome relief from the stifling darkness of the tunnels, but once my eyes grew used to it, we might as well have still been underground, because I felt even more lost in the sunlight than I had been in darkness. Everywhere I looked, there was nothing to see but sand and sky. Matthew dragged the metal disc back in place and scattered sand over it until it was hidden.

Shocked that he had cut us off from the entrance to the tunnel, I cried out in protest.

'How will we ever find our way back into the city again?'

Matthew smiled easily. 'Don't worry. I know how to get there,' he assured me.

For the first time in my life I was outside the city walls. All around us in every direction empty desert stretched away, an unrelieved landscape of tawny beige, beneath a sun that beat down on us relentlessly. Every trace of the city had vanished. Clearly Matthew did not share my alarm. 'So far so good,' he said cheerily. 'And now we have a long walk. Come on, they'll be expecting us.'

It was unnecessary for him to warn me to stay close to him. I had no wish to be abandoned in this vast desert. Now I understood the reason for our sand-coloured cloaks, which kept us hidden from our enemies. Unless I was careful, our camouflage would be my undoing because, with his hood up, Matthew was virtually invisible. Even his weather-beaten face seemed to blend into the sand. Only his eyes showed clearly, as long as they were wide open.

'Are you ready?' Matthew asked.

I nodded nervously, and we each swallowed a hydration pill before we set off. It was a mystery to me how Matthew found his way with nothing to see in any direction but endless undulating dunes of sand, sand, and more sand. After a few steps I glanced back over my shoulder. The entrance to the tunnel had vanished, swallowed up by the desert. Hurrying after Matthew, I had no way of knowing how far we had travelled, since it was impossible to get my bearings. The desert was unlike anything I had seen before. In stark contrast to the city with its labyrinth of narrow streets winding between flat-roofed grey buildings, we were surrounded by a monotonous expanse of ochre stretching out beneath a blazing sky. It was unnerving, but Matthew seemed perfectly relaxed, as if he was enjoying a leisurely stroll. I did my best to walk lightly, but could not help kicking up small clouds of sand with every step. My guide did not seem to disturb the sand at all, and while my feet left shallow footprints, Matthew seemed to glide along without leaving any trace. My legs ached, my head hurt, and still we trudged on across the empty wasteland, beneath a burning sun.

After a long time, for no apparent reason, Matthew raised one arm and started waving it in the air in a circular motion as we continued walking. Too exhausted to question him, I hoped it was a signal that our journey was reaching its end. Unexpectedly, he grabbed my arm. Peering closely, I saw that a wide crater had opened up at our feet. If Matthew had not stopped me, I would have gone tumbling down the steep incline. Standing at the rim of the crater, I could see nothing below us but sand. As I stared, Matthew pointed out what appeared to be sand-coloured shelters packed together on the distant floor of the crater, and figures moving around in sand-coloured robes. It seemed to be a faint mirage, but my guide assured me the camp dwellers had been observing our approach. Lookouts had spotted us outlined against the sky, and they had been watching us walking across the desert. By now they would know that Matthew was leading a stranger to the camp.

'If you were alone, you would have been captured or killed long before you reached this point.'

My guide strode easily down the sheer slope. Attempting to trot after him, I lost my balance, my feet slipped from under me, and I slithered downwards on my back. The sound of children's laughter rang out when I finally bumped to a halt on the floor of the crater. Lying supine on the sand, I looked up at a circle of dirty faces surrounding me, pointing and giggling and chattering.

'Is this it?'

'Don't tell me this is the wife?'

'It doesn't look like a wife.'

'How would you know what a wife looks like?'

'I know it wouldn't look like that.'

'It looks just like us.'

'No it doesn't. Look at its hair.'

'And it's fat! Look how fat it is!'

'It looks funny.'

A stern voice interrupted the shrill clamour. 'Children, go back to school at once.'

My hands were caught in a firm grip and I was yanked to my feet by a sturdy woman. She was probably around my age, although the lines on her sunburnt face made her look considerably older. The skin around her eyes was wrinkled, as though she was used to squinting in bright sunlight. She peered curiously at me through narrowed eyes as, behind her, the children scampered away.

'Are you all right? Please forgive the children's impertinence, they were very excited about your arrival. It's not every day we welcome a trained wife to our camp. I hope you're not too tired after travelling with Matthew as your guide. He's used to walking the sands, and forgets it's not always easy for other people to move around out here in the desert. It takes some getting used to, and this is all new to you.' She smiled sympathetically at me. 'You're accustomed to a very different way of life, but we'll do our best to make you comfortable, and at the very least you'll be safe here with us.'

Longing for a hot scented bath and a soft bed, I assured her everything was fine.

'Come then.' Her smile was spontaneous, nothing like the practised expressions I had seen on every face in The Facility. 'The Elders sent me to fetch you. They're waiting to meet you.

My name's Laura, and of course we all know who you are. Matthew's told us about you.'

As we walked, I studied Laura. Her voice was lilting and, despite her weather-beaten skin, she had a pleasant face, with piercing blue eyes that reminded me of Matthew's. She walked resolutely across the floor of the crater, which was packed with shelters of different sizes, all constructed of the same sand-coloured material. In place of doors, they had an opening on one side, and the thin walls appeared to be made of compacted sand. Some were fairly neat constructions, while others looked lopsided, as though they had been erected in a hurry. There were no clear pathways between them, and we followed a circuitous route.

'The buildings here look as though they're made of sand,' I remarked.

'That's exactly what they're made of.'

I found that hard to believe, and she explained. 'It took our people a long time to form sand into panels large enough to make walls and roofs, but sand is the only material we have to work with. I don't know how it was done, but apparently they used a huge fire pit, and somehow by heating the sand they managed to make enough grains stick together to form huge flat sheets. It was difficult, and dangerous, but the man who supervised the work was very skilled at it. Even so, the walls are quite brittle, so we have to be careful,' she added, glancing anxiously at me. 'Many of us have learned the hard way just how careful we need to be. A couple of huts have been damaged because people were reckless, and these days no one can carry out repairs.'

'Why not?'

'When there was first talk of Guardians searching for us, it was considered too risky to keep the fire pit going, because smoke rose into the sky day and night, like a signal betraying our location. So as soon as enough shelters had been built, the fire was extinguished. And then the master builder died without passing on his knowledge to anyone, so we have to make do as we are. It's not that bad.' She hesitated. 'I've heard the walls of the city are indestructible. Is that really true?'

'Yes. They're made of stone and very thick.'

A few huts were much larger than the others, and Laura pointed them out to me as we made our way through the site.

'That's the school.' She indicated one of the larger constructions. 'I'm afraid you've already seen that some of the children need to learn a few manners. We're hoping you'll be able to help us with that. And there's the hospital. Of course, we don't have much in the way of medical supplies, but the doctors do their best. And we're short on nurses. I don't suppose you've had any first aid training?'

I shook my head. Medical skill played no part in our training as wives. For the rich, there were always qualified staff to treat sickness or injury.

As we made our way to the Elders' hut, Laura explained the camp system.

'The Elders don't have the power to make laws, they can only pass on our ideas to the community. Any one of us can ask them to put a proposal to the rest of the camp dwellers, and the Elders do not have authority to refuse any request. They have to present our ideas to the whole camp, and everyone over the age of thirteen is obliged to vote. The system is very cumbersome and time consuming, but it means no one group of Elders can take control of our lives. Some people think the age for voting should be lowered, but most of us think we already have too many impractical ideas put forward by the youngsters as it is, and there is a vociferous faction who advocate raising the voting age.' She gave a rueful smile. 'It gives rise to a lot of debate, as you can imagine, and we waste a lot of time going over and over the same arguments.'

Unable to imagine what it would be like to discuss the laws that governed our lives I nodded, too tired to try and understand what Laura was talking about. Without responding, I followed her into a crude building in the centre of the crater. A threadbare red carpet on the floor was sprinkled with sand, so that its pattern was all but impossible to distinguish. I guessed that the carpet and a long wooden table beside it had been brought there from the city.

Five men and two women were seated around the table. All but one of them was elderly, with shaggy grey or white hair. The exception was a rosy-cheeked man of about forty, who was broad shouldered and completely bald. Drumming his fingers impatiently on the table, he looked as though he was bursting to spring out of his seat and do something. They all looked up when we entered. The older ones smiled encouragingly at me, while the bald man's eyes burned with some unspoken passion.

'At last!' he exclaimed, half rising to his feet. 'We thought you were never going to get here. What took you so long?'

To my astonishment, Laura chuckled at the bald man's truculence. 'Always impatient, Daniel,' she scolded him.

My training had taught me that men were to be respected and obeyed. Never having witnessed a woman upbraiding a man, I held my breath, waiting to see if Daniel would beat her or banish her from the camp. My surprise increased when he returned her smile.

'This is Rachel,' Laura said, 'the trained wife Matthew brought us.'

'We can see that,' Daniel replied, irascible again.

Staring at my filthy feet, I wished they would stop talking about me as though my escape from The Facility had never happened, and I was still following The Programme, training to be a wife. It was true I had once been elegantly dressed, well-groomed and sweetly perfumed, but that was in the past. Now I smelled sour, my teeth were no longer clean, and my hair was filthy. Dressed in a shapeless tunic and baggy trousers, I could scarcely imagine anyone looking less like a wife. No discerning man would want to come anywhere near me, let alone marry me. For years I had lived as a trainee wife. Now I had exchanged that pampered role for the hard life of a fugitive, wanted by the Guardians for my desertion. With an effort I controlled my trembling and faced my interrogators as calmly as I could.

Six Elders gazed inquisitively at me. The seventh appeared to be asleep, his sand-coloured tunic quivering with every breath he took. No one spoke, but I sensed their disappointment on seeing me. They must have been expecting someone far more glamorous. Having scrutinised me for a few seconds in silence, Daniel asked me to remove my hood.

I hesitated. 'My hair hasn't been oiled for weeks.'

A faint whisper of laughter greeted my apology. The camp dwellers probably never cleaned their hair. Embarrassed, I pulled my hood off and hung my head. Laura had told me everyone in the camp was equal. No one had power over the lives of others. Yet it soon became obvious that Daniel was their leader, and being in charge of the Elders meant he virtually controlled the whole camp. It was evident why they all deferred to him in everything. His energy seemed to give strength to the others. Mesmerised by his rhetoric, I forgot my exhaustion and fear, and felt a new hope and confidence ignite inside me. Life in the desert must be tough, and the camp dwellers needed a leader who could inspire them to keep going. In Daniel they had found such a leader. All of this passed through my mind as I stood before the Elders, my head bowed, listening to what they had planned for me.

Daniel answered my question about my future at the camp

before I could ask, explaining that Matthew had brought me to the camp because they needed my help.

'What sort of help?' I asked, bemused. 'What can I do? I don't know anything about surviving in the desert.'

The old man suddenly woke up and thumped on the table. 'I call this meeting to order!' he shouted.

No one took any notice of him and he closed his eyes again.

One of the old women at the table tapped Daniel's arm. 'Can't you see the poor girl is worn out? Surely this can wait until tomorrow.'

Daniel raised his eyebrows, as though he did not understand what it meant to be tired, but the other Elders agreed with the woman, apart from the old man who had fallen asleep. With an impatient frown, Daniel bowed his head and accepted their decision.

As Laura was leading me away, the sleeper awoke.

'Was that my wife?' he enquired in a querulous voice. 'Why doesn't she come over here?'

'Don't take any notice of William,' Laura told me quietly. 'He likes to think he's in charge. It doesn't mean anything. Most of what he says is complete gibberish, but he's harmless. He suffers from mind slips, you see. Sometimes he follows what you say, and at other times he can't even remember his own name.'

'Why is he one of the Elders, if he's losing his mind?' I asked.

I was amazed when Laura told me that the old man, William, had once been the Leader of the City Council. Ousted by a rival, he had been locked up by the Guardians, and was the only prisoner known to have escaped from the citadel.

'How did he do that?' I asked.

'Allegedly he overpowered a Guardian and stole his uniform.'

'Did he kill the Guardian?'

'I'm not sure. I think that's what happened, but the story is a bit vague and seems to change with each retelling. William is the only one who knows the truth, and his memory is very confused.' Laura lowered her voice even further. 'Sometimes he thinks he's living in the city, and is still the Leader of The Council.'

She explained that William sat at the Elders' table as a symbol of the camp dwellers' freedom from the city, because he had once been the most powerful man on The Council.

'And look at him now,' Laura said. 'It's ironic. We all admire him for escaping from the city, yet half the time he thinks he's still there, in charge of the city that is determined to destroy him, along with the rest of us.'

11

THE CAMP

I spent the night in a hut with five other women. In the clothes we had been wearing all day, we lay side by side under threadbare covers. There was scarcely enough room to turn over without disturbing someone else, and a couple of the women snored all night. It was hardly surprising that I barely slept, in spite of my exhaustion. Apart from being cramped, I was kept awake by the sand. Walking to the camp, I had done my best to keep myself free of it, brushing down my clothes with the back of my hand, and pulling my hood tightly round my face to protect my eyes. Despite all my efforts, sand found its way into my clothes and shoes, as well as my ears and nose. It tickled the back of my throat, and made my scalp itch.

When I had asked Laura how to free myself of the constant irritation, she laughed and told me there was no point in trying. 'You'll never get rid of it, whatever you do,' she said.

'How do you cope with it?'

'I don't even notice it anymore. You have to think before you blink, and whatever you do, avoid rubbing your eyes, but after a while it becomes second nature to be careful with – well, everything really, because the sand gets everywhere.'

When I protested that the discomfort was impossible to bear, she shrugged. 'That's just how it is. You'll get used to it.'

At night we slept on cloaks on the sand, which found its way into our eyes and our hair and between our toes. Scraping it out from under my fingernails, I found more grains inside my shoes. It was maddening. By the time I gave up trying to clear my ears, my fingernails were packed with it again. Running my hand through my hair, I felt grains of sand flick against my face, and thought wistfully of the polished floors and walls of The Facility.

But worse than any physical distress was my mental confusion as I tried make sense of everything I had seen in the camp: rows of sand-coloured huts, laughing children, the Elders who purported to serve the people but in reality ruled them, and their leader, Daniel, who claimed he wanted my help. I wondered what kind of help I could possibly give to people living in such a rudimentary settlement in the middle of a vast desert.

The only answer I could think of was that, as Laura had mentioned, they wanted me to teach their children how to behave. But it was hard to see what my training as a wife could possibly teach them about survival in the desert. Still, I resolved to pretend to agree with the request, until I had worked out a way to return to the city. The deception would not challenge me unduly. My training had made me an expert in feigned compliance.

It was a relief to get up and stretch my legs the next morning. Dawn was only just breaking, but the camp was already warm. The huts afforded some protection from the sun, but were by no means as cool as the stone buildings of the city. One by one we crawled out of our sleeping quarters into the dazzling sunlight. Pulling their hoods over their heads for protection, the other women dispersed to their various tasks. I followed one of them until she disappeared into another hut, telling me she had to start work. Alone and lost in a city of similar huts, with no clear paths between them, I spotted a familiar face and hurried to greet him. Matthew was pulling a small open cart loaded with bulging sand-coloured sacks.

He glanced up, and a faint frown crossed his face when he saw me. 'What are you doing here by yourself, Rachel?' he demanded. 'You shouldn't be wandering around on your own. Who's looking after you?'

I had no answer for his questions. Telling me to wait exactly where I was, he strode off, lugging his cart behind him.

Shortly after that, Laura appeared, hurrying towards me, a worried expression on her face. 'There you are, Rachel,' she called out, flapping one hand in the air to attract my attention. 'I've been looking everywhere for you. Come on, the Elders are waiting for you.'

She did not chastise me, but I had the impression she was upset with me for setting off to explore the camp without her. I wondered whether Matthew was angry with her for leaving me alone, but there was no time to apologise or explain. In their hut, the seven Elders were seated at the table, waiting for me. Daniel sat at one end, with William facing him. The two women at the table looked friendly, but they did not say much. William appeared to have no idea what was going on, and his companions mostly ignored him. The other three men stared curiously at me until I felt uncomfortable. I could imagine what they had been told about trained wives, and realised they must have been disappointed when they saw me with my dishevelled hair, filthy clothes, and unpainted face. I hung my head and remained silent while Daniel opened the meeting with a long speech, most of which I did not understand. He was very direct, and I was not sure what to say when he asked me what help I was prepared to offer the camp dwellers.

'As a trained wife, you must have a lot you can teach us,' he said firmly. 'And a lot you can do for us.'

I looked around helplessly, but the old people merely stared at me in silence. Remembering Laura's suggestion, I offered to teach their children how to behave, but Daniel dismissed that idea with a wave of his hand, without even bothering to consult the others.

'The manners you learned during your training will be of little use in the desert,' he told me. 'In any case, the Elders are not concerned with the children's manners.'

'On the contrary,' one of the women disagreed mildly. 'We are all responsible for the children.'

With a shrug, Daniel turned back to me. 'Well? What do you say?'

'I don't know what to say because I don't know what you want,' I muttered, overwhelmed at being challenged so forcefully by a man.

Daniel stared at me in silence with unnerving intensity, and I lowered my eyes in confusion.

'When Matthew told us you wanted to join us, I thought–' he broke off and glanced around the table before correcting himself. 'That is to say, we all thought you could be a great help to us, if we agreed to allow you to come and live with us. We have offered you our protection. What will you give us in return?' He seemed to be threatening to exile me from the camp unless I gave him what he was demanding, although we all knew that if I left the camp, I would die.

With growing frustration, I repeated humbly that I did not know what he wanted.

'We want to know what those devils are up to,' he replied fiercely, banging on the table with his fist. 'We want to know what's going on at their Council meetings. What are they plotting behind the walls of their blasted citadel?'

'I don't know anything about The Council meetings,' I protested, startled by his severity.

'But you can find out, can't you?'

'How?'

'You're a trained wife, aren't you?'

I nodded. There was no point in denying what I was, or bleating that my training was incomplete.

'You must have contacts inside the citadel,' he went on, 'someone who might know about Council plans. Better still, if you had a husband, you could listen in on his conversations. You could ask him about his work, and pump him for information. We would arrange for you to communicate with us in such a way that The Council would never suspect your hidden allegiance. With your looks, you could easily attract the attention of an important Council Member, and maybe even influence his views about us.'

'You mean you want me to spy on the city Council for you?' I was too startled to protest that there was no way I could attract a husband now that my looks were ruined.

'If that's how you want to put it, yes,' Daniel replied. 'You would be spying for a very important reason. You could help us to save the lives of everyone living in the camp.'

'You don't understand,' I remonstrated when he insisted. 'I could never be chosen as a wife now that I have left The Programme.'

Daniel shook his head. 'You're the one who doesn't understand what's at stake here. We need you to do this. We wouldn't be asking you if it wasn't essential to our survival. It won't be difficult, not for you. We'll take care of everything relating to your passing on information. And don't worry. We'll make sure you're never in any danger. One of us will come and collect information from you in absolute secrecy. If we're caught, any one of us would die rather than betray you. You'd be far too valuable for us to risk losing you. All you need is a husband who's on The Council.'

'But no one's going to marry me now.' I could not help laughing.

Daniel looked at me. 'Why ever not? You're beautiful,' he said. 'You're beautiful, and you've been trained. With a glamorous gown, you'll look as good as ever. All we're asking is that you try.'

I did not feel beautiful. Running my hands through my dirty hair, I felt sand all over my scalp. Remembering what had happened to Naomi, I spoke angrily.

'I could never be a wife, not now. Believe me, it's not that easy to be chosen. I've seen girls far more beautiful than I ever was who were rejected as wives. And look at me now. Seriously, look at me! I'm filthy, my hair is a mess, and I'm not wearing any make-up. My nails are grubby and broken, and I've lost weight. No facility would display me looking like this, let alone expect a Member of The Council to choose me as a wife. No facility would even take me in looking like this. If by some miracle they did, by the time I was sufficiently groomed to be displayed, I would be too old to be chosen. I'm sorry if you feel I've let you down, but it's not my fault. I'm finished as far as The Programme is concerned. That part of my life is over, and can never be resurrected. It just doesn't work like that.' I stopped, my voice betraying a distress I had not been aware of feeling.

Daniel scowled. 'If you're not going to be a wife, how do you propose to help us?'

'I don't know.' My voice shook. 'I was hoping you would let me stay here, and live in the camp.'

'Of course you must stay here with us,' one of the female Elders said. 'Where else could you go? Daniel, you're being too stern with the poor girl.'

With a grunt, Daniel strode to the entrance and instructed

Laura to take me away and find me something useful to do. I had won the argument, but I felt miserable, knowing he was disappointed in me.

Laura took me to the hospital where about a dozen people were lying on the ground. A couple of women were walking up and down, exchanging a few words with the patients as they passed. The atmosphere was calm, and I considered offering to help out in this peaceful place. Laura had told me they were short of nurses, and if I had no idea what to do, I could learn. There was a sudden commotion outside and two men entered, carrying a third man who was struggling to free himself. His arms and legs were bound together so he could do nothing but writhe in their grasp. When they put him down he thrashed around on the floor. His skin was unnaturally pale and speckled with drops of sweat, and his eyes had rolled so far back into his head that only the whites could be seen. He was shaking from head to foot, and gabbling incoherently. Appalled, I asked Laura what was wrong with him.

'He's suffering from sand fever,' a passing nurse answered.

'It's in a fairly advanced stage,' another nurse told us, 'but hopefully we'll be able to sort him out.'

Several people gathered round to watch the man, who was still struggling against his restraints, and someone began snapping out orders in a low voice. A nurse knelt down and forced a pill between the lips of the sick man who gagged and coughed, and abruptly lay still, his eyes closed. No one else seemed particularly perturbed by his condition.

'Will he be all right?' I asked Laura as we left the hospital.

'Oh yes,' she replied. 'It's just sand fever.'

'Does that happen a lot?'

She shrugged. 'It's one of the risks of being a desert walker. He wasn't careful enough.'

'Why does it happen?'

'No one really knows. It's something that happens to the walkers if they spend too much time out in the desert. They usually recover quite quickly.'

The school was a cheerier place. Here the sand offered a variety of opportunities to play and learn. In one area, a group of children were constructing a miniature world of tiny sand hills and valleys, citadels and caves. Other children were scooping up handfuls of sand and digging out small craters in the ground. A scuffle broke out when a small boy smashed another boy's sandcastle. A woman went over and talked quietly to both children, and the aggressor was sent to sit by himself on a low bank of sand at one end of the hut. Other than that outburst, the children played contentedly together, and it was hard to believe their lives were so harsh. Heedless of the sand in their hair, their clothes, their feet and their faces, they seemed oblivious to the dangers that threatened the existence of their community. I wondered how much they knew about the world outside the camp.

When we left the school, we spotted Matthew in the distance, pulling his cart, and I asked Laura what was in his bags.

'It'll soon be time to sleep,' she replied, ignoring my question as Vanessa used to do. 'We need to get to the food clinic.'

The clinic was on the far side of the camp, and we walked there without speaking, our feet padding silently on the sand.

'This is where we come for our pills,' Laura said.

'Where do you get them from?' I asked, voicing a question that had been puzzling me since my arrival at the camp.

'Oh, Matthew brings them here.'

'But how does he get hold of them?'

'It's some deal the Elders made with someone somewhere in the city,' she replied vaguely.

On the point of telling her about my own hidden hoard of pills, I held back. Laura was keeping a secret from me, refusing to disclose what Matthew was carrying on his cart. I resolved to share my secret with her only if she answered my question, but after my first day at the camp I did not see her again for a few weeks. So the opportunity passed, and it was a while before I discovered what Matthew was transporting.

The girl who slept next to me was called Eve. About the same age as me, she was small and wiry, with bright black eyes, very dark skin, and a ready smile. Her tightly curled hair trapped so much sand, it scattered around her whenever she shook her head. She worked at the school, and I was happy to tag along with her. Eve's cheerful nature buoyed up my spirits, and it was not as though I had anywhere else to go. No one paid me much attention anymore, once they knew I could be of no use to them. That was absolutely fine with me. It had done me no good at all being treated as special.

On our way to the school, I asked Eve if Daniel had any children, but she did not seem to understand the question.

'The children belong to all of us,' she replied, with a tolerant smile at my ignorance. 'Including Daniel.'

'No, I mean children of his own. Is he a father?'

She halted and stared at me in surprise. 'A father? What do you mean? We don't have children. No one does. They say people used to, in the old days,' she added a trifle wistfully, 'but now only wives living in the city are able to breed. You must have known that when you were being trained. That's what makes the trainee wives so special.'

Her answer puzzled me.

'I know that's how it is in the city, but I thought it would be different here. Where do the children in the school come from, if only trained wives can breed?'

Eve explained that all the children in the camp had been rescued from the city.

Desert walkers from the camp paid occasional visits to the city at night. When they found an unwanted baby, or an abandoned child, they brought them to the camp where they were looked after. I was shocked at hearing that, but she assured me the system worked well.

'I don't know how they can be unwanted,' she added. 'You'd think a new life would be precious.' She sighed. 'There are few enough of them.'

'Not all trainees become wives,' I told her. 'Some of them are just used for breeding and then discarded. The Council Members who breed with them might not want the trouble and expense of maintaining babies born to women they don't intend to marry.'

'I don't know why they bother to breed with those women at all, if they're not going to keep the babies.'

'Apparently The Council Members like to breed with a lot of women, but they don't always want to deal with the consequences,' I said.

Eve nodded. 'That makes sense, I suppose. Anyway, from time to time the city dwellers abandon babies, and we can't breed, so it suits everyone if we care for them. It's not as if we're taking babies that anyone else wants. I think the mothers sometimes give them to the desert walkers deliberately because if we don't rescue the unwanted babies, they are left to die. The Council probably have no idea that so many babies are being smuggled out to the camp. If they ever found out, they would probably stop the babies leaving the city.'

'But what would happen to the unwanted babies then?'

She shrugged. 'They'd all die, I suppose. Or perhaps the

scientists have a use for them.' She sighed. 'You know, we are the last generation whose fathers were not all Council Members. Women used to breed with other men, any men, but now women are unable to breed. Apart from wives, of course. I suppose trainee wives are given pills to make them fertile?' When I did not respond, she continued. 'I suppose you were able to breed, while you lived in the city?'

I nodded uncertainly and explained how my body bled every month.

Eve grimaced. 'Is it very painful?'

'Not really. It just happens.'

I was glad no one else knew about my secret supply of pills from The Facility. I was given pills in the camp but I resolved to continue taking my own pills at least once a month. They had been issued to me by the clinic in the city, and I was nervous about taking pills given to me in the camp. In the city, it was against the law to swallow anything other than regulation pills, issued by The Council. The punishment for ingesting anything else was death. Although I was no longer living in the city, and had no need to adhere to its laws, my fear was not entirely irrational, because my body might react badly to a drastic change in my diet. But my decision was also sentimental. My fertility was my only link with the past that had not yet been severed. Under the loose tunic and trousers we all wore in the camp, my curvaceous figure and monthly bleeding were easy to hide, and no one ever questioned whether I might still be physically able to bear children.

Working at the school I looked around, wondering whether one of the babies there had been borne by Naomi. Our training as wives taught us nothing about caring for children. The Programme taught us how to please men so that they could breed with us, after which our babies were passed on to other women trained to raise them, leaving us free to return to our beauty routines without any distraction. So I had no experience of children, and was at a loss about what to do with them. The children were very noisy and active. The little ones played, making tiny model camps, pouring sand from one hand to another, and studying how to draw pictures on the ground. Eve explained that older children were taught to walk across the desert without leaving any trace, so that they could not be tracked. They were instructed in the movement of the sun and moon and stars across the sky, so they would be able to navigate their way across the desert where every vista was identical in any direction. Only those who were most talented at sand walking and navigation would ever be allowed out of the camp, but the Elders were keen for them all to learn how to move around the desert. If nothing else, it kept the children busy, and such skills might one day save their lives, and the lives of everyone in the camp.

12

THE SECRET

Working at the school turned out to be unexpectedly enjoyable. Some of the teachers lived and slept at school with the children, but I was pleased to leave at the end of the day, and enjoy a respite from my small charges. The individual children were all very different, and Eve and I chatted about them on our way to the food clinic, speculating about what the future might hold for them.

'Absalom's a born leader,' Eve said.

'Not a very good one,' I replied, laughing. 'He's a bully.'

When he was not pushing other children out of his way, Absalom was grabbing handfuls of sand from them and throwing it on the floor.

Eve grinned back at me. 'He's a strong child, with a forceful personality. Have you noticed how the other children are in awe of him?' She lowered her voice. 'Don't you think Daniel must have been like Absalom when he was a child?'

'I can't imagine Daniel ever being a child,' I said, when I stopped giggling.

'Jacob will be a desert walker,' she went on, more seriously.

'What makes you say that?'

I was still not quite sure what a desert walker was, but was embarrassed to ask.

'Haven't you noticed how the desert draws him?' she replied. 'He loves to explore, and if we don't keep an eye on him, he wanders off and we lose him among the huts. And unlike most of the children, he's not afraid to leave the camp. We've caught him climbing up the slope several times. It wouldn't surprise me if he gets out one day and wanders off into the desert. It's like a magnet for him. But if we manage to keep hold of him for long enough for him to understand what's out there, and how to navigate his way around, he has the makings of a desert walker.'

'What is a desert walker, exactly?' I asked finally, and was relieved when Eve evinced no surprise at my ignorance.

'Sorry,' she said, 'I keep forgetting you haven't grown up here. Desert walkers are the ones who can find their way in the desert. It's like an instinct for them.'

'How do they do it?'

She shrugged. 'No one knows. Even they don't know how they do it, but they just find their way across the desert. It's like they have a map in their heads. It must be something to do with the way they read the sky.'

I would have thought she was joking, had I not seen Matthew striding across the endless monotonous sand, as though he was walking along a clearly marked road.

'Matthew's a desert walker,' I said.

'One of the best,' she replied.

One morning a small girl began to wail because Absalom was throwing sand at her.

'Absalom, don't do that!' I said sternly.

He stopped at once and began to cry, pummelling his eyes

with his fists. His erstwhile victim skipped away happily, and I knelt down beside the little boy.

'Absalom, don't do that. You'll hurt your eyes if you rub sand in them. Do you know why I told you to stop throwing sand?'

Still crying, he peeped at me from behind his clenched fists. 'No one likes me,' he sobbed.

'That's because you throw sand at them,' I said gently. 'You could hurt someone. Everyone likes you, but no one likes having sand thrown at them. Do you understand?'

Dropping his hands from his eyes, he grabbed a handful of sand and threw it in my face before running off. No one else witnessed the incident and I kept quiet, afraid that I might be removed from my duties helping out at the school if the head teacher heard that one of the children had disrespected me. After giving the problem some thought, I resolved to spend more time with Absalom and try to help him feel accepted. I knew what it felt like to live as a stranger in a strange world.

So time passed, each day blending into the next in seamless repetition. There was a sense of peace in the camp, and I soon settled into my new routine. One day, not long after I had begun working at the school, the children were unusually animated. The quiet ones grew talkative, while the liveliest became positively manic. Even the teachers seemed strangely excited and made only half-hearted attempts to calm the children. Puzzled, I asked Eve what was happening.

'Nothing yet,' she replied, with a broad grin, 'but the lookouts have reported a storm on the horizon.'

Ashamed of my ignorance, I asked her what she meant.

'A storm is a great wind that rushes down from the highest dunes and sweeps across the desert. When you look up, the sky is hidden behind a vast moving cloud of sand that covers the sun and the moon.'

'Isn't it dangerous?' I asked, agitated at the prospect of a darkness I had seen only once, in a cell in the citadel. The memory of that experience came flooding back, and I clasped my hands together, fingers tightly entwined, to stop them from shaking.

'It would be very dangerous if you left the camp,' Eve replied, oblivious to the terror her words had inspired in me. 'Only a walker could survive a sandstorm in the desert. Anyone else would be buried alive.'

Her matter-of-fact tone disturbed me, and I shuddered.

Eve must have noticed my anxious expression because she hastened to reassure me. 'There's nothing to be scared about. We're quite safe here in the camp. The sides of the crater slope downwards at just the right angle to make sure most of the sand passes over without engulfing us.'

'But how will we see?'

'That's not a problem. We light torches. And the good news is, we don't have to worry about making a noise. The Guardians never dare leave the city in a storm and, even if some of them were roaming the desert, they wouldn't be able to hear anything above the roar of the wind. So we can make as much noise as we like.'

'What do you mean?' I asked, reassured, but mystified nonetheless. 'What sort of noise?'

'We make music!' she cried out, her eyes gleaming with anticipation.

I wanted to share in her exultation, but I was uneasy. 'Music?' I repeated. 'What is that?'

Eve laughed. 'Come on! You'll find out soon enough.'

There was a clear space in the centre of the camp, where meetings were held. As we approached, we heard a curious beat, fast and regular, which broke the silence with its rapid patterns. Eve began to sway as she walked, swinging her hips to the rhythm.

'Can you hear the drum?' she asked me.

We joined a throng of camp dwellers who were walking towards the clearing, clapping their hands in time to the beat. Without thinking, I began clapping with them. For the first time since my mother's death, I felt a sense of belonging, as though I had finally come home. A sudden shrill note rang out, pure, unearthly and beautiful, and I halted, transfixed by the piercing sound.

'What is that?' I murmured, almost afraid to break the spell by speaking out loud.

'William's playing his pipe,' Eve replied.

We walked on, as the high-pitched note plunged like a man felled by a poisoned dart and rose again, in a haunting melody. We reached the clearing which was lit up by a circle of torches set in the sand. In the flickering light, camp dwellers were wheeling and gyrating to the music. Some danced in pairs, others in small circles, while yet more spun around on their own. All were connected by the music. Like a physical presence, it trapped us in a web of sound. In the centre of the dancers Daniel was seated by a large canister which he was beating with sticks, producing the drumming rhythms. His eyes were fixed on Laura, who raised her arms and waved her hands in graceful spirals above her head.

'What are they doing?' I whispered.

'Dancing,' Eve replied.

Matthew's feet did not disturb the sand as he stamped on the ground beside Laura. Everywhere the camp dwellers gave themselves up to the dance, like people possessed by a spirit of joy. Before I realised it, I was tapping my feet and moving to the pulsing cadence of the pipe, and the throbbing of the drum. Exhilaration coursed through my body and I felt at one with the music, and the dancers, and the darkness of the sky above us. Nothing mattered but the dance, and the dance was timeless.

The music stopped as unexpectedly as it had begun. Exhausted, I followed Eve back to our tent. My mother had told me people were once happy. I wondered if this was what she had meant. Perhaps my mother and my grandmother had danced to music together, in the days before the Great Sickness came and contaminated the earth. Thinking about my mother made me want to cry, knowing that I would never learn the truth about her life. The world in which she had grown up was nothing like the world I knew.

The next morning, the camp buildings were covered in a gritty film of loose sand, a reminder of the storm and our euphoria of the previous night. We spent some time sweeping it onto the ground, shaking it out of our clothes, and brushing it out of our hair.

A few weeks later, Laura came to find me at the school, to say the Elders were asking to see me. That meant Daniel wanted to see me.

'What does he want?'

If she knew, she did not tell me, and we walked to the Elders' hut in silence.

When I went in, Daniel smiled at me. 'I hear good reports of you,' he said. 'You've been helping at the school.'

'Yes.'

'Good. Caring for the children is important, but we have other work, more important work, for you to do.'

I thought about the children, Absalom and Jacob, and the little girls, who were just getting to know me. My disappointment must have shown in my face, because he told me I could go back to my duties in the school once my new task had been carried out. There was no point in arguing with him.

The camp dwellers pretended that everyone in the camp was equal, but in reality our lives were controlled by the Elders, and the other Elders who sat at the table with Daniel were only there for show. Nothing had really changed. The power governing our lives was just better hidden than it had been in the city. Without explaining what he wanted me to do, Daniel told me that Matthew was waiting for me outside the hut.

'It's time for you to learn about my work,' Matthew said, without pausing to greet me.

Manners deemed acceptable in the camp were very different to those expected of trainee wives.

'I know about your work. You're a desert walker,' I replied.

'That's right.'

'How do you find your way?'

'Come with me and I'll show you.'

He strode away towards the edge of the crater and I hurried after his lean figure, my legs weak at the thought of trekking across the desert again. Accustomed to returning to the desert, Matthew strode easily up the steep incline that led out of the camp. I hoped he would not turn round and see me crawling painstakingly up the slope on my hands and knees, slithering backwards whenever I lost momentum. At last I reached the top, and he grunted when I stood up. He must have been irritated at having to wait so long for me to join him, but he did not complain. Instead, he simply walked away, leaving me to trot after him as quickly as I could. Sand dunes rose and fell in front of us, stretching away to the horizon, in a seemingly endless furrowed landscape. Above us the sky glowed clear and white, apart from the sun blazing down on the bronze sand. Within seconds, the slope leading down to the camp had vanished.

We walked for a long time before we reached the end of our journey. On the way Matthew did not speak, and I was too breathless from struggling to keep up with him to say anything.

Our destination was invisible until we reached a slight incline, and saw two sentries guarding a sand-coloured hut. As we drew near I saw there were more figures posted all around the hut. Well camouflaged against the unvarying landscape, they were proof against a stray wanderer, but would put up a poor defence against even one Guardian.

'I'm showing a newcomer around,' Matthew said. 'Orders from Daniel.'

The man and woman standing guard at the entrance nodded and stood aside to let us in, and I saw that unlike the huts in the camp, this one appeared to be several layers thick. We crossed a small outer area and went through a series of heavy sheets of sand, into the main area of the hut. I was already intrigued, but nothing could have prepared me for what happened next. To begin with, I was aware of a potent scent, an exciting mingling of sweet and spicy aromas, warmer and richer than any of Vanessa's delicate perfumes. There were strains of familiar smells in the blend, sweet, sharp and tangy, scents with exotic names that I recognised from bath oils at The Facility: strawberry, lemon, and peach. Long narrow mounds of compacted sand stood on three sides of the hut, and on each one lay rows of bags, like the ones I had seen in Matthew's cart. One bag lay open and I was dazzled by the brightness of the yellow spheres inside it, each one the size of my fist. It was a while since I had seen any colour but the dull bronze of the sand.

'What is all that?' I asked.

'Foodstuffs,' Matthew replied.

'What do you mean?' I blurted out, shocked by the nonchalance of his reply.

'This is what people used to eat. It was all readily available before the earth was contaminated by the Great Sickness. The sickness didn't only afflict people. It poisoned the entire surface of our world, so that all the foodstuffs withered and died. Only a few batches of the food-producing plants were saved.'

What Matthew was telling me sounded crazy, but he looked completely serious. He had saved my life, and I was appalled to think that he was delusional. Yet it made no sense for the hut to be so well guarded, if what he said really was insane. Besides, the smell in the hut was intoxicating, more exciting than the perfume salon at The Facility. If Matthew was not telling the truth, then what were these tantalising scents doing here in the desert, where no one even cleaned themselves, let alone put on perfumes?

'Sit down, and I'll explain,' Matthew said, smiling at my bewilderment.

We crouched on the sand and he talked. It was hard not to be convinced by his low, even voice as he told me that many years ago, before the Great Sickness, the earth itself supplied people with nourishment. The foodstuffs that grew out of the ground were hard to swallow, because they were not compressed into digestible pills. People were forced to ingest vast amounts of different foods to absorb what their bodies needed, and more often than not they got the amounts wrong.

'I know,' I said. 'We learned about this from Hazel, in our history lessons at The Facility. People were all different sizes, and they had all kinds of diseases through eating the wrong balance of foods.'

He nodded, pleased that I understood. 'It probably sounds incredible to you, raised as you were on pills issued by The Council, but that's how it was back then.'

'What I don't understand is how people hydrated themselves,' I said. 'They never explained that to us and I've always wondered about it.'

Matthew nodded. 'That is the oddest thing of all, but I'll try to explain, at least as I understand it. You know about people immersing themselves in oils for cleansing?'

'Of course. We were immersed in oils every day at The Facility, and before that my mother used to take me to the baths once a month.' Recollecting the greasy, scummy oils at the public baths, I wished my mother could have experienced the wonderful baths at The Facility, just once. Recalling the hardship she had endured in her life, I felt like crying, but Matthew was speaking again, and I had to focus on what he was telling me.

'Well,' he resumed, 'before the earth was contaminated by the Great Sickness, a life-giving liquid, softer and lighter than oil, flowed across the land. It moved in great streams, from which droplets rose up into the sky until they soared above the sun. Growing cold, they fell down to earth again, and people collected them in vast pits and used them to hydrate the land and also themselves.'

'I don't understand. How could they hydrate themselves by immersion in pits of liquid?'

Matthew shook his head. 'It wasn't like that. No, it's even stranger than you can imagine. People swallowed the liquid and hydrated themselves from the inside.'

My incredulity must have shown in my face, but he ignored my reaction and carried on. 'After the Great Sickness, fluids stopped falling from the sky, and the great streams dried up and could not be replenished. The soft liquid disappeared from the earth. Foodstuffs that had not already succumbed to disease withered and died, along with many people. Because of this, famine struck, and the human race was threatened with complete extinction. Fortunately, a group of scientists had developed food and hydration pills, and so a handful of us were saved, while the rest of the world perished for want of nutrition and hydration. The Council stepped in to take care of our dietary requirements and, as you know, in the city everyone is now given the pills they need.'

'We are lucky,' I muttered automatically. 'The Council takes care of us.'

Matthew ignored my interruption. 'But there was a problem,' he said. 'A lot of people were addicted to different foodstuffs and were unable to live without them.'

'Couldn't they be cured?'

Matthew shook his head. 'Maybe, but not everyone wanted to be cured. Remember, we're talking about an addiction. They couldn't help themselves.'

I recalled the prisoner who had protested so violently in the cart on the way to the citadel. Other captives had described him as an addict, and one of them had said he could not help himself.

'If they couldn't be cured, and they didn't want to stop, then they should have been locked up,' I said.

'Many of the addicts *were* imprisoned in the citadel, and they died there, but the situation was more complicated than that, because some of the transgressors were Members of The Council.'

I frowned. Of all Matthew's outlandish claims, this was the strangest.

'While the rest of the population ingested only pills, some Council Members carried on eating the old foodstuffs. It had to be done in secret, and it was dangerous to keep a store of illegal foodstuffs in the city. The penalty for transgression was death. When the camp dwellers first went into exile in the desert, they formed a private alliance with The Council addicts, according to which the camp dwellers agreed to deliver foodstuffs to The Council addicts in secret, in return for their protection. But it has always been difficult to keep this quiet, and other Members of The Council are increasingly keen to see rebels stamped out. "Let them go to the wastelands and rot!" is a popular cry.'

Matthew continued, 'So far there have been enough addicts on The Council to keep the camp dwellers safe, but the numbers of our supporters on The Council are dwindling. Some of them have been careless or indiscreet and have been sent to the fire; others have died of old age, and only a few of our old supporters have been replaced by other addicts.'

I stared at him in disbelief. 'Is that true?' I whispered.

He gave a taut smile. 'Oh yes. Most Members of The Council are indifferent to our fate. There is still a faction working to defend us and, in return, we give them foodstuffs. Occasionally a food addict is detected and tortured until they die or, more likely, give up their addiction, and when that happens, they usually turn against us. Several of our fiercest enemies are reformed addicts. For our own protection, we can't let anyone from the city know the location of the camp, so we deliver the foodstuffs to them in secret. That's my job. I make sure foodstuffs get to the right people without anyone else knowing about it. Every month I take food bags along the tunnels to the city.'

'Isn't that dangerous?'

He frowned. 'Of course the work is dangerous, but it has to be done.'

'What would happen to the camp if our enemies found us?'

Matthew looked grave. 'We used to communicate with another camp who had discovered a way to cultivate foodstuffs in the sands of the desert, but they were slack with their security, and made it too easy for The Council to track them down. Guardians were sent to stamp them out. Even the addicts on The Council couldn't save them.'

'What happened to the people living in that camp?'

Matthew heaved a sigh. 'The whole camp was wiped out,

men, women and children. Now we keep to ourselves and only leave the camp to make deliveries to the city. If we stop sending foodstuffs to our supporters on The Council, there will be no one left to protect us.'

I looked around, baffled. 'Is this where all the foodstuffs are made?'

'No, this is just one of our distribution huts. We cultivate our foodstuffs in an underground site far from here. Come on, it's time for you to visit the site and see what goes on there.'

'Are all the camp dwellers taken to see it?' I asked.

Matthew shook his head. 'No one is taken unless it's necessary.' He paused. 'The Elders have a particular mission in mind for you. Now come on, we need to make a start.'

Exposed in the desert again, I settled my hood securely on my head and tried not to think about my mother's tales of wild monsters living in the wastelands outside the city walls. She had described them as huge, man-like creatures with fiery eyes and snapping jaws. As we walked I kept looking around, but there was nothing to see apart from Matthew's tall figure pacing ahead of me. Sometimes he faded into the landscape, and I had to run to catch up with him. The last thing I wanted was to be left alone and lost, a prey to monsters.

We walked in silence for hours. The heat and the travelling made me long to stop and lie down. Physically spent, I looked with loathing at the endless sand, and wondered how Absalom was behaving in my absence. We walked without pausing to rest until the moon rose in the sky, but even then Matthew did not stop. The sun appeared over the horizon and still we plodded on.

Repeatedly I felt my eyes close, and had to force myself to stay awake. 'How much further?' I asked. 'Can we rest yet?'

Matthew did not answer. My eyes were only shut for an instant, but when I opened them again, he had vanished.

13

PLANTS

Alarmed, I spun round, staring in every direction, but there was no sign of my companion. Not only had I lost my guide, but I had absolutely no idea how to find my way back to the camp, and no idea even of the direction to take. Everywhere I looked there was nothing but endless desert.

'Matthew!' I cried out in a panic. 'Matthew! Where are you?'

There was a faint scraping noise, and a head rose up out of the sand in front of me.

'Stop that bloody racket, will you?' an irate voice called out. 'Do you want the whole world to hear you? Come on! Follow me, and get a move on. Some of us have work to do.' Muttering about wasting time, the head sank down into the sand once more. It was a gruff invitation, but I could hardly stay where I was. The monsters might already have heard me yelling. Glancing around fearfully, I shuffled forward. There nothing to be seen but sand until, kneeling down to study the ground closely, I noticed hundreds of small sand-coloured tubes poking out among the grains of sand. Round about where the head had appeared was a circular area free of tubes. Sweeping the sand aside gently, the tips of my fingers felt a flat disc. It was very light and slid aside easily to reveal a spiral staircase leading under the ground.

Slowly I lowered myself onto the steps and was beginning my descent when an angry voice hissed at me to close the roof. Balancing with difficulty, I reached up with both hands and slid the disc back in place. It slotted neatly into position with a faint click. Expecting to be plunged into darkness, I was relieved to discover the staircase was still visible. There was no rail to hold on to, and I descended warily.

Reaching the bottom, I found myself in a spacious chamber lit by sunlight streaming in through many circular tubes hanging down from the roof. Row upon row of bunches of green ribbons hung from sticks poking out of narrow mounds of sand that stretched the length of the vast chamber. Some of them were placed directly beneath a tube in the roof, so that sunlight shone down onto a variety of light and dark green streamers spilling out of the sand. For a moment I was overcome with a poignant sense of joy at the combination of lovely smells that assailed me. Among them I thought I recognised the sharp scent of lemon and a delicate note of lavender. At first the place seemed silent, but listening intently I became aware of a faint rustling. A lithe figure was pacing between the mounds of sand, sprinkling white dust into the green sprays of ribbons, and his activity was the cause of the noise. Matthew, who was striding along beside the stranger, came over to me as soon as he saw me.

'Those are powdered hydration pills,' he explained, with his easy smile. 'Sunlight and hydration, that's all they need.'

'That's all who needs?' I asked.

'The plants we're nursing here.'

'They need more than just sunlight and hydration,' the stranger called out. 'There are minerals from beneath the ground in this powder. Plants need more than simple hydration if they are to thrive.'

'What are plants?'

'These are,' Matthew replied, gesturing at rows of small trailing green pennants sticking up out of the sand. 'All of them are plants, growing out of the sand. You can see they are all very different.'

'Growing?' I repeated, bewildered. 'What do you mean, they're growing? What are they?'

Matthew made it sound as though the green plants were alive, as we were. A memory flitted into my head, of Clare telling me how her grandmother had talked of things that grew out of the ground, covered in living green ribbons. The young man finished dropping powder into a row of plants, and joined us.

Ignoring me, he spoke to Matthew. 'Daylight will be fading soon.'

Matthew nodded and introduced the other man as Gideon. The name jolted my memory, and I recalled meeting a boy called Gideon in the street outside The Facility, when the Guardians had deposited me there several years ago. This man was slim and tall, and the face that had once grinned in mischievous greeting now stared coldly at me. But he had the same grey eyes.

'We've met before,' I said.

Gideon shook his head dismissively. 'She's mistaken,' he told Matthew, addressing him as though I was not present. 'I've not been back to the camp for months.'

It was not surprising that he did not recognise me, and I made no attempt to explain. We had both been children when we had encountered one another briefly outside The Facility, and I had changed a lot over the intervening years.

'I've brought Rachel along to find out what happens here,' Matthew said. 'I want you to show her around. You'll find she's a fast learner. And she has other skills we could use,' he added cryptically.

Gideon glanced curiously at me. His eyes slid away and he gazed around the room. 'Down here is where we grow foodstuffs.' He nodded at the plants all around us. 'What you have to remember is that this place keeps us safe. Without these plants, The Council would have sent Guardians to destroy the camp a long time ago, killing everyone there. Matthew makes a big fuss about what a hero he is, protecting us all, risking his life going into the city to deliver foodstuffs, but down here is where the real work goes on, saving the lives of everyone in the camp.'

'I don't understand what all this means,' I said, looking around helplessly.

With a grunt, Gideon turned his back on me, and went back to sprinkling powder on the plants.

'Don't let us keep you from your work,' Matthew called out to him, smiling.

Matthew did not seem to mind Gideon's insults. I had the impression they knew each other well, and everything between them was a joke, but I had only just met Gideon. There was no excuse for his rudeness to me. Right then and there I resolved to have as little to do with him as possible. He seemed to feel the same. It was left to Matthew to lead me to the nearest green plant and point out its parts: stem, twigs, leaves, and thin white roots hidden in the sand. In among the green leaves he pointed out a variety of blobs, some green, others red or yellow. Most were round but a few were long and thin, and, like the plants, they were of different sizes.

'These plants produce foodstuffs called fruit and vegetables,' he said. 'Some of the foods grow above ground like these, some grow underneath the sand, in another section of the site. We've got a few sites, so if one is destroyed we won't be completely ruined.'

'As long as you or I are alive,' Gideon added. 'We are the key holders.'

'What does that mean?' I asked, irked by Gideon's enigmatic comments.

'No one else would be able to find this place,' Matthew explained. 'Not even the other desert walkers know where it is. We can't afford to risk anyone betraying its location to the Guardians.'

The brilliance of scarlet streaks attached to a small plant drew my attention, and I wanted to know what they were.

'Those are called chillies,' Matthew replied.

Leaning forward, I breathed in a pungent aroma, quite unlike anything I had ever smelled before.

'She won't be able to handle those, not straight away,' Gideon called out, a note of alarm in his voice. 'They're far too strong. They'll knock her head off and make her throat close up.' He gave a bark of laughter and Matthew joined in, as though sharing a memory. 'Start her with something easy, like avocado,' Gideon added.

Moving to another plant, Matthew pulled a small light green sphere from a long trailing tendril. Putting it right inside in his mouth, he showed me how he used his teeth to crush it to a pulp before swallowing it. His face relaxed as he removed a second ball from the plant, peeled back the flimsy covering skin with the point of a knife, and sliced the translucent foodstuff in half. Smiling, he offered one half to me on the flat of his blade.

'Here you are, try it. These are called grapes. Go on, try it. Use your teeth to mash it to a paste before you attempt to swallow it. That way not only will you release the flavour onto your tongue, but you shouldn't choke, as long as you're careful not to breathe while you swallow.'

Reluctantly I took the slimy green blob which glistened on the end of my finger. I watched Matthew pop another one in his mouth and chew. It seemed an odd kind of ritual, and decidedly unhealthy. Pills were far easier to swallow. The thought of putting something so filthy in my mouth made me feel nauseous.

'Go on,' Matthew urged me. 'Try it. That way you'll begin to understand what's happening here.'

Hesitantly, I put the grape in my mouth and bit down on it. At once a peculiar sensation rushed through me. Feeling dizzy, I looked around the chamber but my eyes could scarcely focus and my whole body trembled. The greenery in front of me seemed to glow in blinding rays of light that shone through the holes in the roof, and I felt as though my head was exploding with pleasure. An image of my grandmother flashed across my mind, and I finally understood what she had been doing in the picture I had found, years before, when she had been touching a shapeless pink blob with her tongue. In that instant, I felt very close to her, and wondered what had happened to that picture. More than anything, I wished it were still safely hidden in my pouch. My glorious waking dream ended abruptly as I choked when the grape hit the back of my throat, making me retch painfully. It was worth it. The rapture of tasting food was unlike anything else I had ever experienced, and I knew then that my life would never be the same again. It had taken just one instant to transform me into a devotee of foodstuffs, if not an actual addict.

Matthew smiled at me. 'That was a foodstuff,' he said.

I nodded wordlessly, coughing uncontrollably.

'Are all grapes green?' I enquired, when I had recovered sufficiently to speak.

'Grapes are just one kind of food,' Gideon answered, joining us. 'There are many, many others, and they come in all shapes and colours. What you just had was a fruit, called a grape. Now stop dicking around, Matthew, we can't afford to waste food.'

Ignoring Gideon's rebuke, Matthew plucked a dark green fruit about the size of my fist and cut it open. He removed a shiny black ball from the centre, which he handed to Gideon, who received it reverently. I was mistaken in thinking that Matthew had given the best part of this fruit to Gideon. Frowning with concentration, Matthew scooped a small piece of soft yellow mush from the shell of the fruit, and handed it to me on the blade of his knife. It smelled like the oils the stylist at The Facility applied to our hair to make it shine.

'This is avocado,' he told me solemnly.

'This is what they put on our hair at Vanessa's!' I cried out in surprise.

Gideon scowled. 'Where on earth do you think they get all their fancy oils from, if not from us? Hair oil, what a waste. Go on, taste it and you'll see what I mean. Why would anyone want to squander this on their hair? It's a crime, when avocados are so tricky to grow.'

'You seem to manage,' Matthew said.

This time I was careful to crush the food between my teeth before swallowing. Even so my throat seemed to close up. The soft texture of the fruit somehow made it harder to swallow, and it seemed to stick at the back of my throat, although Gideon and Matthew each ate a larger amount than me without any problem. The taste of avocado was very different to the grape, less sweet but equally delicious. Immediately I wanted more.

'It takes some getting used to,' Matthew told me. 'You have to train yourself to breathe while you're eating. It's best to start with pill sized chunks, because that's what your body's used to.'

Gideon pointed out that if the morsel of foodstuff was too small to chew, it could be gulped down in one swallow. 'In which case you might as well just take pills and be done with it.'

'Yes, you mustn't forget to chew, or you miss the taste,' Matthew agreed earnestly.

A moment before, their comments would have baffled me. Overwhelmed with wonder at the strange new sensations I was experiencing, I stared around the chamber in silence. It was easy to see how people became addicted to foodstuffs. After one brief tasting, it seemed it was going to be impossible to live without them.

'I might be addicted to food,' I said solemnly, and Gideon laughed.

He seemed to be mocking me, and I was almost glad when Matthew told me it was time for us to start the long walk back to the camp. I would have liked to remain there, gorging on foodstuffs, but Gideon was making me feel uncomfortable. As Matthew began to ascend the stone staircase, Gideon slipped something soft into my hand. His eyes met mine and, unaccountably, the touch of his fingers made me tremble.

'Strawberry,' he called out as I followed Matthew up the stairs. 'Remove the stalk before you put it in your mouth, and don't squash the red fruit. It's really soft. And whatever you do, don't forget to chew.'

The strawberry was more sweet and fragrant than either the grape or the avocado. The glorious taste lingered in my mouth long after I finished swallowing it, but the sensation of Gideon's warm hand brushing against mine stayed with me even longer. I slipped the green stalk of the strawberry into my pouch as a memento, a gift from Gideon. Just for an instant, he had dropped his surly façade and reached out to me. I wished we could have spent more time together.

That evening the Elders sent for me, and on this occasion Matthew was seated at the table with them.

'I hope you had an interesting day,' Daniel greeted me, with his customary intense stare.

When I asked him why Matthew had taken me to observe Gideon's work, Daniel smiled.

'I was hoping you'd ask us that. You do know that Matthew makes a regular trip to the city to deliver foodstuffs to our allies on The Council? We want you to go with him on his next trip, so you can make contact with your friends at The Facility, and ask them to help us.'

'How can they help us?' I blurted out, unnerved by Daniel's vehemence.

'I'm talking about when they become wives, of course,' he replied impatiently. 'With a husband on The Council, they will be in a position to pass all kinds of information to us. If The Council is planning a raid on the camp, your contacts can warn us. And with enough wives helping us, we might even be able to convert more Council Members into addicts.'

My only friend at Vanessa's was Judith. I did not know whether she had been chosen as a wife yet, or if she ever would be. But even supposing she was still at The Facility, and in the unlikely event that I managed to speak to her on her own, she would almost certainly not recognise me. Having given Daniel a firm refusal, I waited for the Elders to react angrily to my rejection of their plan, but only Daniel appeared to be annoyed. He was drumming his fingers on the table, his eyes blazing with fury, while the other Elders looked on calmly, and Matthew kept his eyes lowered. It seemed I might not be punished for my defiance after all. All the Elders sat perfectly still, watching me. Only William shifted in his seat, nodding his white head and smiling, as he listened to voices no one else could hear.

Daniel spoke again. 'I don't think you understand how important this is,' he said irritably. 'We hear rumours all the time that The Council is preparing to launch an attack, and these rumours are growing stronger and more credible every day. We accept that you will never be a wife, but you could persuade another wife to confide in you, a wife who trained with you and was once your friend. Any information you can discover might save all our lives.'

'Please,' one of the women said, 'think of the children in the camp. We are all at risk.'

To someone who had never trained as a wife, Daniel's idea might make sense, but with my knowledge of The Facility, I knew it was doomed to fail. It had been a strange day, and my mind was still reeling from encountering foodstuffs. If I refused to agree to Daniel's scheme, I would be sent back to work in the school and might never experience the taste of foodstuffs again. Somehow I had to find a way to return to the plant site.

As though listening to someone else's voice, I heard myself agreeing to attempt the impossible.

At once, Daniel's face broke into a smile. He thanked me, and assured me that the camp dwellers would not forget my courageous decision. But as I was leaving the hut, I saw him nod at Matthew, and had an uneasy feeling that I had been manipulated, because if I had not tasted foodstuffs, there was no way I would have agreed to participate in such a crazy scheme. Outside the Elders' hut, I gazed up at the night sky, trying to convince myself that I had agreed to Daniel's request solely because there was a slim chance his plan could help save the lives of the camp children. But I knew there was a more selfish motive for my decision, and I was ashamed.

14

EVE

The next few days passed quietly. Life at school felt dull after the excitement of my excursion with Matthew, and I tried not to think about my proposed visit to the city. I was working hard to teach Absalom to behave, and the other teachers commented on how much he had improved. It was true he had stopped fighting with other children since I had attached myself to him, and he would sit still, playing with the sand instead of throwing it at his classmates. As long as he had my attention he seemed contented, but whenever I spoke to another child, he would start flinging sand around again. It made me uneasy to know that he was so dependent on me but Susan, the head teacher, was pleased.

'As long as it keeps him happy,' she said, in her soft voice. 'Well done, Rachel. You have really turned that child around.'

I could not help but feel gratified by her praise. Susan was a kindly middle-aged woman who bustled around the school hut, keeping an eye on everyone. Without actually saying much, she seemed to help the other teachers with her comforting presence, and she obviously cared about her young charges. I watched her talking to a group of children, wisps of her frizzy fair hair twitching as she nodded her head, encouraging and praising them.

In addition to my small success with Absalom, I had made a friend. Eve and I walked to school and back every day, and we lay in the dark every night, chatting, until the other girls in our hut called out to us to stop talking and let them sleep.

'You see each other every day. Do you have to talk all night as well?'

Listening to the other girls grumbling, Eve and I would giggle together in the darkness, and continue our conversation in whispers. During the day, my work at the school kept me busy, but once Eve had fallen asleep at night, I worried about Daniel's plan. There was no question a trip to the city would be dangerous. We might run into Guardians. Admittedly, they would hardly recognise me as a trained wife, but apart from the risk involved in returning to the streets of the city, it was a stupid idea anyway. It was extremely unlikely that I would manage to speak to Judith alone. Even if I did, I had no idea how to persuade her to help the camp dwellers. Why would she? The mission was doomed to fail before we even set out, and for that we were going to risk being arrested and executed.

Eventually I summoned my courage and went to confront Daniel, but he refused to acknowledge my concerns. He lowered his gaze, his bald head shiny and bronzed by the sun, and waved a large hand in dismissal. 'You'll find a way to speak to your friend in The Facility,' he said. 'You're a resourceful girl.'

'It's not worth the risk,' I insisted. 'I'm expendable, but you can't afford to lose Matthew. We could both be arrested or killed by the Guardians.'

I tried not to recall my mother, dangling from a Guardian's hand as she fought to breathe.

'You've survived this far,' Daniel replied. 'I have every

confidence that Matthew will take care of you and bring you back to us safely.'

When I did not leave, he looked up in surprise. 'Are you still here?'

Staring into his bold dark eyes, bright with fanatical determination, I knew that he was never going to listen to reason. Helpless to resist my fate, I returned to the school and did my best not to think about my impending return to the city. But Daniel had a point. I had survived against all the odds so far, escaping from Vanessa, recuperating at Saul's home with Helen's help, and finally reaching the camp in safety. All my good fortune since I had left The Facility had been thanks to Matthew, and there was no reason to suppose he would not continue to guide me safely. I resigned myself to trusting in his skills to lead me safely into the city and back to the camp again.

One morning, we heard a commotion outside the school hut. It sounded like many voices yelling at once, and footsteps pounded by as though a crowd of people were all running past in a panic. One of the teachers slipped out to see what was happening. 'It's terrible,' she told us when she returned, her eyes wide with alarm. 'Everyone's frantic out there!'

Calling out to us to carry on, and assuring us the Elders would send word if the school was in danger, Susan hurried our agitated colleague away from the children. Our job was to remain calm while we waited for news, but it was hard to continue as though nothing had happened. Some of us were convinced we were being attacked by monsters that roamed the desert, while others were equally sure the Guardians had discovered the camp. The uproar soon died down, and Eve and I went to investigate. A woman told us what the fuss had been about. A pair of desert walkers had been returning to the camp when one of them had fallen ill. In his frenzy, he had hurled their pouch away. Unable to find their medical supplies or control the sick man on his own, the other walker had been forced to abandon his companion and run back to the camp as quickly as he could. Apart from the risk to his own life, if the sick man found his way to the city we might all be killed. In the grip of sand fever, there was no knowing what a man might say or do.

A team of desert walkers had been sent out to look for him. The rest of us could do nothing but wait. The sunlight faded, and still there was no word from the searchers. In the end, Eve and I went to our hut, too tired to watch any longer. That night I slept badly. Colossal giants roamed my nightmares, dashing sparks of fire from their sharp teeth, while their eyes blazed with flames. I woke in the grey dawn and joined a crowd of people standing at the bottom of the slope, at the place where the searchers were expected to return. Some of the camp dwellers had been waiting there all night.

Daniel was with them, keeping their spirits up with encouraging words. 'They'll come back safe and sound,' he was saying. 'We've sent out the most experienced walkers we have.'

Suddenly the crowd fell silent as a man came into view at the top of the slope, waving his arms in a circling motion above his head. A moment later, a few of the searchers came into view, bearing the sick man between them. He was carried down and taken straight to the hospital hut.

'Will he be all right?' I asked, accompanying his entourage to the hospital.

'They usually manage to sort them out,' one of the searchers replied, although he did not sound very sure.

'It depends how far gone he is,' someone else added. 'He was out there for quite a long time in the heat of the day.'

'We had to knock him out,' one of the bearers said. He looked grim. 'It was the only way we could carry him. He was kicking so hard we couldn't get near him otherwise.' He rolled up his sleeve to show bruises on his arm. 'He was completely demented. I've never seen such a bad case.'

We reached the hospital hut, where the sick man was laid gently on the ground. With a shock I saw his face and recognised Matthew. He looked completely white, and there were droplets of sweat on his forehead, but apart from those telltale signs, he could have been asleep. My immediate dismay was tempered by relief at the realisation that our trip to the city would be delayed, perhaps indefinitely. That feeling that was rapidly superseded by guilt. Had it not been for Matthew's help, I would have died wandering on the streets of the city, or languishing in a prison cell. Whilst I was glad our visit to the city was not going to take place, I regretted the circumstances under which it had been cancelled.

But my relief was fleeting. Daniel had other ideas. 'We can't delay our plans because one man is down,' he said. 'Whatever the setbacks, life must go on.'

'You can't seriously be suggesting I return to the city alone,' I protested. 'I'd never find my way across the desert.'

Daniel announced that I was to go back to the city in accordance with the original plan, but accompanied by a different guide. I was uneasy about undertaking so dangerous a journey. At least I knew and trusted Matthew who had brought me safely out of the city once before, and I had only agreed to return to the city because he was taking me there. But Daniel dismissed my objections with a shrug, and my alarm increased further when I heard who was to be my guide.

'Isn't there another walker who could take me?' I asked. 'Anyone else?'

'What's wrong with Gideon?' Daniel asked.

'Gideon's a dear boy,' one of the Elder women said.

Seeing her sly grin, I suspected Gideon slipped her foodstuffs in secret.

'I never said there's anything wrong with him,' I replied quickly.

It was out of the question to attempt an explanation. They would not understand that the recollection of Gideon's contempt made me balk at the prospect of putting my life in his hands.

'It's just that– well,' I stammered, 'shouldn't he stay here and look after his plants? Surely that's a far more important use of his time. The trip to the city can wait until Matthew is fit again.'

'Recovery from sand fever can take several weeks,' Daniel replied. 'We can't wait that long. There are rumours of an imminent attack, and we urgently need to find out whether they are true.'

'Can't someone else find out?'

'There is no one else. Rachel, you have contacts in The Facility. You are our only hope.'

'But why does it have to be Gideon? Isn't there another desert walker who could take me back to the city? Please, I'll go with anyone but Gideon.'

Behind me, someone coughed. Whirling round, I saw that Gideon had entered the hut and was listening to my appeal, his features twisted in a sour expression. 'So I'm not good enough for you?' he asked, when he saw me looking at him. He was leaning against the side of the hut in a casual pose, but his grey eyes glared furiously at me.

'Now then, Gideon, don't go losing your temper,' Daniel said sternly.

The reprimand only succeeded in convincing me that I was about to be escorted into danger by a man who was prone to fits of rage.

'Calm down, Gideon,' one of the women said, confirming my opinion. 'She's a newcomer. Don't take any notice of her. She doesn't know what she's talking about.'

'That's not what I meant at all,' I said. 'You clearly misunderstood–'

Without waiting to hear more, Gideon stalked out of the hut. Ignoring the interruption, Daniel warned me not to tell anyone about my trip. Although the Elders were not aware that there were enemy agents in the camp, he said it did no harm to be discreet.

'It's common sense to say nothing to anyone, just to be on the safe side,' he explained. 'As long as you don't go gossiping, no one outside this hut will know anything about it.'

'Because you don't want questions asked about what's happened to me if I don't return,' I said. 'If no one knows about my trip, you can always say I must have wandered off on my own and got lost.'

Daniel nodded.

'She's not as silly as we thought,' one of the women murmured.

'Of course you'll come back,' the other woman chimed in, shaking her head. 'Why wouldn't you?'

No one answered her question.

Later that day, Eve and I were walking back to our hut, when she surprised me with a question. 'When were you going to tell me about it, then?' She sounded angry.

'Tell you about what?'

'You're going away, aren't you?'

'Who told you that?'

'Everyone knows.'

I did not answer.

'You are going away, aren't you?'

I was not sure what to say. Daniel had ordered me not to tell anyone, but Eve already knew about my trip. Besides, she was my friend. It did not seem right to keep the plan a secret from her, and lying about it would only make matters worse, because the truth was bound to emerge eventually.

'It won't be for long,' I assured her. 'It's not as if I've never been to the city before.'

I broke off, hearing her gasp, and realised that I had said too much, but it was too late to retract my words. Eve had been under the impression that I was going to walk in the desert, and was clearly shocked to learn that I was returning to the city. Daniel had warned me to tell no one, and I had unintentionally given away the secret at the first possible opportunity. Daniel was right. It was so easy to say the wrong thing, it was best to say nothing. All I could do now was make Eve promise not to tell anyone else.

'Go on then, tell me about it. I won't say anything.'

'I'm not supposed to talk about it to anyone. No one is even supposed to know where I'm going.'

'I'm not just anyone. We're friends, aren't we?'

'Of course we are.'

'Then you can tell me, can't you? Why are you going there?'

It seemed almost impossible to believe that Eve could be a spy and besides, I had already told her where I was going. 'If I tell you what I know, you must promise you won't say anything to anyone,' I said. 'If you blab, you do realise you could endanger the lives of everyone in the camp.'

'Yes, yes, I understand. I've already promised not to say anything.'

'All right then.'

I hesitated, thinking about Daniel's warning. Eve had lived on the camp all her life. After being brought there as a baby, she had never left. It was hard to see how she could possibly be spying for the city Council. All the same, from now on, I was determined to reveal as little as possible about Daniel's plan.

'To be perfectly honest,' I lied, 'I'm not sure why I'm being sent there. But why don't you ask me whatever you want to know, and I'll answer you if I can?' I looked away, hoping she would not see through my duplicity.

To begin with, Eve was keen to know how I was getting to the city, and there did not seem any reason to hide my guide's name. There was nothing to prevent her from watching us leave together, if she was interested. Her reaction surprised me. She stopped and turned to face me, a startled expression on her normally good-natured face. Placing her hand on my arm, she warned me not to trust Gideon.

'Don't worry,' I said, forcing a smile. 'Everything will be fine.'

'Rachel, listen to me. Some men are interested in you, because you're a trained wife.'

'Now you're being ridiculous.'

'I mean it,' she repeated earnestly. 'You've been trained to please men, so naturally men are going to find you attractive.'

'And your point is...?' I challenged her, confused and angry at the same time.

'The point is, Gideon's bad news. He's not like the rest of us. Some people think–' She broke off, biting her lip.

'What do some people think?'

'Nothing, nothing. Just promise me you'll be careful, that's all.'

When I challenged her to explain what she meant, she just shook her head, muttering that it was nothing. She refused to say another word, leaving me to wonder miserably what she had been trying to warn me about.

15

GIDEON

Gideon walked swiftly up the side of the crater, without once looking back to check that I was keeping pace with him. It was hard for me to climb all the way to the top of the steep slope, with sand sliding under my feet at every step. By the time I reached the top he was some distance away, and I had to hurry to reach him before he vanished into the vastness of the desert. Too proud to call out to him to wait, I slithered along as quickly as possible, nearly falling several times. At last I drew nearly level with him and we carried on in awkward silence. We walked for a long time, until I was plodding along almost in my sleep, a few steps behind him. When he stopped abruptly, for no apparent reason, I almost barged into him.

'Is this it?' I asked. 'Are we there? Is this the entrance to the tunnel?'

'We're not even close,' he replied, with his back to me.

'What's wrong then?' I asked.

'Nothing's wrong.'

'Why have we stopped?'

'To look around.'

'What are we looking for?'

'We're not looking for anything. We're just looking.' His voice softened. 'I can look at the desert for hours.'

Gazing around at the seemingly endless desert stretching out in every direction, I felt a tremor of fear in case the monsters were nearby, perhaps watching us as we lingered on the interminable dunes. One man would be helpless against their huge teeth and flaming eyes, and I wondered how Gideon could withstand the terror. There was so much mystery surrounding this desert walker.

'Have you seen them?' I whispered, edging closer to him.

'Who?'

'Them, them. You know, the ones who live in the desert.'

He turned to me then, his grey eyes puzzled. 'What do you mean? We live in the desert, you and me, and the others in the camp. No one else lives here.'

'How can you say that? You know what I'm talking about.'

He shook his head. 'Really I don't.'

I murmured very quietly. 'I'm talking about the monsters who live in the desert.'

'Monsters?' he echoed, laughing loudly.

Petrified by the noise he was making, I wanted to flee, but there was nowhere to go. In every direction there was only sand.

'Monsters who live in the desert?' he repeated. 'Are you out of your mind? Nothing can survive in these conditions, apart from camp dwellers, and it's not easy for us. But I would never want to live anywhere else. It's beautiful out here.' He looked around at the vast emptiness surrounding us, and smiled. When he spoke about the desert, his face glowed with a warmth I had not seen before, and for the first time it struck me that perhaps he felt most lonely when he visited the camp, cast out by the outcasts.

'How do you suppose they survive out here, these monsters

of yours?' he went on, sounding as though he was trying not to laugh. 'Do you think they eat sand?'

Glancing around uneasily, I told him about the monsters my mother had described to me when I was a child. Keeping my voice low, I mentioned their huge teeth, and their eyes that darted flames. Gideon and I were alone in the desert. If the monsters appeared, we would have no chance to escape before they tore us to pieces and drank our blood. My indignation increased when my companion looked amused.

'Monsters,' he scoffed. 'There are no monsters. Don't you understand, that's just a story made up to frighten children so they don't try to leave the city.'

I dared not contradict him. He seemed cheerful, but I had heard Daniel telling him to watch his temper. I couldn't risk antagonising him. What if he abandoned me in the desert?

'At least you had a mother to tell you stories when you were a child,' he said as we set off again, 'even if it was all lies.'

'My mother never lied to me! She believed the stories were true, and so do I!'

'Then you're as stupid as she was.'

'She wasn't stupid,' I protested, struggling to control tears of frustration at his refusal to listen to reason. 'She was told about the monsters when she was a child.'

'So that she wouldn't run away from the city,' he repeated with exaggerated patience, as though he was talking to a particularly slow child. He was the one who was being stupid, but he seemed so sure of himself, there was no point in arguing with him.

'Whatever you think,' I retorted sourly. 'I'm sure you're always right about everything.'

'Is that what they teach you to say, when they're training you to be a wife?' he sneered.

I held my tongue. Once we were back in the camp, he would

find out exactly what I thought of him and his disdain, after which we would never need to speak to one another again. But for now, the prudent course was to avoid provoking him. We walked on in silence for a very long time, until it seemed we must be lost.

'Are you sure you know the way?' I asked at last.

Gideon scowled. 'Of course I know the way.' He quickened his pace, and we did not speak again until, eventually, we reached the entrance to the tunnel and climbed down the stairs, still without exchanging a word. By the time we reached the bottom, my legs felt weak from my exertion. Struggling behind my guide in the flickering shadows cast by his torch, I had to force myself to follow him along the metal rods as far as the first wide platform. On the point of collapse, I was relieved when he put his torch down and said it was time for us to stop for a rest.

'If you like,' I replied, doing my best to sound as though I did not care whether we stopped or not. My legs were shaking so violently I could hardly stand. Only pride kept me on my feet.

'We can press on if you like,' he said.

Too tired to keep up the pretence that I possessed enough stamina to keep going, I shook my head. 'No,' I murmured, as I sank to the ground. 'Let's rest for a while. You must be exhausted too.'

We both knew he could walk continuously for days on end, but he nodded and sat down without contradicting me. Sitting side by side with our backs against the cold wall, we each took a pill.

'You are a good walker, for a trained wife,' Gideon remarked.

No longer a trained wife, I was free to respond to condescending comments from a man, but I needed Gideon's protection, and could not risk alienating him. I wished Matthew was with me to guide me through the tunnels, instead of Gideon. Still, there was nothing to be done, so I decided to try and make the best of the situation and be as obliging as I could. While we rested, my companion asked me what it was like to be trained as a wife. I shook my head. Following The Programme was such a contrast to living in the camp, it was almost impossible to describe.

'Life in The Facility is as different to life in the camp as pills are to foodstuffs,' I replied at last. 'Only I'm not sure which is the pill and which is the food.'

'I know which I prefer,' he said.

'I mean, Vanessa was kind to us in many ways,' I went on. 'We were clean and sweetly perfumed, and we had our own beds – proper soft beds – and we bathed in scented oils every day. Our hair was styled for us, and we wore beautiful clothes.' I broke off, momentarily lost in memories of glossy satins and silks, delicate pink lace, white netting, and soft velvets. 'Our clothes were gorgeous, and the fabrics were so soft. And you have no idea how many colours there are in the world, and we had fashionable shoes to match every gown. But it wasn't only our clothes,' I added, seeing his lips curl in disdain.

Gideon grunted. 'You sound as though you miss your life in the city.'

'In a way, I do. That is to say, I miss certain aspects of it.' I sighed. 'We were clean and fresh, and now every part of me is irritated by sand. All the time. It gets in everywhere. I liked wearing beautiful dresses, and the bath oils and perfumes were lovely. But in spite of everything they gave us, I wouldn't go back there, even if I could.'

'Why not?' He sounded genuinely interested. His attention comforted me.

'Because we were prisoners,' I replied more fiercely than I had intended. 'They told us how to walk, how to sit, what to wear, what to say, what to think. We were never free, not even in our minds.'

'No one can tell you what to think,' Gideon said solemnly.

'I don't expect you to understand. They told us what to think all the time. It was a constant barrage of commands, until we lost the power to think for ourselves. I'm telling you, we were never free. But none of us are ever truly free, are we?'

'I feel free when I'm alone in the desert.'

'You can't live your whole life alone.'

'Why not? Don't you think it's better that way?'

'It would be a pretty miserable existence.'

'No, that's where you're wrong. People ruin everything, with their greed and selfishness.'

'You're a person,' I said.

'I mean other people.'

'Life would be very lonely without other people,' I insisted.

'The desert is the only companion I need. The desert never changes, and it never lets you down. It's hard to explain what I mean, but the desert just is what it is and it's always there.'

My aversion turned to sympathy for this man who had known nothing but the harsh life of the desert, and had never learned to value the warmth of human company. He passed his time in solitude, with only dumb plants for company. Curious to know more about him, I asked if he had been found as a baby. He had told me I was lucky to have known my mother, so it came as a surprise to learn that he had spent his childhood in the city with his own mother, the wife of a Council Member.

'What happened to her?' I asked.

'I've no idea. She could have been locked in a cell by the Guardians, and left there to starve to death, or thrown alive into the fire pit, for all I care. They do that to people who transgress, you know. She deserves worse than anything they could do to her.'

His bitterness shocked me.

'Gideon,' I said gently, 'you don't have to talk about your

mother if you don't want to, but you shouldn't speak
disrespectfully of her. She was still your mother.'

He shrugged as though he really did not care. 'The painted
bitch denounced my father for being an addict. And of course
the other addicts on The Council refused to help him. Cowards,
every one of them!'

'What happened to your father after she betrayed him?'

'What do you think happened?' he replied roughly. 'He was
arrested by the Guardians and sentenced to death. My mother
and I had to witness the spectacle, along with all the Members
of The Council, including many secret addicts. One day they
were sharing food with my father, the next day they were
smiling at his execution, cheering as we watched him die.'

He fell silent, brooding over his dark memories.

'I can see why you hate The Council so much,' I ventured at
last. 'But how did you manage to find your way out of the city?'

'I couldn't have done it alone. It was only by luck that I
escaped at all. After I ran away from home, to get away from the
foul witch, my mother, I lived on the streets for a few months.
Starving and begging, I did my best to stay out of sight of the
carts that patrol the city, day and night. Then a desert walker
found me, and he took me to the camp where I've been ever
since. It was Matthew who saved me,' he added. 'If it wasn't for
him I'd have been caught by the Guardians years ago.'

'Me too,' I said. 'I owe my life to him.'

Gideon listened in silence as I told him about my escape
from The Facility, and how Matthew had left me with Saul until
I was strong enough to walk to the camp. When I finished my
account, we stared into one another's eyes, and I experienced an
unexpected rush of happiness. Gideon and I were both misfits in
our own ways. Perhaps that was what drew us to one another, as
though we were meant to be together. Without noticing how it
happened, I realised we were holding hands. His calloused palm

felt warm against mine, in a promise of affection I had not experienced since my mother died.

'How did you end up working with plants?' I asked.

'You're surprised they don't use me as a carrier, delivering food to The Council, since I know my way to the city. But I am still the son of a Council Member, even if he was executed for his addiction. Not everyone in the camp trusts me.'

'That's really stupid.'

He shrugged and his arm brushed against mine, warm and comforting. 'It doesn't bother me,' he said. 'I like tending the plants. I prefer them to people. I feel safe with them.' He stared at the ground, unconsciously tightening his grip on my hand. 'People can't be trusted. And besides, I could never live in the camp for long, not now I've discovered the freedom of the desert.'

My next question had puzzled me ever since Matthew had led me out of the city.

'How do you find your way around in all that sand?'

Gideon shrugged again. 'I can't say. I don't want to sound secretive, but it's just not something I can explain. Navigating the terrain comes naturally to a desert walker. It's easy enough to follow the stars at night, and in the daytime there's the position of the sun and the lay of the sand that never changes. Even after a storm it's only the surface of the sand that's disturbed. The shape of the landscape doesn't alter, not really. It's a kind of instinct, really, to know where I'm going. It's just the way my mind works.' His voice grew soft. 'It's the only time I'm at peace, when I'm walking the sand with no one else around for miles and miles.'

'I can't believe they still don't trust you in the camp, when you do so much to protect us all.'

'You're forgetting, most of the camp dwellers don't have any idea what I do. Only the Elders and the other desert walkers know about my work.' He hesitated. 'I don't think anyone really believes I'm a spy, but there are people who don't need a reason to turn against someone who doesn't fit in. It was Matthew who suggested I move to the plant chamber, away from the camp, for my own protection.'

'Did you really not mind having to leave?'

'Honestly, I was pleased. It suits me fine to spend my time with the plants. I'm not like Daniel. I don't care about being popular. The less time I have to spend with people, the happier I am. And growing plants is where the real work is done. As long as we keep supplying the city with materials for food pills, and send them fancy oils for the rich wives, we'll be protected by the established members of The Council who understand how the system works. But we're living on borrowed time. Future Council Members might not be so sympathetic towards us.'

I was doing my best to follow what he was saying, but something still puzzled me. 'How do they make the food pills?'

'They use chemicals which they dig up from under the ground, and combine them with particles of the foods we produce. So you see, they depend on us as much as we depend on them. For now.'

'But if everyone in the city depends on us, they can't let anything terrible happen to us. Not if they need us,' I said.

'In theory, yes. That's what's kept us alive so far. The Council is split into three groups. The addicts support us whatever happens, but they have to be careful how they go about it, and make sure they keep their addiction hidden from other Members of The Council. If they are too vocal in their support of us, they risk being exposed, and they can't afford to let that happen, not unless they want to follow my father and be consumed by fire. Then there are the fanatics who want to stamp us out, regardless of the role we play in keeping them alive. They don't care about the food we supply, they just hate us for living outside the city where they can't control us. They want power at any cost, and nothing less than absolute power over everyone will satisfy them. They are too blind to see what would happen to the city dwellers without us. The problem is, they think they can make pills without us.'

'Is that possible?'

'I don't think so. Not yet. But maybe one day they will succeed and, for all we know, it could be very soon. When that happens, we're done for. Once they no longer need foodstuffs for their pills, we will lose our protection from everyone on The Council. Only the addicts will continue to need us, and they won't be able to admit they support us.'

'But why do we need protection?' I asked. 'Why can't we just carry on as we are? We don't pose any threat to the city.'

Gideon frowned. 'That's where you're wrong. Our very existence is a threat to The Council. As long as there are still people living outside the city walls, resisting their control, there's always a possibility more people could rebel against them. They can't afford to let us survive a moment longer than they need us. At any moment The Council could vote to send an army of Guardians out into the desert to track us down, and then it would only be a matter of time before they found us. At the moment, our friends on The Council are managing to prevent that happening by arguing that the Guardians cannot be spared from their other duties, maintaining civil order within the city walls, and patrolling the streets to stamp out insurgents. And of course they are all aware that they still need a supply of our foodstuffs to help them produce enough pills for everyone in the city.'

'What about the other group on The Council? The ones who are neither addicts nor fanatics who hate us. Who are they, and how do they fit into all this?' I asked.

'Those are all the others, the ones who are neutral. They

probably hate us as much as anyone, but they're not afraid of us, and they don't really care what happens to us. They are constantly being swayed by the other two factions. The addicts do their utmost to befriend them, and persuade them the Guardians are needed inside the city, while our opponents argue that the Guardians should be sent out into the desert to hunt us down. That's why the Elders are so keen to find out what's going on at Council meetings. We're living on the edge of a precipice, never knowing when the Guardians will be sent out in force to find the camp and destroy us all.' He sighed. 'If it wasn't for all this trouble, I'd be busy tending the plants right now.'

'You really do like looking after the food plants, don't you?'

'Too right I do. It's really important work. Anyone can be a carrier, all it takes is stamina and cunning and courage. Growing plants is skilled work. You need to be patient, and kind, and plants won't let you down, not like people.'

We were silent for a while after that, each absorbed in our own thoughts.

'From what you've said, it's only a minority on The Council who really want to destroy us,' I said at last.

Gideon leaned his head back against the wall. He looked grim. 'At the moment, but the real problem for us is that The Council has scientists working on making nutrition pills in a laboratory. Once they can make a pill that doesn't need foodstuffs at all, we'll be finished, whether we have friends on The Council or not.'

I had been brooding over this possibility, ever since I had first been told it might one day be possible for scientists to make pills without foodstuffs. 'We need to persuade the addicts on The Council to sabotage the work of the scientists,' I said.

'They do what they can, but they can't obstruct the scientists' progress indefinitely, not without being discovered. They can only slow them down. It's just a matter of time.'

I thought about the children living in the camp, and shivered.

'Are you cold?' Gideon asked me. He put his arm around me, and I did not move away. 'You're beautiful,' he whispered.

Seeing me tremble at his words, he leaned down and kissed me lightly on the lips. Once again, I did not move away. Lying down in each other's arms, we crossed an unspoken barrier as our bodies moved together in harmony.

'You should have seen me before, when I really was beautiful,' I said wistfully, when we had finished making love.

'What? You mean when you were all done up, like a painted doll? No, thank you.' He sounded so indignant, I could not help laughing.

'But all men like to see women wearing tight-fitting gowns, with their hair styled, and their faces painted to look perfect,' I replied.

'No, they don't.' He half sat up and leaned on one elbow to gaze at me as he spoke. 'A trained wife is a status symbol. That's all she is. Only The Council can afford wives who are fat and painted, with long eyelashes and dyed hair, and the members use their wives to show off how rich and successful they are. No one really thinks the wives look attractive, with their false smiles and fake faces. But you–' He broke off and stroked my cheek with his free hand. The touch of his hard-skinned fingers was soft as sand settling after a storm. 'You are truly beautiful.'

He leaned forward, and the touch of his lips on mine was gentle. As we lay down again together, I would not have swapped the hard ground beneath me for the softest bed. But we could not stay there forever. All too soon, Gideon announced that it was time to carry on. He stood up and grabbed my hand, and I scrambled to my feet. Gripping Gideon's hand tightly, I told myself that if our plan did not work, at least I would die trying. I was about to risk losing my life, just as it had become almost unbearably precious, but I forced myself to think about the children in the camp, whose lives might depend on the success of my mission.

'If anything happens to me before you're safely back in the camp–' Gideon began.

Pressing my finger on his lips, I silenced him. Losing Gideon was not possible, not now that we had found one another. Not ever. 'Don't say it,' I murmured. 'I'm not going back to the camp without you.'

'But if–'

'No,' I interrupted him firmly. Neither of us spoke again as, hand in hand, we walked along the dark tunnel towards the city.

16

JUDITH

As Gideon led me through the city, we passed several people. Heads down, dressed in filthy rags, they shuffled by, their eyes averted. With a shudder, I recalled walking around the city as a trainee wife, constantly aware that other people were staring at me. Now not a single person even glanced up to look at us as we passed. Although it was a relief to attract no notice, it was also strangely disconcerting to feel invisible. In the city where I had been trained to feel special, I was now just another insignificant citizen, scurrying along, trying to avoid attention. At one point, we heard a cart rumbling by. Without a word, Gideon grabbed my arm and yanked me into a narrow side street before I could shriek in alarm. Pressing ourselves against the wall, we listened to the cart pass by.

'Come on,' Gideon whispered to me when they had gone. 'Let's get you to your Facility.'

He left me at the corner where we had first set eyes on one another, all those years ago, when the Guardians had left me in the street for Vanessa to find. I hoped our first meeting place would not turn out to be the scene of our final moment together. Every day people who instructed and groomed the trainee wives went in and out of The Facility. The other trainee wives and I had occasionally overheard our teachers complain about the indignity of being forced to enter the building through the narrow side door, but Vanessa was adamant. The wide front door was reserved for trainee wives and visitors. The side door was supposed to remain bolted, as a security measure, but Vanessa tended to leave it unlocked during the day, to save her having to go downstairs every time one of our attendants arrived. If it was unbolted now, I would be able to gain access to the building. Nervous about my mission, I fervently hoped the door would be locked, giving me an excuse to withdraw from the task ahead of me. To my dismay, the door swung open easily.

It occurred to me that I could tell Daniel it had proved impossible to enter the building unobserved, but the thought of the children in the camp spurred me on. There had always been a strong chance I would be prevented from carrying out Daniel's plan. Voluntary withdrawal was a different matter altogether. I imagined Guardians slaughtering everyone in the camp, after I had fled from an opportunity to prevent such a catastrophe. Cursing Vanessa's sloppiness in leaving the door unlocked, I slipped inside the building and hid behind a pillar, my heart pounding. If I was caught, my punishment would be brutal.

The ground floor corridor was empty, as was usual at that time of day. Even so, I stole from one stone pillar to the next, doing my best to move quietly in case anyone came along unexpectedly. There was no sound, apart from my stealthy footsteps. Reaching the bottom of the stairs, I was hit by a dizzying perfume. A light citrus scent mingled with a sweet fragrance that I could not identify. Closing my eyes, I shivered with longing, but I could not remain standing in the vestibule. Another aroma reached me and my eyes watered. Resisting the temptation to pause, breathing in the heady mixture of lavender and rose water, I pulled myself together and crept upstairs.

Judith was unlikely to be on her own in the bedroom we had once shared. My best chance of catching her alone was to wait for her to pass me in the corridor. In the meantime, I would be exposed should anyone else walk by. While we were in the tunnel, Gideon and I had tried to think of excuses to use if I was found lurking in Vanessa's house.

'I didn't know where I was,' and 'I was lost,' were the best we could come up with.

Gideon hoped Vanessa would believe me, or at least forgive my intrusion, but he had never met her. Having brought shame on her facility, I could expect no mercy, but would be handed over to the Guardians without hesitation. If she failed to recognise me, as seemed likely, my fate as an unknown intruder would be equally cruel. I had all but forgotten about the Guardian's mask at the top of the stairs, and my legs nearly gave way when I caught sight of it glaring blindly at me from its plinth. Once a cause of terror, it now became my shield, because there was space for me to crouch out of sight beside the plinth, hidden behind the helmet, until my legs ached and my eyes grew tired.

Several instructors and a small group of trainee wives passed me in the corridor, oblivious to my presence, their strong perfumes covering up my stench. After they had gone, all was quiet again. I was beginning to despair when, at last, I saw Judith gliding along the corridor. Thankfully she was alone, or I would have been forced to wait for another opportunity to waylay her.

'Judith!' I whispered.

She turned and saw me, hiding behind the plinth.

'Hello,' she said evenly, without any appearance of surprise. She bestowed on me the smile of welcome we had all perfected, and dipped her head gracefully, seemingly blind to my filthy appearance. I recognised her instantly, although she had filled out since we had last seen one another. Compared to the gaunt figures of my companions in the desert, she looked curiously bulky. Her painted cheeks were puffed out, and her body bulged with voluptuous curving hips and a full bosom. Her limbs were mostly obscured by her gown, but I could see her plump fingers and small rolls of fat around her wrists. It was hard to believe I had once looked like that, or that I had considered her beautiful.

'You must be new here,' she said, her smile fixed, her voice smooth. 'You shouldn't be standing by yourself in the corridor like this. Come along, and I'll take you to Vanessa who will see that you are thoroughly cleaned, and shown to your dormitory.' Her smile grew faintly perplexed. 'How old are you?'

'Judith, wait,' I called out in an urgent undertone, reaching out to grab her arm as she turned away.

Although she drew back in alarm, her smile did not falter. 'How lovely to meet you,' she said. 'How do you know my name? Have we been introduced?'

'Judith, I'm Rachel,' I hissed frantically. 'You must remember me. I used to live here. I shared a dormitory with you and Naomi. We trained together. Hester was here when I arrived, and Vanessa sent her away because she wasn't putting on weight. And then Leah joined us. She's probably still here. You must remember me. My name's Rachel.'

Judith's eyes seemed to mist over, and her smile became rigid. 'Rachel?' she echoed faintly. 'There was a trainee wife called Rachel, but she died. It was very sad. We learned how to mourn without creasing our faces.'

It was unnerving to see her smiling while she talked about my death. In my indignation, I almost forgot to keep my voice low. 'What is supposed to have happened to Rachel?' I asked, barely able to conceal my agitation at the lies she had been told. 'What did they say to you?'

'It was a long time ago. Rachel swallowed too many pills in an attempt to increase her sexual allure, and that was what killed her. It made the rest of us feel sad. She had not intended to end her life but her independent choices killed her. As trainee wives, we have to do exactly as we are told, or the consequences for us can be grave. Our curves must be allowed to develop naturally. We cannot speed up the process. Rachel's impatience was a lesson to us all.' Still smiling serenely, she smoothed her gown over her ample hips.

'No, no, it's not true. I'm not dead,' I cried out in a fierce whisper. 'It's me, Rachel. I'm still alive. You must remember me. It's not that long ago. I know I've changed, but it's still me. Don't you recognise me? I ran away and left you at the clinic.'

As I described leaving her at the clinic, a flicker of recognition crossed her face, vanishing at once beneath her tranquil smile, like a drowning body surfacing only to disappear again beneath the surface of the water. It was enough to reassure me that Judith had remembered me, if only for an instant, before the years of indoctrination clouded her mind again.

She spoke very rapidly. 'Well, even if you are who you say you are, you can't come back. Look at you! All that hard work gone to waste. It's a terrible shame. Vanessa will never take you back looking like that. You have to deal with the consequences of your perversity. There's no place for you here. Leah's training now, and Martha and Ruth, so there's simply no room for you. The best thing you can do is go away before Vanessa sees you and summons the Guardians.'

Still smiling, she glanced up and down the corridor.

'I don't want to come back and live here,' I replied. 'I just came to see you. No one else. Judith, we were friends once. Listen to me.'

'I'm going to be a wife,' she said, with a careful smile.

Her eyes grew wary, and she edged away from me. Still her smile did not falter. My congratulations stuck in my throat. Judith's news reminded me why I was there. Upset at seeing her all painted and puffed up, for a moment I had almost forgotten the reason for my visit. This meeting with her in the corridor might be my only chance to ask for her help, but my hopes faded as I stared into her glazed eyes.

'I've just been trying on my wedding dress,' she said, while I was trying to think of what to say next. 'It's white, of course, with delicate lacy sleeves, and glittering jewels all around the neck and cuffs. It's so long I'll have to be carried to the wedding hall so the hem doesn't get dirty.' She gave a coy giggle. 'My husband hasn't seen it, so you're not to say anything about it, not to anyone. Promise me you won't say a word.'

I had no time to listen to her chattering foolishly about her wedding arrangements. Someone else might come along at any moment and see me. 'Judith, I'm sure your dress is lovely, but I can't stand here like this right now.'

She sounded faintly offended, although her smile did not falter. 'It's my wedding dress,' she said, emphasising the words as she spoke. 'I've been chosen to be a wife, and you know what that means.'

It struck me as odd that she had not thought to ask me what I was doing there in my dull dirty clothes.

'Did you hear me? I'm telling you about my wedding dress.' She nodded complacently. 'My veil is going to be very long, longer than my dress, but that's all right because I won't walk on the ground at all. Did I tell you, I am going to be carried all the way to the wedding hall? My future husband will be waiting for me there. He's extremely rich and important and he looks very distinguished. I'm going to live in luxury. These are such momentous considerations for a bride, aren't they? I suppose it must be hard for you to hear this, but it's your own fault if you're jealous. You had the chance to be a wife, and you threw it away. And look at you now. You look hideous.'

'Judith, stop talking about your wedding for a moment, and listen to me.'

For a second she looked almost startled, but she recovered quickly and carried on, speaking in an even tone. 'I can see you're not listening to me. I'm telling you about my wedding. You could have had all of this, you know. You could have been chosen by now. Your birthday's not long after mine, and you too could have had a wonderful husband. Mine is one of the richest husbands we've had here, so Vanessa's very pleased with me. It has taken me a lot of hard work to get to where I am, and of course I appreciate how lucky I am. Not everyone succeeds in finding a husband.'

'Judith, you're going to be a slave to a man you don't even know,' I said bluntly. 'What if he mistreats you? What will you do then? You know there will be no escape.'

'I'm going to have a wonderful life as a wife,' she replied. 'My husband is a very important man.' Her voice faltered. Just for a second her eyes betrayed the bewilderment she was feeling, but she regained her composure and continued. 'I'm so happy. I'm happy, I'm happy, I'm happy. I must be the luckiest girl in the world.'

There was no time to waste, knowing Vanessa might appear at any moment. I reached out to take Judith's hand but she drew back, looking disgusted. It was the first sign of genuine feeling she had shown since we had started talking.

'Get away from me, you filthy creature.'

'Judith, we were friends once, weren't we? Good friends. Don't you remember how we used to laugh together, you and me and Naomi? Listen to me. Please, you have to listen to me. I left because I didn't want to end up like Naomi, forced to breed with a man who disgusted me.'

'Naomi wasn't chosen to be a wife,' Judith responded primly. 'She was not as fortunate as me.'

'No, you're wrong. Naomi *was* chosen, but she didn't want to marry the man who had chosen her. She told me he was old, and ugly, and he hurt her. He beat her. She said she would rather die than spend the rest of her life being touched by him. He disgusted her.'

Judith gazed over my shoulder and shook her head smoothly, so as not to disturb her hair. 'I don't know what you're talking about. Go away and leave me alone. You don't belong here in The Facility. You don't deserve to be here.'

'Judith, I've joined the people who live in the desert. We live in a camp beyond the city walls, where we're free to live how we want, and to love any man we choose.'

Judith's eyes met mine and she stared at me as though she did not understand a word I was saying. 'How can you choose a man?' she murmured.

'Well, we can, and what's more, no one can tell us who to marry or what to wear or how to think.'

'What to wear?' she echoed, staring at my dirty tunic and cloak.

It was a mistake to mention clothes. I should have remembered how important they were to wives.

'You have to look beyond my clothes, and forget what I'm wearing. It's me, Rachel, your friend. I came here to see you because I need your help, Judith. We all do. There are small children in the camp whose lives are in danger.'

'Only trained wives can breed,' she said flatly. 'Only the lucky ones are chosen to be wives.'

Naturally I had expected it would be difficult to convince her to help us, but I had arrived prepared to put rational arguments to her. It had not occurred to me that she would not understand what I was telling her. All the time we had lived together at Vanessa's, I had never noticed how stupid she was. There were no ideas of her own in her brain; she was capable only of repeating other people's words. Despairing of getting through to her, I made one last attempt to convince her to take me seriously.

'Judith, I need your help to save the lives of some little children, just like the baby you're going to have soon. Will you help me?'

She gave me a gracious smile. 'It is my duty to breed with my husband and do whatever he wishes.'

Being a wife was what she deserved. She would be taken care of, and fed, and washed, and would never need to think about anything but maintaining her appearance. I was bitterly disappointed that she did not understand there could be more to life than those shallow considerations. Yet staring at her painted face, brittle as a doll's, my anger melted into pity for her narrow-minded view of life. When I had lived at Vanessa's, I had been exactly like Judith. I had been stupid to believe her capable of helping us. She was never going to share Council secrets with an outcast, not even with one who had lived and trained with her. The truth was, if she could have stepped out of line, she would never have been chosen as a wife. She would have been discarded long before she reached the end of The Programme, as I would probably have been had I not left of my own accord before then.

It had not occurred to me earlier that I might have to find my way out of The Facility by myself. Even if Judith refused to help us, I never thought she would stand by and watch me get captured. I should have known better. My friendship with Judith had been a sophisticated masquerade. She cared nothing for me. All she was interested in was her wedding dress, probably the one part of her marriage she was going to enjoy. But I did not have time to worry about Judith's happiness.

'Listen, I've got to get out of here.'

She looked straight at me, but the small part of her memory

that had fleetingly evaded her indoctrination had shut down, and she no longer recognised me. 'Well, goodbye, and thank you for visiting The Facility,' she said. 'Now I must go and prepare for my wedding. It's only three weeks away and there is still a great deal to be done. We have already chosen my dress and shoes, but my tiara has not been agreed on. The other girls are all very excited, as you can imagine. Thank you for your congratulations, and good luck with your own marriage.' She smiled courteously and turned away.

Her words chilled me. She must have known I would be arrested if anyone else discovered me inside The Facility.

'Judith, help me. I have to leave here without being seen. I need your help, please.'

She shook her head carefully, and I wondered if she remembered me at all. 'There's a side door for staff, or you can use the main door, which is down the staircase and straight ahead,' she said. 'That is for visitors.'

With that, she turned gracefully and glided away, leaving me alone in the corridor to make my escape or be captured.

If anyone found me, I would be tortured for information before my execution. I could only hope I would be strong enough to deny my enemies the satisfaction of hearing my voice before they silenced me forever.

17

RETURN

S ince I had been relying on Judith to smuggle me out of the
building, I had no escape plan, and my situation felt
hopeless. Hearing the padding of footsteps on the polished
floor, I ducked down behind the plinth at the top of the stairs
until the immediate danger passed, but I could not hide there
forever. I was trapped. Peering out, I saw Vanessa go down the
stairs, and waited. A young girl trotted lightly up the stairs and
scurried past me, on her way to a training session. Her perfume
lingered in the air long after she had disappeared, making my
eyes water.

All at once I was gripped by an overwhelming desire to be
clean, and free of the sand that irritated my still delicate skin.
Eve had assured me that I would grow accustomed to the sand,
and my skin would become hardened to it, but it was hard to
resist the lure of the girl's sweet scent. A wave of nostalgia swept
through me and I almost cried out recklessly.

The slam of the front door restored me to my senses.
Cautiously looking down, I noticed Vanessa's long black cloak
was no longer on its hook by the front door. She had gone out,
meaning Judith would not be able to tell her about my visit just

yet. I had been given a brief respite, but Vanessa might return at any moment and I had to find a way out of the building before anyone saw me. A couple of attendants in white uniforms were talking in the hall, preventing me from running down the stairs and making a dash for the side door.

'We'll wait for Vanessa to return and then we'll see what she has to say about it,' one of them said, folding her arms across her chest.

Listening, I was dismayed to discover they did not intend to leave until Vanessa had returned. With the two women waiting at the bottom of the stairs, I could not hope to slip away undetected. As I crouched out of sight behind the plinth, a desperate plan began to form in my mind.

By the time Vanessa returned, my legs were stiff with cramp and I felt as though I had been crouching there in the shadows for days. If my legs had not been strengthened by walking across the sand of the camp and the desert, I doubt I would have been able to maintain my position for so long. I listened to the muffled voices of the two instructors talking to Vanessa. From what I could make out, they were complaining about the quality of the oils they had been given. Eventually, they departed through the side door.

Vanessa locked it behind them, before crossing the hall to slide the great bolt shut on the front door. The chains rattled. Vanessa was locking up for the night. At last she climbed the stairs and headed off to her sleeping quarters.

There was no time to waste. I had to be away before dawn, when the cleaners would arrive to polish the floors and walls. Slipping silently down the stairs to the main hall, I hurried to the plinth and lifted the helmet. It was so heavy I almost dropped it. Clutching it awkwardly under one arm, I went to the main door and grabbed Vanessa's cloak from the wall. My trousers were sand coloured, but Vanessa was short and her cloak reached nearly down to the ground. With the helmet out of sight beneath the cloak, there was a chance anyone who spotted me in The Facility might mistake me for Vanessa, at least from a distance, unless she herself caught sight of me crossing the vestibule. That was a risk I had to take. Once outside, with my face concealed inside the helmet, I might be able to carry off my disguise, as long as no one challenged me. After that, I would just have to hope that Gideon would be waiting at the corner where we had arranged to meet. Without him, I would never find my way out of the city, and my escape from The Facility would not save me.

Cautiously I pulled the heavy chain from the front door. It was not easy to remove it quietly with one hand, but I held on to the helmet with my other arm. I had a wild notion that it might be possible to use it as a weapon, if someone confronted me. Careful though I was, the chain jangled until I thought everyone in the building was bound to hear it; the heavy bolt squealed as it slid across. At last the door swung open, and I stepped outside. Pulling the door closed behind me, I hurriedly put the helmet over my head. It was far too big for me, and very heavy, and it was dark behind the visor. Unable to see anything, I descended the front steps of the building, feeling my way with my feet. A couple of times I stumbled and nearly missed my footing, but managed to regain my balance before I fell headlong down the stairs. Clumsily I shuffled around to the side of the building where Gideon had agreed to wait for me. Turning too soon, I collided with the wall, hitting my head painfully against the side of the helmet. There was no one to observe my clumsy progress and at last I felt the corner of the building with my outstretched hand, and turned into the side street that ran along the side of The Facility.

'Gideon?' I whispered.

There was no reply.

Alone in the city, a fugitive wife poorly disguised as a Guardian in a stolen cloak and helmet, it was hard to see how my situation could be worse. Abandoned by the only person I cared about, for the first time that night I was ready to give up. Squatting on the ground, I pulled off the hated helmet. There was no point in wearing it any longer, and the weight was making my neck ache. A night patrol was bound to find me sooner or later. In the meantime, I gazed up at the starry sky and tried to savour my last moments of liberty. Without a sound, a pair of sandals appeared in front of me, and I looked up to see Gideon staring at me.

He swore softly. 'I thought you were a Guardian. What were you doing in that foul thing?' He nudged the helmet with his foot, and it rocked gently on the ground.

'Let's get away from here,' I said in a shaky voice, too relieved to say more.

'Are you all right?' He crouched down, still staring intently at me.

'Where were you?' I blurted out. 'You were supposed to be here waiting for me. That's what we agreed, wasn't it? Why weren't you here?' I bit my lip, determined not to break down in tears. 'I thought you'd left without me.'

'I was waiting right here, just as we agreed, until a solitary Guardian came marching round the corner, so I hid. How was I supposed to know it was you, disguised in one of their filthy helmets? If you had turned up just then, I would have rescued you somehow, or died in the attempt. Obviously, I was hoping the Guardian would go away before you arrived, or that you would see him and hide until he left. Only the Guardian didn't go away: he sat down on the ground, and removed his helmet. I couldn't believe it when I saw it was you! Now come on, we need to get away from here. You can tell me all about what happened later. We can't hang around. We need to get away.'

Apart from the danger that we could be discovered at any moment by a passing patrol, we had to get away before the missing helmet was noticed, or Judith spoke to Vanessa. Even now, Vanessa might be hearing about my visit and preparing to report it to the Guardians. I wrapped her cape around me as protection against the chill air of the night, and grabbed Gideon's hand, pulling him into the shadows on the other side of the street. He allowed himself to be dragged along, muttering that we should not have left the helmet behind. It could have been useful.

'Come on,' I said, 'we need to get as far away from here as possible. And the last thing we want slowing us down and betraying our identity is a stolen Guardian's helmet.'

Gideon nodded, but it was already too late to avoid being seen. We heard marching boots, and a second later a line of Guardians appeared round the corner, their black helmets gleaming in the light from their torches. Gideon let go of my hand, and I sensed him tense beside me. But what could we do, two of us pitted against a dozen monumental brutes? They were trained to fight, and each of them rested a gloved hand on a deadly blow pipe. Gideon and I both knew something of the torments that lay ahead of us if we were captured. Once we were arrested, there could be no escape.

The Guardians came to a halt right in front of us and one of them stepped forward. 'What are you doing outside after curfew?' he demanded.

Beside me, Gideon cleared his throat nervously. 'We came out to see what was happening. We heard someone running away, and then you arrived.'

'Did you see a girl on the street?' a second Guardian asked. 'She is wearing a tunic and trousers. Tell us where she is.'

The bellowing voice sent a shiver of terror through me, and I recalled the prison where they had thrown me after killing my mother. Too frightened to speak, I stood with my eyes lowered, hoping this would all end quickly.

'We didn't see anyone,' Gideon said.

The Guardian turned to me. He made a rumbling sound in his chest. 'Who is this?'

'She's my sister,' Gideon said.

The Guardian was silent, contemplating me. I hoped he would not notice how fine-spun my cloak was.

'We haven't seen anyone,' Gideon repeated firmly. 'Who are you looking for? Perhaps we can help you search. We heard someone running along the street before you arrived, going that way.' He pointed up the street, away from the entrance to the tunnel that would lead us back to the camp.

'We are wasting time,' one of the other Guardians called out. 'These citizens have not seen the one we seek.'

'We are not interested in you,' the first Guardian said. 'Move aside.'

'Do not defy the curfew. It is not an option,' another one added loudly.

'Leave them. They are not important. We must find the fugitive wife,' the first one roared.

Without another word, the Guardians marched on down the street, and the sound of their stamping boots faded into the darkness of the night.

'Come on,' Gideon said, taking my hand.

We walked quickly away from the Guardians, and Vanessa's Facility, to the tunnel that would take us out of the city. Neither of us spoke again until we were safely underground.

'That was a close call,' Gideon said, when we reached the foot of the ladder. 'We're lucky they let us go.'

'I thought they were going to trample us into the ground.'

'They were too focused on looking for you to notice you,' he said, with a chuckle.

All at once, he flung his head back, laughing with relief, but I felt more like crying. Noticing my sadness, he put his arms round me and held me close so that I could feel his heart pumping against my chest as though it was beating for both of us. I wanted that moment to last forever. He bent down and kissed me gently on the lips.

'Tell me what happened,' he said softly. 'I take it none of the trainee wives were willing to help us?'

Briefly I explained my dismal encounter with Judith, and he nodded.

'I should have known that anyone who has the independence of thought to be sympathetic to our plight is never going to be chosen as a wife,' I concluded. 'Just the ability to think for herself would rule her out. It took me a while to learn to think about anything, and I'm not as stupid as some of them.'

'You mean there are trainee wives who are even stupider than you?' he teased me. 'But you're right. This was a futile plan, really.'

'It was worth the attempt, I suppose,' I replied. 'At least from Daniel's perspective. He didn't know there was no chance we would succeed. I don't think Daniel has any understanding of the way trainee wives' minds are controlled. But I think we knew all along that we were bound to fail. Did you really believe it was going to work?'

'There was only ever a very slim chance the plan could succeed,' he replied. 'If it had been possible, you would have managed it. And the risk was too great,' he added, reaching out to stroke my filthy hair as reverently as though I had just come from the hair salon.

We walked along the tunnel in silence until finally, tired and aching, we made our way back up the ladder and across the desert sands to the camp. This time, Gideon walked down the slope at my side, cradling my elbow in his hand and steadying me when I slipped. We went straight to the hut of the Elders, who were eager to hear what had happened. I struggled to appear miserable about the failure of our mission, although the trip had, unexpectedly, been the most wonderful experience of my life.

'It's just that I'm so pleased to be safely back here,' I replied, when Daniel wanted to know why I was looking so happy. 'I'm so grateful to Gideon,' I added, truthfully.

'So it was all a complete waste of time,' Daniel concluded when we finished.

I looked around at the circle of old people who had listened patiently to our sorry tale. Disappointment was visible in their faces, but I no longer cared what they thought of me. Only one person's opinion would ever matter to me again. All I wanted was to be with Gideon.

'Don't be too hard on them,' one of the women said.

'They did their best,' the other woman agreed.

'And they did well to get away from the Guardians,' another Elder said.

'Yes,' Daniel agreed, 'that was quick thinking.'

'Where are the Guardians?' William asked, suddenly alarmed. 'Where are they?' He had become increasingly agitated while we had been describing our encounter with Guardians in the street. 'Where are the Guardians?' he repeated, rising to his feet. Shouting out in a reedy voice, he banged on the table with a clenched fist. The other Elders quietened him with difficulty.

'There are no Guardians here,' one of the women told him.

'That's what they want us to believe,' William replied, glaring around the room, his white hair sticking up in clumps. 'But I tell you, they are on their way. They will be here soon. We must prepare.' At last he settled back in his chair, silently sucking in his cheeks and puffing them out again, like a small child making faces. It was hard to believe he had once been Leader of the City Council, responsible for laws governing the lives of thousands of people. I wondered how many people he had sentenced to rot in prison, and whether he had ordered any executions. I glanced at Gideon, but if anything he appeared as concerned as the Elders about William.

Despite the failure of our mission, the Elders agreed that Gideon and I had done our best. We were each given a pill to revive us, and sent away to rest after our journey. My hope of sleeping in Gideon's arms was scotched when he offered to walk me back to the hut I shared with the other women. In spite of my disappointment, I was relieved to be back in the camp that had become my home. Before we parted for the night, Gideon reached out and touched my hand, in a silent promise of future intimacy.

Exhausted, I slept soundly that night.

18

HANNAH

Gideon came to see me at school the next day, to tell me he was on his way to tend to the food plants. When I replied that I was ready to accompany him, he said that was impossible. The other teachers began looking curiously at us as we argued, so we stepped outside. Close to tears, I begged Gideon to take me with him, but he insisted the Elders would never agree.

'I have my work to do, and you have yours,' he said.

Even if the Elders agreed to let me accompany him, he added, he could not risk thinking about anything apart from his work, while he was at the plant site. My presence would be a distraction. He was worried that many of his plants might have died while we had been away, especially as Matthew was in hospital. Although everything he said made sense, I remonstrated with him. We had only just found each other, and now he was leaving. Once he left the camp, I might never see him again. Even if I wanted to, I would have no way of finding him.

'I know the plants are important, but doesn't my happiness matter to you at all?' I asked. 'I won't get in your way, I promise, and you can spend as much time as you want with your plants, and give them all the attention they need. I just want to be near you, and know that you are close by, even if I can't see you. I can't bear to be parted from you.'

Despite my pleading, he remained adamant.

'What about the children?' he replied. 'If the plants die, we'll all die. I can't stand by and let that happen.'

'I'm not saying you shouldn't go, only let me come with you, please.'

'What about your work here at the school?'

'They don't need me here. It's not as if I'm the only one looking after the children. They were fine before I came here, and they can all get on just as well without me. I don't suppose the children even noticed I was gone when we were away.'

That was not entirely true. Absalom had resumed his old habits in my absence, throwing sand at the other children and knocking their castles down, but I could hardly be held responsible for his misdemeanours. He would have to learn to behave sensibly without me one day.

'I could help you with your work,' I insisted. 'You can teach me what to do. With two of us working there, we can do twice as much and cultivate twice as many plants.'

Gideon shook his head. 'You don't belong underground with the plants,' he said. 'It's dark and dirty at the plant site, and the work is physically demanding.'

'I don't mind how arduous it is, and I don't mind getting dirty, only please don't leave me here without you. I couldn't bear it.'

He avoided looking at me directly. 'To be strong enough for my work takes years of hard physical labour. I'm sorry, Rachel, really I am, but it's just not sensible for you to come with me.'

He hesitated, but as he turned away, I saw his expression and understood what I ought to have realised from the start. As an addict, Gideon was eager to leave and return to his foodstuffs.

Even his feelings for me faded into insignificance compared to his desire to satisfy that craving. But I did not care. He should have known it would not change my feelings for him, and if living with him meant I would have to become an addict too, then I would accept that happily.

'I don't care what it takes, it will be worth any sacrifice or hardship to be with you. We have to be together.'

'We are together,' he replied. 'We may not live in the same place, but you'll always be in my thoughts and dreams, a part of my life.'

'Not if you go away.'

'Yes, wherever I am. We have to get on with our jobs. We both have responsibilities, and that means we can't choose where we live. That's just how it is. I don't like it any more than you do, but I need to get back to my work, and there's no place for you there. It's too dangerous. Goodbye, Rachel.'

'Please don't go without me. Don't say goodbye. Take me with you.'

He gave me a fleeting kiss on the lips and stepped away from me. I reached out and held on to his hand. 'When will I see you again?' I asked, careless of the tears that would make my eyes red and swollen.

'Soon.'

With that, he turned and left. I stood watching him, until he disappeared from view behind a neighbouring hut. He did not look back.

Back in school, I caught Eve staring at me. She dropped her gaze when she saw me looking at her but, although I tried to hide my feelings, it must have been obvious to everyone that something was wrong. Absalom took my mind off my misery when he grabbed a fistful of sand and threw it at a little girl, who promptly started wailing. But it was hard to stop thinking about what had happened in the tunnel with Gideon, and several times I was recalled from a daydream by Absalom's hot little hand tugging at my sleeve.

'Rachel, Rachel,' he nagged me. 'Look what I made. Look at my sand man. Look at my sand man. Look, look!'

On our way to the food hut that evening, Eve asked me about my trip to the city.

'It's a long story,' I replied. 'I've been through it already with the Elders. Basically, I met one of the girls I trained with. We used to be friends, but when I asked her for help, she pretended not to understand what I was talking about, and perhaps she really didn't. But in any case, she refused to help us.'

Eve interrupted me. 'I'm not talking about that. I want to know what happened between you and Gideon.'

'What do you mean?'

'Don't pretend you're not upset about what happened to you. What did he say to you on your journey? Was it really awful? You needn't worry. He's gone now, and he won't be back in a hurry. Gideon's not like the rest of us. He stays away from the camp. Everyone says he's not to be trusted.' She broke off, seeing my face.

'What are you talking about?' I asked, struggling to control my temper.

Puzzled by my angry response, Eve hesitated. 'It's just that everyone thinks he's strange, keeping to himself like that. No one at the camp trusts him. Come on, Rachel, you don't have to be shy with me. I know he's got a violent temper. Quite a few people have said so. If you ask me, the Elders should never have sent you off with him like that. You're lucky you got back here alive.'

'You don't know what you're talking about,' I snapped. 'You're just repeating stupid ignorant gossip.'

Eve's eyebrows rose in surprise. 'They say it's because of the food.' She shuddered. 'Susan says it's not his fault. It's because he's so close to food all the time. I've heard he sleeps in a tent filled with stuff they make pills from. Susan said no one would have been able to resist becoming addicted, if they worked with food all day, but it was his choice to live like that. What sort of a person would choose that? It's asking for trouble. Anyway, the point is he's not like us and all I'm saying is, you're lucky he's gone and we can get back to normal.'

I was furious. Eve was talking about Gideon as if he was some kind of monster. She was no better than Judith, with her mindless acceptance of lies and propaganda.

'You don't need to worry about me,' I told her coldly. 'Worry about yourself. And stop listening to pathetic gossip. You'll only succeed in turning yourself into an idiot, believing every stupid story you hear.'

'It's more than just gossip,' Eve protested. 'You can't deny he's not like us. For a start he grew up in the city.'

'So did I.'

Eve gave me a curious look, and was silent. She had been my best friend, but we barely spoke to one another for days after that disagreement. Gideon was never out of my thoughts for long but, for all I knew, he had forgotten about me. Sooner or later everyone I trusted abandoned me. Judith and Gideon had both deserted me, and now Eve had turned against me too. She might have been right when she said that Gideon was not to be trusted, but I refused to believe that was true. None of the other women in our hut asked why Eve and I stopped chatting in bed at night, but they must have been pleased.

After a few days of hostile silence, Eve approached me outside the school. 'You've changed,' she said.

'What are you talking about?'

'Ever since you went to the city you've been different. You're mean to me and you don't seem interested in anything anymore, not even the children.'

She was right. I did not care about the children anymore. All that mattered to me was seeing Gideon, and I was waiting impatiently for him to return.

'Something happened to you, didn't it?' Eve pressed me.

'What's it to you?'

'I thought we were friends?'

But I no longer cared about her friendship. She had no inkling about what had happened between Gideon and me while we were away from the camp, and she would never understand my feelings. No one but Gideon could understand, and he had gone away. Waiting was agony. It did not help that my best friend and I had fallen out, making me feel more isolated than ever. One day I overheard Eve chatting with Susan. Neither of them knew that I was standing nearby, listening.

'I hate seeing her looking so miserable all the time,' Eve was saying. 'She used to be really kind to the children, especially Absalom. I don't know what's happened to her, but she doesn't seem to care about anything anymore.'

'Do you think she's sick?' Susan asked. 'Sand fever can manifest itself in different ways.'

'This isn't sand fever,' Eve replied. 'She's been odd ever since she went to the city.'

'Didn't she go with Gideon?'

'Yes.'

'Well, let's hope she doesn't go the same way as Hannah,' Susan said.

They moved away and I could not hear what they said after that. Matthew had been looking for someone called Hannah when I first met him, years ago, in the city, and now the mystery surrounding Gideon's alienation from the camp seemed to hinge on a woman called Hannah. Although I desperately wanted to find out who she was, I was reluctant to ask for fear of making myself look foolish. Worse, I was afraid of what I might discover about Gideon.

All I could do now was settle back into my life at the camp and forget about the past. The Facility and The Programme were behind me, and out of my life. Never again would I return to the city. I had moved on from being a trainee wife, and now I had to forget about Gideon as well. Not only my way of living and my thoughts were different: my body was changing. Despite still taking a pill from The Facility once a month, in a probably vain attempt to maintain my fertility, my monthly bleeding had stopped. Perhaps it had something to do with the foodstuffs I had ingested. In a way it was a relief not to have to deal with the inconvenience, but I could not help feeling sad, knowing I would never have a baby of my own.

It was a couple of months before I had an opportunity to find out about Hannah. Laura, the woman who had first initiated me into life in the camp, was walking past the school one morning as I arrived. She had grown up in the camp, and knew everyone who lived there. She answered my question straight away, without enquiring why I wanted to know. Her lined face softened and her eyes stared through me, as though she was gazing at a melancholy memory.

Laura told me that, like most of the camp dwellers, Hannah had been brought there as a baby. With large blue eyes and blonde curls, she was extraordinarily beautiful, even as a small child. If she had grown up in the city, everyone said she would have been chosen for training, and become a wife.

'It would have suited her,' Laura sighed. 'Hannah was exquisite, and she was fascinated by the city and tales of fine living. She pestered anyone who delivered foodstuffs to the city to tell her about it. Mostly she wanted to hear about clothes made of soft shiny fabrics, and wonderful perfumes, made for the wives. To tell the truth, she never had to ask anyone twice. The desert walkers competed with one another to oblige her. We all did. It was hard to resist spoiling her, she was so captivating. One time a desert walker brought her back a scrap of bright blue silk from the city. She kept it with her for years and wept when she lost it. We searched everywhere for it, but we never found it.' She smiled wistfully at the memory. 'We all fell under Hannah's spell. We couldn't help it.'

'What happened to her?' I asked.

When she was fourteen, Laura told me, Hannah ran away with a young man. I did not have to ask his name. The two of them had been seen together, holding hands and putting their arms round one another at the edge of the camp, and one night they both disappeared. No one saw them leave the camp, but in the morning they had gone.

'Did she ever come back?'

'No. After a while we learned from one of our allies on The Council that she had been accepted as a trainee wife, and ended up married to an important Council Member. And that was the end of Hannah, as far as we were concerned. We knew we would never see her again. Anyway, some time after that the young man returned, alone, and the Elders sent him away. That is, there was a vote in the camp,' Laura corrected herself, 'and it was decided that he could not stay, not after he had chosen to leave us and return to the city. He told us Hannah had mesmerised him, but he had finally realised that she was corrupt and depraved. He claimed it was his misfortune that the woman who cast her spell on everyone had fallen in love with him. Some of us felt sorry for him, because his only transgression had been to fall for Hannah's charms. Hannah had that effect on people. She could persuade anyone to do anything she wanted. So some of the camp dwellers were sympathetic towards him, and saw him as a victim, but others insisted he be exiled from the camp. Many of us were worried that Hannah might be able to find her way back to the camp and would lead the Guardians to us.

'So he was sent away, and a message was delivered to Hannah to let her know that he had been exiled from the camp. In that way, any personal animosity she felt towards him would be deflected away from our community.' She lowered her voice. 'I think some of the men were jealous of him, and could not forgive him for having been chosen by Hannah. You have no idea how beautiful she was. But I don't know what happened to her after that. She may still be living in the city, but most of us believe she must be dead, because we've heard nothing more about her.'

'What happened to the man who ran away with her?' I asked, although I already knew the answer to my question.

'He was sent away to the plant site. He developed an affinity with the plants, and he's been living with them ever since, tending them and taking care of their fruits.' She stopped speaking abruptly, as though she had remembered something, and stepped away from me. 'I must get on,' she said. 'And you should be at school. The other teachers will be wondering where you are. This is where you belong now, Rachel, and everyone here has to work to support the community however they can.'

Laura turned and walked rapidly away, leaving me devastated. Eve had been right to warn me, and I had been a fool to ignore her. Whatever had happened to Hannah, I now knew that Gideon had loved another woman enough to run away from the camp with her. He did not even love me enough to share his work with me.

19

WARNING

I had never been so miserable before. Even when the Guardians had taken my mother away and locked me in a dark cell on my own, somehow I had clung to the belief that life would improve. But once Laura told me about Hannah, jealousy tormented me. There was no one I could confide in. Feeling alienated from everyone else in the community, I envied Eve and the other camp dwellers, cheerfully carrying out their duties.

Slowly I withdrew into myself, preferring my own company to anyone else's. The children I had learned to care for now irritated me.

Absalom's shrill voice followed me around the school, 'Rachel, Rachel, look at me,' and 'Rachel, look what I done.'

'Why don't you go and play with the other children?' I would answer wearily.

Deserted by everyone I had ever cared about, I resigned myself to a joyless future. Gideon preferred his plants to me. It seemed ironic that I only really understood him now that our relationship was over and we would never see one another again. Picturing him pacing up and down between rows of plants, at peace with himself, I tried very hard to hate him. Yet if he returned to the camp, I knew my bitterness would melt away in the warmth of his embrace. We knew that foodstuffs were addictive; I wondered if people could have the same effect.

Meanwhile, Matthew recovered from his sand fever and was able to work again. Returning from a trip to the city, he brought worrying rumours, and I forgot about my falling out with Eve in the general panic, as we heard that the Guardians were planning to attack the camp within the next few days. Daniel summoned the entire camp to a meeting in the early evening, after the heat of the day had died down. This was the first time I had seen all the camp dwellers gathered together in one place since the dance. The mood among them was very different now as, fidgeting and muttering, we waited anxiously for the Elders to address us. There must have been at least 300 people there, all impatient to hear what Daniel had to say. Only a few women were absent, supervising the smaller children who were asleep in the school hut.

At last Daniel climbed up onto a creaky box, and gazed fiercely around the crowd. A few people shuffled and jostled, and then everyone fell silent, watching him. His blue eyes glittered as his voice rang around the meeting place, telling us that it seemed the rumours we had been hearing were not exaggerated. The threat was real.

A few grew restless, listening to him. 'How do we know it's not just more scaremongering?' a man shouted angrily, and several voices called out in agreement.

'We've heard it all before,' someone else said.

'Why should we believe it this time?' the first man asked.

'Because this time the rumours have been confirmed,' Daniel said, raising one hand for silence. 'Are we all agreed that Matthew and Gideon are trustworthy?'

There was an uneasy murmur of assent.

'They both independently reported overhearing a

conversation between Guardians. So unless Matthew and Gideon hatched a plot together to fool us all, then we have to believe what they are telling us.'

The crowd grew still when Daniel began to talk about evacuating the camp. 'We need to start preparing to leave now, while there's still time. There are too many of us to delay until the last minute. We won't be able to set off in a hurry. We have to work things out properly, without panicking.'

Several people began calling out in alarm. Some of the crowd agreed with Daniel, others shouted out that we should not hang around to work anything out but must leave at once, while yet others cried out that they were not going to run away and abandon the camp where the Guardians would never find us.

'We can't just pack up and leave.'

'Where can we go?'

'We have to stand up to them.'

'What about the children?' someone asked, and the murmur of voices swelled to a roar.

Daniel raised his hand and waited for the commotion to die down.

'Shut up and hear what he has to say,' a loud voice cried out, and the crowd fell quiet.

'We need to take this threat seriously,' Daniel repeated firmly.

'I say we stay and fight. We can't run away forever,' someone yelled.

Everyone started shouting again. Once again, Daniel held up his hand for silence, and the people stopped talking and listened. 'This is not only based on what Matthew overheard from Guardians. Our supporters on The Council have sent us a warning as well. Two of them have told us that The Council is planning an attack, and it's coming soon.' He paused and looked down at a small group of people standing just in front of him. 'Go on, tell them what you told me, Matthew.'

Daniel stepped down. Matthew leaped up onto the box, looked around, and cleared his throat. The crowd were very quiet, watching him. Matthew was popular, and everyone knew he had contacts on The Council.

'Matthew should be our leader,' someone called out.

'Shut up, will you, and let's hear what he has to say.'

Matthew had little to add to what Daniel had already told us. A Member of The Council had told him an army of Guardians was standing by in readiness to attack the camp. The offensive was being orchestrated by our enemies on The Council. Either they had all gone mad, he added, or else they had successfully made pills in a laboratory and no longer needed our plants. Either way, we were in imminent danger of extinction.

'They won't be able to find us,' Laura said uncertainly.

'The word is they have a guide,' Matthew said quietly.

For a moment, the crowd was quiet, shocked by this, and then a few people broke the silence. A low muttering rose to a crescendo by the time Daniel climbed back onto the box, but no one shouted at him when he raised his hand for silence.

'Our enemies might not attack,' he said. 'The warnings might be mistaken, or exaggerated. Or perhaps a raid is being planned, but it won't go ahead. We don't know what is going to happen.' He paused and looked around the crowd, which was now completely silent. 'But we have to be prepared for the worst. The Guardians could arrive at any moment.'

'What are we going to do?' someone asked in a trembling voice.

'There is only one course of action open to us. We must pack up immediately, and prepare to leave the camp. There is no time to lose. We will leave as soon as possible,' Daniel said.

People started calling out. 'Isn't it time we stopped all this talking and got going then?'

'Yes, yes, let's get out of here!'

'Where are we going?'

'What about the hospital?'

'What will happen to the children?'

Suddenly everyone seemed to be shouting out at once, asking questions, and making suggestions. Daniel raised his hand again. This time it took a few moments for the crowd to settle down. People were upset, and everyone wanted to talk.

At last it was quiet enough for Daniel to speak. 'When I said there's no time to lose, I didn't mean we should leave the camp right this minute, nor even tonight. Everything must be done in an orderly fashion. That way we won't make a hash of it. So don't panic. We must begin our preparations so we're ready to leave as soon as possible. There's enough time to get everything done that needs to be done.'

'You keep talking about being prepared and making plans, but what exactly are we supposed to do?' Susan asked. 'We have the children to think of.'

Before the crowd could grow restless again, Daniel started issuing instructions, and it was soon clear that he had given this a lot of thought. We were told to pack everything we possessed, and bring only what we could carry. In my case, that was one change of clothes, and my pouch with the dried-up strawberry stalk Gideon had given me. No one else had many more personal possessions than me. The Elders would abandon their prized wooden table, concealing it in the sand along with everything else we could not take away. Children were to be led out of the camp first, just after dawn, since they would travel more slowly than the adults, and people too old to carry anything would travel at the rear, sweeping over the sand to ensure we left no tracks. Meanwhile some of us would remain to cover up any signs of the camp. While we were preparing to evacuate, lookouts would be posted from the camp all the way to the city. As soon as the Guardians set off, a message would be relayed back to us along the line. By the time the Guardians searched the area, all traces of the camp would lie buried in sand. The Guardians would return to the city, and report that they had been unable to find the camp, if it even existed, and we would survive to set up a new camp somewhere else, far away across the desert.

'It's not ideal, but that's the best we can do,' Daniel concluded. 'Now, are there any further questions before we disperse to start our preparations?'

Gazing around, I saw my own fear reflected in the faces surrounding me, yet in spite of our desperate plight there was an atmosphere of excitement too. The threat of an attack had been hanging over us for so long, in a strange way it was a relief that the time for action had finally arrived.

'What if it's already too late?' a voice called out.

'Then we'll all be dead before sunrise,' Matthew replied in his even tones.

'We must prepare to leave at first light,' Daniel said grimly.

No one asked the question that must have been on everyone's mind: without a desert walker to guide them, how could the Guardians find the camp? There was only one possible answer. One of the desert walkers had betrayed us to The Council. We were sent to our huts to pack, and Eve and I stared at one another in dismay, our quarrel forgotten.

'The school,' Eve stammered, 'let's see if we're needed there.'

I nodded, and we hurried to the school hut. People rushed past us, and everywhere we looked the scene appeared chaotic. But there was a sense of purpose in the faces of the men and women who were scurrying around, and a growing sense of exhilaration that, for better or worse, the anxious wait might finally be over. As we walked through the camp, we caught snatches of other people's conversations as they charged past. One exchange in particular caught my attention.

'If you ask me, it could only be Gideon.'

'It was obviously not Matthew.'

'No, it wasn't Matthew.'

'I agree, it must have been Gideon.'

'Yes, it all points to Gideon.'

'Where is he anyway?'

Listening to the camp dwellers filled me with dread, not least because I was afraid they were right. There were other desert walkers who might have betrayed our location to the Guardians, but they all lived with us at the camp. Hard though it was to accept, it seemed that Gideon must be the traitor. My fantasies about him one day returning to me evaporated in the harsh reality of the situation.

The calm atmosphere inside the school felt surreal after the alarm outside. As soon as they saw us, the teachers who had been left watching the children hurried over to us, demanding to be updated. As briefly as she could, Eve told them what was happening, while the children slept on, oblivious to the danger we were facing. Susan summoned all the adults together and we huddled in a corner, to make plans. Somewhere in the room a small child began to cry. No one took any notice. While we talked in lowered tones, Susan dithered. Good at organising the school day, she seemed helpless in this crisis. The rest of us gazed at one another in dismay. There was nothing we could do to avert the disaster, but we had to do our best to protect the children.

Recalling Daniel's advice to bring with us only what we could sensibly manage, I suggested we might carry the smaller children away from the camp, if they were too tired to walk. They could take it in turns to be carried. Susan grasped at the idea gratefully and, now that we had a plan of sorts, she took control once more.

'We need to work out a rota,' she said. 'The strongest must be prepared to carry children when we are all exhausted. And we have to be ready to set off as soon as we are told to abandon the camp. This is not a drill.'

She broke off as the import of her words sank in. The rest of us muttered in fervent agreement. The team of lookouts posted on the route to the city would hopefully have time to warn us when the Guardians set out in our direction, giving us time to leave the camp before the enemy arrived. Whatever else happened, we were determined to save all the children from the onslaught. Nothing else mattered. Even my disappointment in Gideon was forgotten. Susan sent two of the teachers back to their own huts to pack. As soon as they returned, Eve and I were sent to collect our belongings.

'I haven't got much,' Eve admitted, as we hurried through bustling pathways between huts. 'All I own is a spare tunic, and a blanket I was wrapped in as a baby. It's quite small, not much use really, but I keep it because it's mine. I suppose you've brought things with you from the city?'

Without even a blanket to call my own, all I had was my one set of clothes, my pouch, and a memento from the strawberry that Gideon had pressed into my hand when I had left the foodstuffs production site. Surreptitiously I dropped the shrivelled stalk on the ground and kicked sand over it with my foot. It had nestled in my pouch, as a kind of talisman, helping me cling to the belief that one day Gideon would return to me, embrace me, and promise never to leave me again. That dream was over.

Meanwhile, there was a frenzied commotion in our sleeping hut. Women were rushing around in the small space, crashing into one another, tripping over each other's feet, and generally causing havoc.

'Get out of the way, will you?'

'Excuse me!'

'Hey, watch where you're putting that.'

It was impossible to move without barging into someone tugging at a bed cover, or grabbing a tunic, and sand was flying everywhere. We were all on tenterhooks, waiting for a message to reach us that it was time to flee. A sudden yelp startled us, and I felt my heart racing in my chest. It turned out that someone had taken Eve's blanket.

'You stupid idiot! I thought the Guardians were here,' someone cried out.

A chorus of voices joined in, chattering with a mixture of anger and relief, all agreeing that Eve had been thoughtless to frighten us over something so unimportant.

'It's only a blanket,' someone said.

A few people laughed, and the mood in the hut grew oddly cheerful, as though the danger had passed, even though Eve's outburst had changed nothing. The Guardians might still be ready to attack the camp at any moment, and within a few hours we could all be dead. But this whole scenario felt unreal, and I doubt whether any of us really believed the Guardians would find us. Apart from worrying about the lives of the camp dwellers, I had a personal reason for hoping the muttered accusations against Gideon would prove unfounded. I regretted having thrown away the shrivelled strawberry stalk he had given me, but it was too late to retrieve it. My memento was lost forever, buried in the sands of the desert.

20

BATTLE

The sun had not yet risen when a deafening racket woke us from uneasy sleep. Outside, we could hear people screaming and yelling. Eve and I exchanged a terrified glance and ran out of our hut. The camp was in chaos, with shadowy figures dashing about in the darkness, running in every direction. In the eerie moonlight, I made out several bodies writhing on the ground, while the air rang with the clamour of many voices, shrieking and moaning. A few paces in front of me a man dropped to the ground. Sick with fear, I watched his fingers scratching at a black dart in his neck. It was too late to help him.

I almost lost my footing as a pack of men barged past me, waving their fists and bellowing wildly, a desperate fury in their faces. Daniel was leading them, shouting encouragement over his shoulder at the men behind him. 'Follow me!' he was bawling. 'Up the slope while there's still time!'

One of his companions fell to the ground, a dart in his eye. Daniel yelled at the others to keep going. 'Stay together!' he yelled. 'We have to stop them coming down into the camp!'

Looking up to where they were heading, I saw a ring of

Guardians posted around the rim of the slope, black helmets outlined against the lightening sky. Our escape route was blocked, and the crater that had offered us protection had now become a trap.

One of the Guardians caught my eye. Shorter than the others, while the other Guardians lifted their feet slowly and clumsily on the sand, this one moved around with ease, passing in and out of their ranks as though at home on the slippery surface. It made no sense for a Guardian to be comfortable walking on the desert sand, and a terrible thought struck me. Gideon had failed to recognise me in a Guardian's helmet, and I wondered if that had given him the idea to adopt the same disguise, in order to lead the Guardians to the camp without being recognised by the camp dwellers. The idea made no sense, really. Given that we were all going to be killed, he could have no reason to worry about revealing his identity. All the same, it was true that, years before, the Elders had exiled him from the camp. Perhaps he had been harbouring a growing resentment, which had finally erupted in this terrible betrayal. The thought was painful to contemplate, but there were even more pressing matters at hand.

Lifting their blow pipes to their lips, the Guardians released a shower of deadly darts. Their lungs had been trained from an early age to blow their deadly missiles at unbelievable speed, too fast for a man to dodge, and the poison from a single arrow from their blow pipes would kill a grown man almost instantly.

Stunned, I turned and ran towards the school hut. My one thought now was to protect the children. A sudden blow to my shoulder knocked me off my feet. I was aware of a dart flying past my face before I was crushed by the weight of someone hurling themselves on top of me. Had I remained upright for another second, the dart would have killed me. Twisting my head round, I could not see who had saved my life, but even with the noise of battle all around us, I recognised his voice as soon as he spoke.

'What are you doing, exposing yourself like that?' he panted in my ear. 'Do you want to be killed? Have you been hit?'

I was too shocked to answer. Gideon repeated his question, more urgently, and I assured him I was unhurt.

'Keep your head down,' he warned me. 'You can survive a dart in the arm or leg, even the body, as long as you suck out the venom straight away, and are careful to spit it all out. It works quickly, so you have to act at once. Get a dart in the head and you're dead. Understand? The poison has to be removed before it reaches your blood, and you can't suck the poison out of your own head or neck. Try to stay out of sight and whatever you do, keep your head protected at all times. Here, take this in case you need to cover your head and make a run for it. It's not much, but it's all I've got, and it's better than nothing.'

He shoved a piece of rough sand-coloured fabric into my hand, and his grey eyes glared at me with the fervour of a desperate man. 'As long as a Guardian doesn't spot you're alive, then you've got a chance of surviving this madness,' he went on. 'The best thing you can do is lie still and don't move a muscle, and hope you don't get trampled on. If they think you're dead, they're not going to waste their darts on you.'

'Was it you who betrayed us?' I demanded.

'What are you talking about?'

Before I could answer he had gone, and a moment later I caught a glimpse of him halfway up the slope, kicking at a Guardian's legs in a vain attempt to fell him. I stared, horrified, as the Guardian swivelled his huge head and raised his blow pipe to his lips. Watching, dry-eyed, I felt only a dull numbness as I lost sight of Gideon, and knew that he must have fallen in the terrible slaughter. It no longer made sense to believe Gideon had led the Guardians to the camp. Having saved my life, he had died defending our community, and the last words I had spoken to him had been an accusation of the most terrible treachery. But he was dead, and it made no difference what had passed between us. Nothing could ever make any difference to him again, and nothing mattered to me anymore. I clambered to my feet, careless of the poisoned missiles raining down into the crater. All around me, people staggered and crashed to the ground, but I was not hit. Dazed, I made my way back to the children, determined to do everything possible to comfort them, while I was still able to move.

Inside the school hut, children were wailing in terror. Susan dashed over to me, wringing her hands. I almost did not recognise the screeching maniac confronting me. Her eyes glared around wildly, while she chattered to herself, hair flapping around her face. Her fingers closed suddenly on my upper arm, pinching my flesh, and spittle sprayed from her lips as she shouted at me above the noise. 'We cannot stay here! It's too dangerous! We must get the children away! There's no time to lose!'

I shook my head, shocked at the change in her.

'The children,' she insisted. 'We must save them! You've got to help me. We have to get away!'

'It's too late,' I told her. 'The Guardians have surrounded the camp. No one can get away.'

'Then we'll all be killed,' she shrieked. 'We'll all be killed.'

I did not tell her that many of the camp dwellers were already dead. We gathered the children together as quietly as we could, but it was difficult to make them hear us above all the groaning and yelling that reached us from outside.

'We have to stay calm and work out what to do next,' I called out firmly.

Susan pounced on two small boys. Clutching them to her chest, she began rocking backwards and forwards with her eyes closed, muttering to herself. The two children swayed with her pitching motion, their terrified eyes staring up at me. We could not hope to get the children past the Guardians. All we could do was try to hide them if our enemies came down into the camp. None of us would survive if they saw us so, for now, the children were safest staying exactly where they were in their hut in the middle of the camp. The roof of the school offered us protection from the Guardians' darts, and as long as they continued shooting at us from the top of the slope, we might have a chance of surviving the attack with all the children unharmed.

Frantically, I came up with a plan. To have any hope of success, we had to keep the children still and quiet. Once the Guardians knew we were alive, they would find a way to slaughter us all. On the other hand, if they thought they had succeeded in killing everyone in the camp without having to descend the steep slope, they might leave and go back to the city. I was not sure if my plan would work, but it was the best I could come up with, and no one else seemed to have any idea what to do. I explained my proposal to Susan, who stared blankly at me. It was not clear whether she understood anything I said. For my plan to work, first we had to shift all the children to one side of the hut, so that we could dig out a long ditch in the sand along the opposite wall. Once we had moved the children into the trench we had dug, we would dismantle the school building, using one wall to cover the children, and leaving enough space above us to allow us all to breathe.

Working with Eve and two other teachers, I managed to shepherd all the children along one edge of the hut, apart from the two boys Susan was cradling in her arms. Taking the older children with us, we ran over to the other side of the hut where we dug a trench. As soon as it was deep enough, we laid all the children in it, below ground level, and instructed them to keep perfectly still. They cowered in a row, terrified into silence.

'We need to get these boys into the trench,' I told Susan, shaking her by the arm and indicating the two children she was clutching. 'We have to make sure there's as little of the school building showing as possible. That way the Guardians might not notice we're here and leave us alone.'

The two children whimpered at the mention of the Guardians. One of them threw his little arms around Susan's neck and hung on to her.

'Take them to join the others,' I urged her. 'They'll be safer there.'

'Don't worry, little one,' Susan crooned. 'I'll look after you.'

We could not dismantle the hut while Susan remained crouching by the entrance. Without warning, she sprang to her feet and I had the impression she had understood my plan after all, and was going to help me.

'They won't hurt the children!' she shrieked. 'They won't hurt the children!'

Before anyone could stop her, she dashed out of the hut, with the two small boys in her arms. If any of us attempted to follow her and drag her back inside, we risked drawing attention to the school, and all the other children might die too. Our only hope of keeping them safe was if they remained hidden and the Guardians failed to target them. Susan had fled the safety of the school, and there was nothing more we could do for her.

Now came the most dangerous part of my plan. Covering my head with the cloth Gideon had given me, I crawled out of the hut on my stomach, tore at the entrance and punched the wall violently. The teachers inside understood what I was planning, and were ready to prop up the wall that fell on top of them as the whole edifice came crashing down. Hoping they had succeeded in preventing the falling wall from causing any injury, I sprinkled sand lightly over the ruins of the school.

Within seconds, the school hut was fairly well camouflaged.

A stray dart glanced off my head covering and fell harmlessly on the sand. Sliding back under the fallen walls of the hut, I rolled into the trench beside the children and helped my colleagues to prop up the wall above our heads.

After that, there was nothing to do but wait, and listen to a rain of darts bouncing off the outside of the hut. We comforted the children as well as we could, and urged them to remain calm.

Gritty sand stung my eyes and irritated my throat, and close by I heard a few of the children moan, and teachers exhorting them in hushed tones to be silent, while the sounds of battle roared all around us. With a faint tapping and scraping, darts continued to hit the hut above our heads. As far as we could make out, the Guardians had not yet made the descent into the crater. Once they did, we would probably be crushed beneath the weight of their marching boots. The wall of the hut above our heads trembled under the barrage of darts, but we managed to prop it up on shattered segments of the roof, and keep it in place, a shield against the enemy's weapons. But we knew it was a temporary reprieve.

It was hard to ignore the shrieks and groans that rose and fell in a horrible chorus all around us. It was poor comfort that the voices all sounded human; I knew that once we heard the Guardians' stentorian tones nearby, everything would be over. I imagined watching Guardians trampling on my dying friends, before a dart ended my life. But I was alive, most of the children might survive, and there were others from the camp who had not yet given up. I could hear them fighting on.

Eventually I could no longer lie hidden, like a coward, leaving others to engage in mortal combat against the Guardians. It was better to be killed resisting, than die in hiding while everyone around me lost their lives. Cautiously I edged out from under the wreckage of the school. The view that greeted my eyes was more horrific than anything I had imagined. In every direction, bodies were strewn around the camp. Some were groaning in their death throes, but most lay still, their limbs twisted in awkward positions. Those whose faces were not buried in sand seemed to stare at me, their eyes glassy, their skin pale. With a cry, I recognised Susan lying nearby, her face fixed in a rictus of fear, her frizzy hair packed with sand, and her arms reaching out towards the small stiff bodies of the two children she had carried with her in her insane bid for freedom.

A couple of Guardians began a clumsy charge down the steep slope into the camp. The leading one slid and lost his footing. Waving his arms wildly he crashed to the ground, tripping up his companion who was following closely at his heels. At once a gang of camp dwellers ran up the slope and set on them, beating them with their fists and flinging handfuls of sand at their helmets.

'Bury them! Bury them!' a strong voice rang out above the din. 'It's our only hope.'

A few men began shovelling sand over the fallen Guardians to suffocate them, and within seconds their heads were buried. Their arms and legs beat frantically on the ground for a moment and then they lay still. A cheer broke out among the men even as they dropped one by one, felled by darts.

William was standing on the box Daniel had used at the meeting. His white hair flapping around his face, his hands held high above his head, he raised his thin voice to rally the camp dwellers. 'Forward, men!' he howled, flourishing a sand-coloured scrap of cloth above his head like a pennant. 'Forward! Revenge on the Guardians! Revenge against the city! Fight on! Fight for freedom from tyranny!'

He had never looked so animated. All at once the fabric fell from his grasp, and his frail arms flailed in an arc as he plummeted forwards, a dart stuck in his forehead. He must have been dead before he hit the ground.

There was a roar as another Guardian attempted the descent, and a group of camp dwellers swarmed around him. One of them dashed the blow pipe from the Guardian's hand while the rest tripped him up on the slippery sand and buried his head. A second Guardian followed, and a young woman leapt on his back, clutching him round the throat. The Guardian shook his head in an attempt to dislodge her, and dropped his blow pipe. At once, other camp dwellers ran forward and the Guardian fell to the ground with a crash, surrounded by people scrabbling at the sand around his head. As they fell in a hail of darts, more ran forward to replace them, until the Guardian lay inert, his head buried in sand. This time no one cheered. Too many camp dwellers had lost their lives fighting to overcome him.

A mob surged up the slope, with Daniel at the front. They raced forward in a hail of darts, individuals dropping to the ground around their leader. A few of them, including him, made it all the way to the top. With a loud roar, he lunged and his fist made contact with a Guardian's helmet. Daniel was a powerful man. The Guardian shook his head several times as though dazed by the blow, staggered, and regained his balance. Daniel dropped to the ground with a dozen darts in his head. At once, Laura dashed over to him with a piercing cry. Kneeling beside him, she leaned forward and began desperately sucking poison out of his wounds. An instant later she was lying spread-eagled across his body, victim of a shower of darts.

Matthew began leading a small party of men up the slope at another point, where several Guardians were lying still, their heads buried in sand. If Matthew's group succeeded in breaking through the line of Guardians, I hoped they would have enough sense to flee and save their own lives. If they did not make a run for it, they would perish, along with the rest of us. Remembering Gideon's advice, I lay down motionless on the sand. This was no time for heroics on my part. Any attempt to defeat the Guardians was futile, but there was a chance they would leave once they thought we were all dead, and if that happened, the children were going to need my help. For their sake alone, I had to survive this destruction.

21

AFTERMATH

A faint whimpering roused me from a stupor of despair. In the moonlight, I gazed out over a horrific scene, worse than any nightmare. The crater had become a mass grave. Bodies were strewn everywhere. Close by I heard muffled sounds coming from children concealed beneath the fallen wall of the school. With an effort I forced myself to raise my head and sit up, flinching in expectation of the dart that would end my life. No one responded to my movement and I saw that the Guardians had left their post at the top of the slope, unaware that a few of us remained alive, hidden in the sand. Hoping we were safe from further attack, I cautiously raised the wall that was still in place, protecting the children. Whining and crying, they clambered out of the trench, coated in sand. Their hair was smothered in sand, their eyelashes were encrusted with it, while tears formed narrow channels in the sand that caked their cheeks. I comforted them as well as I could. None of the other teachers were in view so we huddled together helplessly, with our backs against the remnants of the school. Around us there was little other movement.

Leaving a couple of the older girls in charge, I made my way to the site of the pill store. Keeping my eyes nearly closed, in an attempt to shut out the ghastly consequences of the battle, I did my best to avoid trampling on any of my fallen friends and neighbours. At last I completed my dreadful journey and reached my destination. Where only a few hours earlier smiling women had been handing out pills, there was nothing to be seen but corpses lying on the sand.

Scrabbling around, my fingers felt the edge of a wall of the buried hut. I had to push a dead woman aside before I could dig down to the store. Her sightless eyes seemed to stare at me in wordless reproach as, gritting my teeth, I rolled her over. The touch of her dead body made me recoil, but the situation offered me no choice. She was dead, and the children needed my help. Although the woman was only slight, I was almost overwhelmed by the effort of moving her. Weeping, I murmured a pointless apology as I heaved her out of the way.

Frantically, I dug down into the sand, searching for pills, until at last I uncovered a corner of the buried hut. Rummaging around inside it, I stumbled on a stock of pills and stuffed as many as I could into my pouch. It was nowhere near enough. Using my head covering, I made a crude pouch which I filled with pills. Then I made my way slowly back to the children, trying to avoid stepping on sprawling limbs and staring faces. Worried we might not be seen by any other survivors, I led the children to the central meeting point, hoping the remaining camp dwellers would join us.

I had no idea what to do if the children and I were the sole survivors of the battle. We now had enough pills to sustain us for weeks, but we would be leaving the mass grave of the camp dwellers to end our days starving to death in the desert. If by some miracle we found our way back to the city, only the babies would be allowed to live, if they survived the journey. Alone with the group of children, it was impossible to conquer my despair. In finding pills, I had only prolonged their agony. It would have been kinder to simply end all of our lives straight away, instead of finding a supply of pills so I could force the children to clamber up the slope and struggle to stay alive for another few weeks of suffering with no hope of rescue.

My relief was almost overwhelming when I discovered that a few other adults had also managed to survive the attack. Slowly they came limping towards me to gather at the meeting place. My relief intensified when Matthew joined us. He sank to the ground, barely recognisable. One eye was swollen closed and his face was bloodstained. We waited in silence, while a slow trickle of people joined us.

After a while, Matthew glanced at the stars and heaved himself to his feet. It was dismal work, drawing up a list of survivors. Daniel was dead, along with the other Elders, Laura, Susan, and almost all the rest of our community. Over 300 people had been living in the camp. Less than thirty of us were still alive, including nearly a dozen children. We gazed at one another, stunned, reluctant to express the terrible truth aloud as though by not talking about it, we could somehow will it undone.

With the Elders dead, the decision that Matthew should take charge was unanimous. Apart from the fact that we trusted him, Matthew was the only one who could lead us away from there, and we all knew we had to leave soon. The Guardians were likely to return before long to check that we were all dead. In addition to any practical considerations, no one except Matthew was willing to assume responsibility for our future.

A couple of people wondered aloud how the Guardians had found us.

'It could only have been a spy from the camp,' someone said. 'There's no way the Guardians could have found us without help.'

'It must have been a desert walker.'

There was no time to sit around arguing about what had happened, and I was relieved when Matthew interrupted the discussion. It was painful for me to know that my friends blamed Gideon for the massacre, although my private anguish went unnoticed in the general misery.

'How the Guardians found us is not the issue right now,' our new leader said. 'They could have been out looking for us for weeks, and stumbled on us by chance, or they might have followed an inexperienced walker. We knew this might happen at any time, and we should have been better prepared. We had been here for so long, we allowed ourselves to become complacent. But now is not the time for regrets or speculation. We need to save ourselves, and that means we have to leave this place as quickly as possible.'

There was a murmur of agreement, but everyone fell silent when Matthew announced that our first task must be to bury the dead. No one liked the idea, yet we knew that we could not leave the bodies of our friends exposed. If the Guardians returned, they would no doubt carry the corpses back to the city as a warning of what happened to anyone who rebelled. Even in death, we understood that camp dwellers would not want their bodies to be used to bolster the power of The Council. Most of the children had fallen asleep, worn out, their dirty skin speckled with blood and sand. A couple of old women watched over them while the rest of us set to work, digging a large hole at one side of the crater. By the time we finished, my back and shoulders were aching, but we could not rest. What followed was a grisly task. We worked in pairs, dragging the corpses over to the pit and laying them in it as gently as we could, side by side. At last they were all in place. Only a few were missing, including Eve and Gideon.

'Let's hope they got away safely,' someone muttered, and a shiver ran round the group as we thought of our absent friends.

Given that one of those missing was a desert walker, Matthew expressed the hope that other members of our community might have survived. 'Gideon's probably led them back to the plant site,' he said, forcing a grim smile. 'The Guardians won't find them there.'

'The Guardians found the camp,' someone muttered. 'If Gideon brought them here, he's hardly likely to want to save any of us.'

Matthew drew us back to our task. In silence we prepared to throw sand over the bodies of our friends. At first we sprinkled handfuls of sand into the pit we had dug, weeping and murmuring their names. We dared not shout aloud for fear our voices might carry. After a while the men knelt down and began shoving sand over the edge in larger quantities, until at length there was only a low dip in the ground to indicate where our friends lay. Our sombre task completed, we climbed up the slope and hacked at the barrier of compacted sand that had been holding back the sand at the top. The hardened fortifications cracked and crumbled and slid down into the crater in huge chunks, gathering momentum as they fell, until they shattered at the bottom. We kicked as much sand as we could after the smashed barricade, and turned to leave the place that had been the only home many of the camp dwellers had known. It would take only one storm for the desert to reclaim the site, and all trace of the camp would be lost.

Unexpectedly, a familiar voice reached us. 'What are you doing? The Guardians are bound to come back. You should have left a long time ago. Why are you all still here?'

We turned to look at the figure striding easily across the sand towards us. Gideon was leading more than a dozen people, including Eve. As soon as they reached us, they all began talking at once. Gideon took Matthew to one side and they stood apart, deep in conversation, while Eve told us how she and another woman had managed to crawl up the slope unseen, and sneak through a gap in the Guardians' line. Once they had left the camp, they were lost. They had escaped the terrors of the battle, only to perish in the desert, so they decided to return and die with their friends. They had a wild hope they might manage to kill a Guardian from behind, before they were spotted. But although they could hear distant sounds of battle, they had been unable to find their way back to the camp. When the noise of battle ceased, they had not known whether the fighting had stopped, or they had wandered too far from the camp to hear it any longer. Either way, the outcome could hardly have been worse for them.

They had given up hope of ever finding us, when Gideon appeared, having picked up their trail, which they were making little effort to conceal. With a desert walker to guide them, they easily returned to the scene of our defeat, gathering other lost camp dwellers on the way.

'We would have been here sooner, but Gideon insisted on following every track. He was determined to leave no one to wander, lost in the desert,' Eve explained. 'We were afraid we might return too late to find anyone still here, but Gideon said it didn't matter if you'd already left by the time we returned, because he would follow the trail and find every single survivor, however long it took, and bring us all back together again.'

I made no attempt to hide my joy. Happier than I had been in a long time, I could not take my eyes off Gideon. Like Matthew, he had not escaped the battle unscathed. One of his arms was crusted with dried blood from a wound on his shoulder, his top lip was split, and his face was badly bruised. But he was alive and talking animatedly with Matthew. The sight of Gideon's battered face made me feel quite giddy. He had saved my life, and those of other camp dwellers, and our survival depended on his and Matthew's skills as desert walkers.

'You did well to bury our dead, but we need to conceal the Guardians that remain exposed,' Gideon pointed out. 'Otherwise, others are going to search the site and dig up the bodies you hid under the sand.'

In our zeal to bury our friends, we had not thought about covering up the bodies of the Guardians who had fallen near the top of the crater. Thirteen of them had been killed in battle, of whom only three had made it all the way down to the camp. Some of the remaining ones had lost their lives at the top of the slope, while others had been overpowered halfway down. All of their heads were buried in sand, but apart from the three who had reached the floor of the crater, their bodies lay exposed, pointing the way to the fallen camp dwellers. We clambered back down the slope, pushing and dragging the exposed bodies until they all lay sprawled side by side. No one objected when Matthew suggested we remove their helmets, as a mark of respect for the defeated warriors. What no one admitted out loud was that we were curious to see their faces. For as long as I could remember, I had lived in fear of these inhuman brutes, without ever knowing what they looked like. Perhaps they were the monsters my mother had described, with eyes that flashed fire, and teeth as long as daggers.

We laid the ten bodies in a row, as far away from the resting place of our friends as possible. Even the children were silent, watching Matthew kneel down and tug a helmet from a dead Guardian's head. He set it on the sand beside its owner, and shuffled on his knees to the next body. With icy blue eyes glaring up into the sky, a long straight nose, and thin lips clamped shut, even in death the Guardian looked menacing. It might have been my imagination, but there seemed to be a pitiless expression on his face that made me shiver. But although he was gigantic compared to a normal man, he looked human.

Eve was as surprised as me. 'But– but it's a man,' she stammered. 'I don't understand. He's a giant.'

Gideon scowled at her. 'Some male babies are selected at birth to follow a programme of pills that enhance their growth, and their lungs are trained so they can blow darts at more than human speed and power.'

'That must be why their voices are so loud,' I said.

'Not all of the trainee Guardians make the grade,' Gideon went on. 'Only the very largest and strongest are chosen. Unless they have every vestige of compassion trained out of them, they are not accepted.'

'How can you train someone to be inhuman?' one of the women asked.

Recalling my own training, and how potent the indoctrination of The Programme was, I frowned. 'People can be brainwashed to believe anything.'

'Not everyone,' Gideon countered, staring at me.

'What happens to the ones that don't make the grade as Guardians?' someone asked.

'Who knows?' Gideon replied. 'And, honestly, who cares?'

I thought about Naomi's fate, and shuddered at the cruelty of the system.

The next Guardian in the line had similar features. He looked younger than the first one, and his eyes were dark, but his face bore the same cruel expression, with heavy lowered brows and lips pressed together in a curious pout. Perhaps he had been preparing to blow a dart when he was felled. Gideon went to the far end of the row and began removing helmets. He and Matthew worked on in silence for a few minutes, each making his way along the line of Guardians from opposite ends, while the rest of us stood watching.

Suddenly Matthew let out a yell of surprise. It was unlike him to be startled by anything. Afraid one of the Guardians was still alive and dangerous, I felt my heart pound as I turned to see what had prompted his cry. If Matthew was killed, we would lose one of our two surviving desert walkers.

In a way, the truth was even more shocking. Looking down, I blinked several times, struggling to believe my eyes. In among the row of stern looking Guardians, the helmet of the smallest one had been removed to reveal the loveliest face I had ever seen. Glossy blonde hair framed her exquisite features in soft curls, and her huge blue eyes seemed to gaze around in wonder, as though questioning why anyone would want to destroy such perfection. Her skin had taken on the pallor of death, giving her an ethereal quality, and her beauty drew my gaze with a seemingly irresistible power.

'That looks like Hannah,' Matthew said.

'It *is* Hannah,' Gideon replied in a hollow voice.

'I'm sorry,' Matthew muttered.

A few of the older camp dwellers mumbled condolences, as though Gideon had lost someone close to him. After so many of our friends had been killed in battle, it made no sense for anyone to feel sorry because a Guardian was dead.

'I didn't know there were any women Guardians,' I said, disturbed by this turn of events.

'Hannah wasn't a Guardian,' Matthew replied.

Rising to his feet, Gideon kicked at the sand beside the dead woman, spraying it over her pale face. I studied the stylish cut of her hair and the traces of paint on her face, noting her skin which was smooth as though she had just finished a treatment.

'She looks like a wife,' I murmured, staring at the face that could have been carved out of marble.

'She *was* a wife,' Gideon replied, kicking at the ground again.

A shower of sand descended on the dead woman, covering her in a gritty shroud.

'Well, now we know how the Guardians found us,' Matthew said, sitting back on his heels and gazing at Hannah's still face. 'It's hard to believe such beauty could conceal a spirit so vile. How could she betray us like that?'

'Even knowing there were children here, she still accepted a bribe to betray our location. What price did she put on all our lives, I wonder?' Gideon asked bitterly.

His voice broke and he turned away. He did not hint at it, but I wondered if he suspected Hannah's betrayal was an act of revenge against him for abandoning her. My heart beat fast as I went over and slipped my hand into his. Briefly his face relaxed into a faint smile, as though the touch of my hand comforted him. Then he stepped away from me.

'Come on, everyone!' he called out. 'We need to get away from here before dawn. We don't have long. Let's deal with this as quickly as we can.'

We did not cover the corpses of our enemies tenderly, as we had done with the bodies of our friends. From the top of the slope, we shovelled sand down into the camp area until no trace of the Guardians remained. Even the children helped to bury all vestiges of their home. There was not enough time to fill the crater in completely, but it blended into the desert nonetheless.

If the human race survived, no one would ever know that hundreds of people had lived together peacefully on that site for many years. And once the sand had blown across the crater floor, our enemies would never know that a few outcasts had escaped the massacre.

MOUNTAIN

Matthew and Gideon stepped away from the group and began talking together in undertones once more, out of earshot of the rest of us. Before I could sidle closer to listen, Eve approached me.

'I was wrong about Gideon,' she said. 'He saved my life, and it looks like he and Matthew might save us all – all of us who are still alive, that is.' Her face contorted briefly with grief, but she recovered herself and carried on. 'Anyway, the point is, Gideon's a good man and I never should have doubted him.' She gazed anxiously at me.

'I know he's a good man,' I replied coldly. 'I didn't doubt it for an instant.' That was not strictly true, but no one needed to find out that I had suspected Gideon of treachery, along with everyone else.

'Look, I'm sorry I misjudged him, and I'm sorry we argued. I just hope we can be friends again, like we were before – before all this.' As she gazed at me, her black eyes pleading, she reached out and placed her hand on my arm in a gesture of supplication. 'Please,' she whispered.

'It doesn't matter,' I said, my hostility melting away. 'We all make mistakes. And I think we're both going to need all the friends we can get from now on. With so few of us left, we can't afford to fall out. We have to work together, if we're going to make it. There's no point dwelling on the past. We have to think about the future.'

'If we have one.'

'We have,' I said firmly.

'How can you be so sure?'

I nodded at the children huddled together on the ground. Some of the little ones had fallen asleep clutching each other's hands, the sand on their faces streaked with tiny runnels from their tears.

Eve glanced at them and turned back to me, smiling uncertainly at my optimism. 'There will be another time, won't there?' she asked. 'After this. Life will continue for us, won't it?'

I nodded, desperately hoping I was right. 'It has to. We'll move on and make another camp. We have to carry on. For all we know, this may not be the first time this has happened to our people, but we're still here, aren't we? Some of us, anyway. If we give up now, they will have won. And of course we're still friends,' I added as she started to turn away.

To my surprise, she threw her arms round my neck and we clung together, enjoying a brief moment of comfort in our grief.

The children who were still awake were tired and some of them began whingeing.

'Save your energy,' Matthew told them. 'You've got a long hike ahead of you tonight.'

Eve and I sat down with the children and tried to soothe their fears which was not easy, since we were as frightened as they were. In a state of shock after the night's events, we were all terrified the Guardians would return to finish their undertaking. We did our best to reassure the children that the danger had passed.

'We sent them packing, didn't we?' Absalom shouted, hitting the sand with his fists. 'I'm killing a Guardian! I'm killing a Guardian!'

Another boy joined in, punching the ground and laughing. Beside them, a little girl began to cry, rubbing her eyes with her fists.

At last, Matthew and Gideon called us all together to present their survival plan. They gazed at us gravely, as well they might, but at least they had a strategy for us to consider. Matthew's proposal was that he lead us across the desert to a distant mountain where he claimed a tribe of people survived on foodstuffs growing wild on the rocky slopes.

'Now that we've cut off contact with the city we can't rely on pills to keep us alive,' he said solemnly. 'So we are going to have to depend on foodstuffs instead.'

A gasp of dismay ran round the listeners. 'We'll become food addicts,' someone protested.

'We'll all be obese.'

'It's that or starve to death,' Matthew replied, 'and we won't become obese if we don't ingest more than we need.'

'It's more likely we'll all lose weight,' Gideon said. 'At least to begin with, while we're establishing our supplies.'

'And learning how to eat,' I muttered.

When he added that he and Matthew had both been food addicts for a long time, several of the listeners looked shocked, while others merely shrugged as though they had suspected as much, or perhaps already knew.

'We don't know if it's possible to cultivate foodstuffs without hydration pills,' Gideon said. 'But we have to try. There are no other choices open to us, and we can't just sit around here, waiting for the Guardians to return.'

Hearing that, several children began to wail, and Eve went

over to reassure them that the Guardians were not on their way yet. I hoped she was right.

Gideon carried on speaking. 'If it's true about the tribe living in the mountains, that means it must be possible to cultivate foodstuffs there. If they can do it, so can we.'

Some of us agreed with the proposal, but several members of the group expressed reluctance.

'Why don't we go back to the city?' one woman suggested. 'At least we know there are pills there.'

Other voices chimed in, agreeing with the woman.

'Gideon's idea is crazy.'

'We can't survive without pills.'

'Are we really going to cross the desert on the strength of a fable about people living on a mountain?'

'Has anyone ever seen them?'

'I don't believe a word of it.'

'What if there isn't any foodstuff when we get there?'

'And no pills.'

'This is madness.'

Admittedly, the idea of setting off without knowing where we might end up was daunting, but others argued that we could not return to the life we had known before. Whatever happened, the future was going to be a leap into the dark. Many of us trusted Matthew and were prepared to accept his suggestion, but others remained wary.

'Has anyone actually been to this mountain?' someone asked.

Matthew told us he had seen it in the distance. 'It's a long way from here,' he admitted. 'But that means it's a long way from the city. There's a chance we may be safe there. I don't believe the Guardians would venture that far.'

'Why would they?' Gideon asked. 'They'll think they wiped us out.'

'Where is this mountain?' a woman asked, muttering that it probably did not even exist since no one but Matthew had ever seen it. 'Food can affect the brain,' she added darkly.

'Many days' walk from here you'll see it towering over the landscape, like a vast black wall rising out of the desert,' Matthew replied.

I gazed around and saw nothing but endless desert stretching out wherever I looked.

'But where is it?' the woman persisted. 'I can't see any sign of it.'

Other voices joined in. 'If it's so far away, how do you know there are people living there?'

'If it exists.'

'How can a wall rise up out of the ground so far from the city? Where does it come from?'

'Someone must have built it. What if they're hostile to us?'

'Yes, we'll be leaving the Guardians for a worse problem.'

'How can anything be any worse than our current situation?'

Matthew raised his hand for silence and everyone listened intently as he described how he had been exploring, many years ago. As a young man he had crossed vast tracts of desert, which rose and fell across the land. In the distance he had spotted a small boy playing in the sand, in the shadow of a high mountain.

'But what *is* a mountain?' someone asked.

'A mountain is the opposite of a crater,' Matthew explained. 'It's an area of land that rises above the desert, reaching up towards the sky.'

'Get back to telling us about what you saw,' another voice interrupted impatiently, and others joined in, urging Matthew to continue.

As Matthew had been approaching, a dark-skinned woman ran up to the boy, jabbering in a shrill voice. Without understanding a word she said, Matthew guessed that that she was scolding the child for wandering off into the desert by himself.

'What happened then?' Eve asked.

Matthew shrugged and said the woman had scooped up the child, who had clung to her as she loped off towards the mountain.

'So you never spoke to her?' I asked.

'There was no time. She was there and gone in an instant, while I stood dumbfounded, wondering whether to approach her or duck down out of sight. In any case, I didn't know her language. But the point is, she was with a child, and the pair of them can't be living there on their own.'

'That's true. The child must have a father,' Gideon remarked.

There was silence for a few seconds as everyone pondered the implications of what we had heard.

'She must have come from the city in the first place,' someone said. 'The Guardians will be looking for her.'

'Not necessarily,' Matthew replied. 'And if she did escape from the city, she would have been given up for dead a long time ago. But the point is that the mountain is a long way from the city, and those people must be surviving on something. They didn't look malnourished. The little boy was quite chubby, but not unhealthy.'

Gideon spoke decisively. 'Well, if other people can survive on the mountain, so can we.'

'She must have stolen the child from the city,' Eve murmured.

'What if she created the child herself, out there on the mountain?' I wondered aloud. It seemed a reasonable supposition, and I was taken aback when everyone turned to stare at me.

'Rachel, what are you talking about?' Eve demanded.

'If the woman is ingesting healthy foodstuffs, it's possible she might be fertile,' I said.

Eve stared at me as though she couldn't decide whether to laugh or be angry. 'Don't be ridiculous,' she said. 'Everyone knows that only wives can produce children.'

I looked away. I could have been mistaken, but there was another possible reason why my monthly bleeding had stopped. Beneath my loose desert clothes, I thought my belly had begun to swell gently.

'If we travel away from the city, we will never be brought another unwanted infant,' Eve said, gazing sadly at the children.

'If we stay here, we will be killed,' Matthew replied solemnly.

'Never mind all that, what if the other tribe is hostile?' an old man asked.

'Yes, what if they're hostile?' a woman echoed.

At once a few more voices joined in.

'What makes you think they'll share their foodstuffs with us?'

'They could be savage.'

'If they really exist. We only have Matthew's word for it.'

'Don't you trust Matthew?'

'Anyone can be mistaken.'

Gideon interrupted their chatter. 'They won't need to share anything with us. We're not going to depend on anyone else to feed us. We're going to cultivate our own foodstuffs when we get there. The point is, if others have done it, so can we.'

'If,' someone muttered.

'Does anyone have a better idea?' Gideon asked, sounding impatient.

Matthew interrupted anyone who would have spoken up. 'We don't have time for any more discussion.' He outlined the plan. While he led us west over the desert to the distant mountain, Gideon would return to the plant site. Gathering up as much as he could carry from there, he would follow us to our destination where he would set up a new plant site, producing enough food for us all. We would have no need of pills.

'What if your plants don't grow there?' Eve asked.

'They will,' Gideon replied calmly. 'Some of them are hardy and if they survive on sand, they'll thrive anywhere.'

'You don't know that.'

'Gideon knows as much about growing food as anyone, and if he's confident it will work, that's good enough for me,' Matthew said.

Studying Gideon as they presented their plan, I suspected he was not as sure of himself as he appeared, but we really had no other choice. We had to leave, which meant we had to go somewhere. Matthew's mountain was as good a goal as anywhere. Whether or not the mountain existed, we could not stay where we were. We were in the hands of the two desert walkers, without whose guidance we would wander blindly until, one by one, we breathed our last, lost in the desert. Eve suggested we all go to the plant site together on the way to the mountain. She was afraid that once we split up, Gideon might never find us again, but he reassured her that would not happen.

'How can you be so certain?' she asked.

'I'll find you,' he replied.

Afraid of losing Gideon again, perhaps forever, I agreed with Eve that we should stay together. He could track us across the sand, but in the mountain everything might be different. Matthew explained it was not possible for us all to take a detour to the plants, which were in the opposite direction to the mountain. With children to carry, and elderly people who could not walk swiftly on the sand, we would be moving too slowly to go to the plant site and then reach the mountain before we ran out of pills. There must be more pills buried in the food hut under the sand, but it would be impossible to dig them up now.

We stared at the sand, appalled that we had buried the sustenance of our lives along with our dead.

'Don't worry,' Matthew reassured us. 'We've got enough pills to get us to the mountain and wait there for Gideon to join us. He can cross the sand more quickly than us. But we need to get started on our journey soon. Apart from anything else, it will soon be light and the Guardians may return. We really can't stay here talking any longer. Come on.'

Gideon nodded briskly at Matthew and then turned to me. 'I'll see you soon,' he promised, his grey eyes staring earnestly into mine.

'I'm coming with you,' I replied, without thinking. 'Between us we can carry twice as much as you can manage on your own, and we're going to need as many of your seeds and plant roots as possible.'

I had made my choice without pausing to consider the implications, but as I was speaking, I knew it was the right decision. Gideon did not answer, but I thought he seemed pleased. To my relief, Matthew agreed it would be sensible for Gideon to take a companion with him.

Eve turned on me with a frown. 'You can't be serious,' she exclaimed. 'You're not going all the way back to the plant site. Why on earth would you want to do that?' She lowered her voice, struggling to control her indignation. 'One of the men can go with Gideon. I don't get it. What if the Guardians are already there? What if you run into monsters on the way? You can't do this, Rachel. It's suicide. You're coming with us and that's all there is to it.'

'I've made up my mind.'

'It's– It's such a long way,' she protested. 'Think about what you're doing. If someone has to go, it doesn't have to be you. Come with us. Let one of the men go with Gideon. They're stronger than you.'

Realising she was not going to talk me out of my decision, she appealed to Matthew. 'You can't let her go with him, it's too dangerous. She has to come with us. The children need her. Tell her,' she pleaded.

'It will be dangerous,' Matthew admitted.

'Exactly!' Eve cried out. 'Tell her. Tell her that what she's suggesting is madness. Any one of the men could carry more than her. Someone else has to go with Gideon.'

Matthew looked at me and gave an almost imperceptible nod. 'One volunteer is worth ten who are chosen,' he said calmly. 'Rachel has freely offered to go with Gideon. And now we need to get moving, so come on, everyone. We're running out of time.'

The sky was beginning to lighten as we gathered up our few belongings and prepared to depart. Eve put her arms around me and held me close, unaware that my resolution was already weakening. If she had appealed to me right then, I might have yielded to her entreaty and gone with her, but she merely gazed at me solemnly and begged me to look after myself. Matthew swung a young boy onto his shoulders and nodded, a signal that it was time to leave. Carrying an infant in her arms, Eve turned and followed Matthew.

Hand in hand, Gideon and I watched the other outcasts walk away. Just before they melted into the landscape, Eve turned and raised one arm in farewell. I waved back, murmuring, 'We'll see you again.'

The other outcasts were too far away to hear me, but I knew we all shared the same hope for the future.

THE END

ACKNOWLEDGEMENTS

I would like to express my appreciation to Betsy, Fred, Shirley, Maria, and all the amazing team at Bloodhound Books for their expertise and support. My thanks especially go to my brilliant editor, Clare, and to Tara - not only for her expertise, but for her kindness when dealing with my ignorance of technology.

I would also like to thank Bill Goodall, my agent who has helped me through the process of producing a book. Above all I am grateful to Betsy for believing in Rachel's Story from the start. This book is a significant departure from my usual crime and thriller genre but, as any writer knows, we do not choose our stories. They find us.

A NOTE FROM THE PUBLISHER

Thank you for reading this book. If you enjoyed it please do consider leaving a review on Amazon to help others find it too.

We hate typos. All of our books have been rigorously edited and proofread, but sometimes mistakes do slip through. If you have spotted a typo, please do let us know and we can get it amended within hours.

info@bloodhoundbooks.com

Made in the USA
Las Vegas, NV
04 April 2021